Son of the
Morning

TOM ANDERSON

Published by Accent Press Ltd 2016

ISBN: 9781783757947

Copyright © Tom Anderson 2016

Acknowledgements

With thanks to Max Romeo and Charmax Musix for approval to mention the lines from Mr Romeo's song 'Chase the Devil'; and with thanks to Cambridge University Press for permission to quote from the King James Bible, Isaiah 14:12.

Part 1

Chapter 1

I saw my first ghost when I was four. That was eleven years ago, when life was simple. That's why I know there's nothing to worry about now. Really not a big deal. I've always seen things no one believed, so why would it be any different now?

Idiot Dr Wentloog, though, has decided all the stuff that has happened was down to 'limited emotional literacy'? Not being able to understand your own thoughts, in other words. He's wrong, of course. I understand exactly what goes on in my head. The only problem is getting it all into words.

Apparently that's where the *literacy* bit comes in.

'Draw me a picture, then, Luca,' he said, looking around the most barren room you'll ever see, as if maybe there was something in our surroundings I might like the look of. 'Show me how you're feeling.'

This was his big idea of how to solve all my 'problems'. D'you realise how much these idiots earn? It's like five times more than my mum and dad combined – and the rest.

Mind you, my dad would have an issue with me saying that. He's going to make a fortune for himself one day soon. Something big is just around the corner. All he needs is for the rest of us to believe it. As well as for the thing to actually exist.

So anyway, back to Dr Wentloog. He reckons I need to try and work out how I came to be here, in this stupid situation. Get my stuff in order, he's told me. Knock up a sort of log, even, if it helps. Do I get a choice? Apparently not. Especially since he can probably lock me up and ruin my life far more effectively than my parents ever could. And they're not bad at it either.

To tell the truth though, I don't really know the story, anyway. He says that doesn't matter right now, and maybe he's right. What's important, they're telling me, is that I'm *trying* to tell it, wrong or not.

This probably is all wrong, but here goes anyway. I don't know what I'm meant to say anymore, so when you really thing about it, what have I got to lose?

Nothing at all.

Chapter 2

So the first really important thing I saw was about three months ago. That's when the whole world started whirling for me.

It was a freezing night, but the fizzing of the sea kept me sort of warm. D'you get that too, or is it just me? That noise the water makes when it scratches the shore – it stops me worrying about cold, or the other stresses in my life. Skint parents, fighting friends, even danger. And in the dark it's even better – the noise of the water.

Tell me it's not normal to sit on the shoreline in the middle of the night? Who's anyone to say what is 'normal' anyway? After the day I'd had, it was the best place to head. I mean it.

During the morning I'd been listening to an old, old man, Bunny Wailer, on my way to school. He's the guy who just about set Bob Marley up with all his earliest, best music. Did you know Bunny's first band was *Bob Marley and the Wailers*? Well, that's why.

Anyway, that freezing morning Old Bunny was wailing in my ears for me and only me to hear about how dawn is breaking as you approach the gates. As always I'd chosen my lyrics perfectly to help me through the bits that make me all anxious. This particular day I had it perfect, too. I rounded the corner just as Bunny sings about the gatekeeper and how I mustn't arrive late, and there was Mr Kleener, as always, ready to hold me back and put me on litter duty if I was thirty seconds slower.

Now, before we go any further, it's really important you understand how important this kind of music is to me. I know it's a bit old-school and the rest of the kids in my year think I don't really like it and am just trying to be the odd one out. But that's not it at all. I like reggae more than anything on earth because it's got some sort of magical connection to my blood. Maybe my heart pumps on that off beat, or my brain fires with that same, slow wobble. Whatever it is, though, if I get it right, it makes me invincible – even if *people* still mess me around. It's a medicine to me.

Cool Runnings, wailed the title of Bunny's song, secretly in my ear, as Mr Kleener glared at me. I knew he was a bit gutted that I was on time. He'd probably get someone else in a minute, anyway. *Cool Runnings*.

*   *   *

I do my best not to be on too many people's radars in school. My main friend at Chapel Shores Comprehensive is probably a girl. Gabrielle is her proper name but she's got like three versions and she'll tell you which you're allowed to use.

'Like the way it works in French,' she explained once. 'You've got *tu* and *vous* or in Welsh you've got *ti* and *chi*. Well, I go by different names depending on your position to me.'

She's made it work well, too. She's 'Gaby' to friends and family, 'Gabe' to the people she calls 'close-close friends'. The third name she uses, 'Gabo', was given to her by a few of the boys who wound her up, but she took it on and made that into a kind of nice-sounding name, too. Apparently her favourite Latin American writer is called that, too. Gabo is what she goes by if you only know her a bit.

'I'm "Gaby" to you,' she tells me. 'You probably need to be a girl before I'm "Gabe".'

That's kind of silly coming from her, because she's got short, light hair and often dresses like a boy. It's not spiky – just a basin cut, and it's probably dark originally but you never see roots. She's got a big thing about how it's her *right* to look like a boy if she wants. Easy for her to say, because even though she doesn't really know it, she's pretty hot. She's never gonna be at any risk of looking like a boy. Trust me.

'Your hippy parents can call me Gabe though,' she used to say.

Now, the bit that's always been odd about our friendship is that I was kind of banned from showing it in certain places. I think it's probably beyond that now, after this little episode and the whole Dr Wentloog nonsense, but back then the rule was properly in place. That's what set me off, in fact.

Anyway, Mr Kleener had failed to get me into his late club, which left me in Reg with nobody bothering me. My other two mates were in another form, so I sat there trying to listen to more Bunny and his song about the land across the sea, without our supply form teacher seeing the earphone. All good. But then came PSE.

Now you know no one really wants to take PSE seriously, right? Okay, occasionally someone comes in to talk about drugs, and we listen then – even though everyone knows everything they're telling you and the nicknames for things are several years out. Also, there was a bloke who used to be a girl who spoke to us once and everyone was quiet then, but I think that was because they were so scared. The sex-ed classes are the same. The idiots are too embarrassed to say much, while the cool kids who want to pretend they've done it already stay quiet to look like they're over it. But generally, for the other topics that make up ninety percent of the course, it's a free-for-all.

I can't remember what the lesson was on. Think it was fair trade, maybe. Anyway, they'd mixed our tutor groups up so I ended up sat across the room from Gaby who'd been put in our class. It was horrible. Her form has some of the biggest thugs in the entire school and they were flaring up really badly. There was stuff getting thrown every time the supply looked away – kids shouting at kids, the supply shouting, people shouting back at her – and then out of nowhere Gaby suddenly lost it.

'Just SHUT UP!' she yelled with no warning whatsoever, and the whole class went dead quiet. 'It's all the time! The noise and the *hating*! It's horrible. HORRIBLE! I can't think. I don't want to be here…'

And then she started sobbing. No word of a lie. The ice-cool Gaby, salt water draining down the edges of her normally spiked out eyelashes.

'Look what you've done,' the supply said to the boys in the middle of the room. It's brutal, but to the supply Gaby's meltdown was something to be used for personal gain.

Gaby just sat there, still trembling, head in her hands.

'That's okay,' added the supply, realising it might actually be wise to try and do something about this. 'I'll get someone now. Can one of you go and fetch a teacher from next door?'

Nobody moved an inch.

'Okay…' She turned back to Gaby. 'Well, would you like to go across to Reception? What's your name?'

Gaby didn't reply because by now she must have realised she was having a crying fit in front of a whole class. Her face probably was best left out of sight behind those palms.

'Gabo,' yelled one of the cheesers from behind me, and a low, hooligan chuckle bounced around the room, gentle but sinister.

Almost out of ideas, the supply said to Gaby, 'Is there someone here who you know well? Someone who can take you over.'

I looked around. No answer from anyone. No answer from Gaby either, so I did what I simply don't do. I put my hand up. I volunteered as tribute.

'I know her, miss. I'll go.'

And like that, I was committed to the course of action. Next I know, my bag was packed, notepad away along with the pen everyone knew we were never going to use, and I was leading a sniffling Gaby out into the foyer.

The boys behind were chuckling again, and as the door closed I heard one say, 'Too easy! She flips like that all the time, honest, Miss.' I wanted to go back, to tell the supply that it was bullshit, but the moment for that action came and went in an instant.

By now Mr Kleener had got onto our block and he'd seen us come out. I don't know if he was alerted by hearing Gaby freak out, or – and this is probably more likely – if it was the *silence* that followed which warned him something wasn't normal. Either way, here he was, taking over without a word and she was on her way towards the part of Reception Block which people don't tend to come back from within the same day.

'Go back to class, Luca Lincoln-James,' he said. First name too friendly for him, surname too long – so he always went for the whole lot.

And off Gaby walked.

Back in class and not brave enough to challenge the view that Gaby had meltdowns like that routinely, I was drifting and trying to be forgettable again. I'd probably done about the right thing, but still, I was now fully stressed at how something must be massively wrong with her for Gaby to be like that. Then the buzzer went and it was off to Maths.

Little did I know I had been lined up for a proper grilling, too. And not from any teacher.

The boys had been staring from the second I got back in the room. They'd gone a bit quieter and I'd kind of thought it was just because they'd finally got the crap out of their system after making Gaby spin out like that. I got my head down and started reading a loose copy of a worksheet we were meant to be doing, one of the few that hadn't been ripped or scrunched up yet.

The eyes stayed on me, though. And they were whispering. D'you ever find that *worse* than a heavy din? Bad kids whispering… It means they're using their brains.

I forgot how idiots like that think, didn't I? Forgotten that in their world everything is always about them and no one else.

In their minds, I'd been outside telling Mr Kleener in perfect detail how it was *their* behaviour and *their* actions that made the class the kind of place a girl like Gaby would freak her way out of. It probably was, in fairness, but I walked out because I cared about her, not because I was looking to report what anyone else in the class was doing. And anyway, as I just told you, Mr Kleener didn't even give me the chance to breathe before sending me back to PSE again.

'Luca! Lukalukalookaa!' one of them shouted as we all made our way towards the Maths rooms.

I kept on walking, just ahead, steady pace.

'Lookalookaa. LUCA!'

Now it sounded kind of aggro. I walked on, no turning round, that chesty feeling coming up on me like there was some side-pipe carrying the air back out of me when I breathed. My shoulders started burning and my neck and eyes felt tight.

The only reason I didn't fall over was because there were people in front who broke my tumble.

One of the boys behind had timed it perfect, kicking my right foot sideways when I was taking a step, so that it clicked against my heel. I grabbed the bag of some Year 10 kid in front of me to keep my balance, and saw the look of fear in his face when he turned round. The whole group of trouble makers from PSE was right up behind me. The stumble meant I'd slowed down and whirled, face to face with them.

'Walking out of class like that?' said Joseph Poundes, the biggest, largest, most popular and least sensitive of the lot. It sounded like a question.

In my head I was telling him to piss off, but the breathing thing was now fully on me. Chest was sore, throat dry. He grabbed my head on each side with his hands.

'If Kleener comes after *any* of us now, I'll paint the floor with you. Or even worse.'

Then he planted a kiss hard against my forehead and the others all laughed, deep and forced.

* * *

There was nowhere to go but to get dragged by the current to Maths, where I sat trying to get the breath back right. To do that, I had to think about Gaby again. What she might need. She would almost certainly be missing lessons now. I couldn't imagine what someone like Mr Kleener could do for her, or what made her blow her top, but my head was saying I'd done the right thing by helping get her out of PSE.

Then I started thinking how I kind of hoped she *was* putting down some big statement about what it was like in lessons here, how scary it could be for the rest of us to try and be anything at all with Poundes and his crew making the air thick with their fake bravery. It must be so much worse for girls to sit through that stuff than it was even for me. And you wouldn't believe how they talked in subjects like PE, either – when there were only boys around and they got to say the uncensored, 'lad' version of what they thought about girls. Or what they were *pretending* to think about girls, anyway.

Anyway, they had chucked me in with the girls as some kind lesser species a long time ago now. And d'you know what? I was fine with that. At least I knew where I stood – or stumbled, maybe. As my throat warmed again and my heart steadied, I kept repeating to myself that Gaby had needed the help back there. Her horrible morning might be slightly more bearable because of what I'd put myself through.

Or so I thought, anyway. Maybe *I* don't read anyone right at all, though. Only minutes out of Maths and it was all on top of me again. The whole world was trying to cave in. I don't know what I was expecting when she phoned during break – I mean, she *never* phoned me – but it wasn't this:

'What the HELL were you DOING?' Gaby yelled at me.

'I, er, I…'

'Well? D'you realise how much WORSE you made that? I've told you. Stay OUT of my business when we're in those big classes. What makes you think you can just announce you're one of my friends like that?'

'But I am,' I tried to tell her. 'Gaby…'

'Gaby NOTHING,' she was fuming. You could feel it down the phone. 'I TOLD you. It's your weirdo parents that make me like you. That's all. And it's not a case of "liking" anyway. I'm the one being kind to *you*. Get it? I don't need no hero to the rescue like that. If I'm having a crap day then STAY AWAY.'

'Okay, I'm sor…'

And she was gone. Hung up. Cut off. Home. Off the radar. Out of contact.

Leaving my warped Luca mind to have to get itself through the rest of the day, which was only about another four hours of noise, and Joseph Poundes, and his mates, and movement, and heat.

* * *

Now, the one thing I *cannot* handle is doing things wrong. That's often why I don't do things in the first place. (Wow. There's one thing this *has* just made me realise! Scrub that last comment before this goes to Dr Wentloog, then.) Seriously, though, I hang behind when things need to be done because if I put my foot in it then my head can't come back.

Getting pegged in the corridor and then threatened by the prop forward in the rugby team might sound scary to you, but it was the Gaby thing sent me over the brink that day.

You can see it coming a mile off, and then there's like this sort of lightning-bolt moment when it's on me and there's nothing I can do. My face heats up. I want to scream but can't because my breath has gone. It lasts no time at all, but when it leaves it kind of empties my head and my heart with it. It floors me.

Gaby didn't know back then, of course, so who can blame her? But what she said to me at break, so soon after I'd had that boily-blood feeling? Well, it must have helped get the cycle going, right? And what a cycle. The rest of the day's a write off – it's not even about survival anymore – and then I'm sitting there at dinner, watching my parents laugh at nothing, and I'm thinking how I want to make them feel like I do. I start wanting to vanish, go away, like that will do it. They wouldn't notice, anyway.

As if Gaby hadn't filled my head with monkeys, that night my dad was on about this deal he's gonna do, again.

'I *think* I know someone now who can lend me the last two G,' he was telling my mum.

'Wait,' she was saying back. 'Do it properly. Sell those boxes of shoes and you'll get half of that anyway, without causing yourself more trouble.'

'They're going slow,' he told her. 'Plenty of watchers. But only got a bid on one of them that's going close to the reserve price I set.'

This was the kind of stuff my dad spent most of his time doing – and it was why we were skint. From time to time I got something nice out of his deals, like the iPhone which a poor kid like me should never have. The only trouble is that getting some little sweetener present off him is never straightforward… also like my iPhone, which was obviously nicked from somewhere because of all the weird messages it would get from people who must have still had the number of its old owner.

'Can't you stick a *buy it now* option on those shoes?' asked my mum.

'Yeah, but that would be even higher if I'm gonna get a decent return. And it makes people not bother bidding, too.'

'Well, if you will buy up all the sizes no one wants.'

He looked at her with that gaze he uses to say, 'You're right but please don't be right'. Then he went on:

'Seriously, though. Two G and I could buy in then. This is a really good chance to make a *lot* for once. Two grand. I know how to get it. That's all I'd be short if I could just go up with Jeff the next time he goes.'

I'd heard enough. He was on about the same thing again. He'd been trying to get his mate Jeff Rafferty to take him to some jewel market for at least a year but was always needing a little extra before he could buy anything there. Story of his life. Well, story of the pair – mum and dad.

You're welcome to them, Gaby, I thought.

And so came bed. Without sleep, of course. Sometimes, when I get that brain flu, it's enough to wipe me out and I get whacked by this full-on heavy sleep, right through until I get shaken out by my mum and have to run past Mr Kleener with the wrong Bunny tune in my ears.

This night was a proper restless one though. I kept wanting to Facetime Gaby and try to talk my way out of it. Wasn't brave enough, of course. So the only place I could go was deeper into Luca Land.

And it was dark enough there, too. Like always.

Chapter 3

'Think of it as a diary, Luca. You can trust a diary. It's only yourself as an audience so you can tell a diary exactly how you're feeling, or how you did feel at a time and place. You can teach yourself about your own thoughts.'

'Except you'll read it,' I said, sitting up further back into the bed, as if I might be able to crawl away from him.

'I won't read anything you write, Luca. Not unless you're comfortable with it, first.'

Dr Wentloog was sitting side on, so he could stare at me without looking like it. I was probably trying to crawl the wrong way. There wasn't going to be any escape by clawing through the mattress. Seemed my days of being able to pass through stuff like I was made of gas were done. The window though... Nah, I'd never make that drop. Plus it was locked, and double glazed, and reinforced too, probably.

No option then. I'd have to listen.

'We've got you this dark blue notebook,' he went on, producing what was certainly, beyond doubt, something very like a notebook that had a dark blue cover. 'Apparently you like having notebooks for Christmas and birthdays?'

'Love it.'

'Good. What do you put in them?'

'Nothing.'

'Nothing?'

'Yeah. Nothing.'

'You mean that you don't see the contents as being worth much to anyone else?'

'No. I mean *nothing*. Blank pages. I don't write in any of them.'

This was a little bit of a fib, but this guy doesn't deserve the full truth.

'I see,' he said.

But he doesn't see. I can promise you that.

*   *   *

What I've always loved, more than any other part of the human world, is the night. Mind you, it's not really the human world, when you think about it, is it? That's probably *why* I'm so into it.

You know the way most kids get scared of the dark when they're very little? Didn't happen to me. No way. I've gone into the night since as young as I can remember. First I used to just get up in secret and watch out my bedroom window for hours. I remember the orange street lights and waiting for ages to see tiny things happen, like a cat go past or the milk floats that used to come round in Chapel Shores. I remember the noises and how the dark would amplify them.

One time I waited for hours for a far off engine noise to grow closer. In the end it grew and grew so loud that by the time the winter gritting truck trawled its way down my street it was as if a jumbo jet was landing overhead. It gives me chicken skin to think of it now.

Those are the little things. If you're a proper night-watchman, you'll see bigger deal things sooner or later, as well.

In my case, sooner – but everything I saw as a little kid is old news now, right? What's the odd talking animal, flash of light, UFO or gap in the clouds when you think about it, anyway? Even the ghosts I reckoned I'd seen as a little child. None of them ever really did anything to me anyway, so who cared?

That night, though. The night I'd been thumped away by Gaby like that. That night I didn't even try to nod off before heading out. No point. There was and always would be one solution to feeling as hollowed out as that. One thing that would make it go into the background for a little while…

Heading into the night – well, I'd done that for years too. It's as if it lets you figure out the world when it's not looking. Like going onto a pitch, a court or a track after some huge race or tournament and seeing it silent and bare, all the fuss gone for good.

You can walk streets and the cold isn't even cold. It's too exciting for that. Roads are so empty you could lie in them, gardens and driveways are still and sleepy. You can stare at things, step on things, sit next to them. Nothing replies or tries to make you feel uncomfortable. Going out into the night, if you time it right – the darkest, darkest hours – makes you think the world was made for you. The same world that spends all the waking day trying to crush you and to hold you back. Seen in darkness with nothing but that frosty mist and the strange glow of street lamps, it's *yours* to play in.

It was somewhere past two when I slipped out and made straight for the dunes and the bridle path to the sand and rock behind my house. My parents genuinely had no clue I did this, and so the front door key was always under the phone and easy to slip silently around in the lock.

The Council drop the streetlights sometime around then, too, so it was just a matter of feeling out the pavement underfoot, before the point when it turns to long grass and I'd hop that little broken fence. I could see the outline of

17

the dunes and crops of longer, spiky grass before the thin stretch of pebbles leading to the beach. And then there I was: miles of freezing, moonlit ocean ahead of me.

It was high tide, and I tried humming something that kept rhythm with the little shore-pound that was rolling the pebbles every couple of seconds. The moon was at about three-quarters and right over the far-off horizon. Below it, a wobbling shape of lunar reflection shook gently on the silk surface. At the point where the water met the shore, that sheen of light would fold inside the little breaking waves and then jump around on the angry water getting flung up the beach.

Just above the tide mark, where the ground was cold but bone dry, I sat down and thought of nothing at all. There was so much space around me, I didn't need to. Anything living that wanted to disagree was sound asleep – deep under, out for the count, off in dreamland, too far away to matter.

That rhythm I'd been looking for started to look for me instead. The cold ground felt good, and I wanted to lie back on it and look at the sky. That was when the first figure began to break the surface.

At first it didn't stop the emptiness in my mind at all. I watched that little arrow of water rings disturb the sea as if it was just a nosy fish – or even a sea turtle, except they only like warm water. So when a dark lump began to rise out, I watched it and waited as if I had been expecting them.

It was when that lump kept pushing out of the water, kept rising steadily, twenty metres away, then nineteen, then eighteen, that I realised it was a human head, and that below it the head had shoulders.

Wow-wow-wow-wow-wow, went a voice in my head. *Stand up, run away.* But I didn't need to do that at all.

The figure was rising out of the water at such a steady pace it felt as if he wasn't going to be any threat at all. It was all so slow that it looked like the sea had turned to oil or become some sort of black treacle. I could see the saltwater draining off his clothes, a dark and shiny gloop. They were a properly odd shape, too, his clothes. That's how I knew he wasn't from our time.

When the first man got his feet onto the sand the second figure was already rising behind him. Now I could see better what they were wearing. There were little bits of seaweed hanging out of the neck of the leader's jacket, and under that was a slightly lighter shirt. It was old, though, and baggy. Maybe more of a tunic than a shirt. His trousers were sagging and tucked into knee-length socks. He had a beret hat on too, which the sea hadn't knocked at all. It was perched neatly towards his forehead. The jacket had long tails, and the water was draining off them, faster and lighter now he was on dry land.

I scrambled softly across the floor, backwards, to the pebble line and wedged myself against a rock that shaded me from the moonlight. He *had* to have seen me. I watched his shadow quiver up the beach in front of him as he walked, same pace as always, up the sand.

The second figure was now out of the water to his waist, and he was dressed exactly the same.

And there was a third one – a third man, rising gently from that spot on the surface. Over and over again, that little circle of ripples would begin, then break into another dark, moving object, another head, another hat, another wide-shouldered jacket. The forth was exactly the same distance behind, too, and the fifth.

By now the leader of this procession was about to go right past me, and without moving my head I glanced up towards his face.

There was no expression at all. His eyes, white in the moonlight with tiny dark pupils, were focussed dead ahead. His square chin had a tracing of dark stubble across it, and his mouth was closed tight. Every step, on sand, pebbles, rocks or the grass, was the same distance – feet the same length apart, and at the same speed. All he did was move forward, as if pulled towards something behind my housing estate at the end of the dunes.

The second guy trudged along just like him, brilliant, bright eyes gazing straight ahead, no notice of me at all.

By now I had begun counting them. Besides the two to pass me, there were four more making their way across the dark sand, one more almost free from the water and still another pair of head and shoulders rising from the glassy surface behind.

And still, each had the same clothes, the same weight of water running off them, the same seaweed and grime around their clothes and hair. One had a small crab clinging to his trousers, and another a few barnacle shells on his back, but you could see the way they'd all put the clothes on. Their hats were at an angle, the undershirts baggy, the socks high and tight. A uniform, identical – like they were all meant to be part of the same body.

I had slipped back into that rhythm in my mind that the lapping waves had made when I first arrived. The figures kept passing, and I kept watching, staring – following them with my eyes as they all, one at a time and equal distance apart, slipped up over the dunes and back into the night, headed for the streets where I lived.

It was the most natural thing in the world. I felt like I knew them right away. I'd seen them, somewhere before, far, far away in the deepest bits of my own head. And now here they were, doing what seemed like just the right thing for them to do.

I leaned back against the damp rock, felt sea water starting to strain up through the sand, wetting the seat of my jeans. Still the cold hadn't got to me. I watched the shining surface slow down again, as the patch of water they'd emerged from healed and smoothed over. The horizon was marked out by the end of that white strip of dancing moonlight. Uneven edges of moving foam slipped up the sand in gentle layers, thinning out as the tide dropped back. I knew exactly how long I'd been here, exactly when to go back. The image of each of the men strolled on and on into my memory as I looked at the footprints they had left. My house and the warmth of bed could wait a little longer.

I hadn't lost the count at all, either.

There had been nineteen of them.

Chapter 4

It was nearly five in the morning when I got in, and a few yellow upstairs lights were just pinging on in my street. I was back in bed straight away, two and a half hours before my mum woke me for school. Or, as she puts it, checked I'd managed to wake up for myself.

'Luca… That's you up, right?'

'Yeah.'

'Good.'

I'd been doing a better job of the whole waking thing anyway. I'd put my iPod into a speaker port in the evening and set it to fire up with Toots and the Maytals singing *45-56 That's My Number?* which is the only song that gets me out in the right way. It's gentle. It drumrolls you in and then gets going gradual enough to make you just about happy to wear another day on the chin.

Maybe it was the two hours' sleep. Maybe my mum giving me hassle about being politer to my dad as she drove me to the corner. Maybe just bad timing, but this next morning, like I knew he would, Mr Kleener got his wish.

'Luca Lincoln-James. Registration started three minutes ago. Stay right where you are! Line up by the fence.'

It was brutal. He doesn't get me that often, but when he does it makes you want to curl up and fall into a pit with no bottom. You can tell the guy loves it, too.

'Your excuse?'

'You know I have none, Sir.'

'Excuse. Now.' He doesn't let you just be late.

'Uh... Traffic?'

'Leave earlier, then. You know that. You need your attendance figure. You're missing out otherwise.'

'I did.'

'Did what?'

'Leave early Sir.'

'Think of all the money that goes into your education,' he began. 'All the work and all those people running it, all getting up, all making it here on time themselves. Kids to care for, milk to buy, car tanks to fill. But *they* still make it. And then this is how you thank them? It's rude of you!' He had the whole speech off by heart.

'I know,' I told the floor.

'So... Let's get on with it. Inside, Reception, sign in then wait for me.'

I love the way they punish you for 'missing out', by making you miss out more. Anyway, that day it was fine. I waited for him to catch a few more latecomers in his net, thinking how it was okay not to be in assembly at least. Plus it was a good chance to think, awake, in the daylight about those weird men from the beach.

What I'd seen the night before had done the job of pushing crap from the day into the back of my mind. Did it really matter at all if Joseph Poundes was in today, or if Gaby was, or if either of them had any interest in me? Technically, that's what I should have been caring about. Gaby especially. But now I had something better to fill my head with.

No sleep does great things for a kid my age, by the way. It means I can't think about anything that adults want me to, like Maths or English for example. It also makes everything seem kind of unreal. Mr Kleener was back at Reception with two more kids, arranging to have them call our parents about lateness and to get us on this attendance e-monitoring thing he loved.

For me though, it was all about what was in my head. There, if I squinted, or rolled my eyes into my head, were those figures I'd seen. It was like I was looking at them all over again. I tried working out how many hours ago they'd happened to me by now. And then came the job of wondering what they were.

'Make sure all three of these leave for lessons before nine,' Mr Kleener was saying, to someone. 'Get them booked in to spend lunch here, though. They owe us extra time. I'll send them out to litter-pick, maybe.'

I wasn't tuned in to that business, though. I had a bigger question to deal with. Who or what were these shapes – men or shadows of men – that I'd seen on the shoreline last night? Were they alive? Of course not. Or not in the way we consider being alive, anyway. And who *walks out of the sea*? Sailors? Ghosts? Ghosts of sailors? Maybe they were wreckers or smugglers from some of the folk tales people in this town tell kids. Visitors from a time when this was an exciting place to live. And where were they going?

The slip was in my hand, confirming my lunchtime appointment back here for Mr Kleener's late club, and so I walked, distracted, towards lessons. I knew the one thing the figures in the dark *couldn't* be, though. I knew it from the start. The one thing they definitely weren't was a one-off. They knew what they were doing. You could see it in their eyes, in the perfect distance of their paces, in the straight line they cut across the dune. They would be there again another night, too. I was sure of it.

* * *

No surprise; Gaby wasn't in. And Poundes? Of course he'd be around, but for now he didn't seem too interested in holding onto yesterday. That had nothing to do with forgiving or forgetting, mind you. It was just that he had his interests elsewhere. When I saw him, he was hassling a couple of the best-looking girls in our year with this creepy smile and his loudest voice. Oh well, at least two people on site had the power to draw some sort of cave-man warmth out of him. Fine, I thought. Let *them* have his attention.

I wondered for a minute what it might be like to be someone like Joseph Poundes. His sort probably overlooked how intimidating it was to get singled out like he did to me yesterday. They move on like it's nothing, but the heat of that moment is still left to affect the weaker one. Joseph Poundes probably hadn't thought once about my existence since, a comforting thought, almost.

It was no consolation for how worried I was about Gaby, though. I had to try and reason with her in some way, and since she wasn't in school it would mean one of two things. Either trying to call her, or just suffering and being patient enough to wait for her to get in touch with me.

I'm not good at doing either of those. To call her would be a step of bravery that went *way* beyond anything I had in me. But then again, waiting and worrying wasn't going to be much fun either.

Waiting and worrying did actually involve doing nothing on my part, though, so it was just about the easiest option.

I lasted until break.

Then I slid out my phone and went to dial her number. My head throbbed with dread at that, so I went for the middle ground and sent her a text:

'Sorry u not in today. Hope u okay. Let me know if u need anything.'

She replied nearly straight away.

'Thanks. NO. Fine.'

Then she followed it with another message which I think sort of helped lift a bit of my gloom: 'Not gonna stay in house all day. Might need bunker to hide away in. U should come too.'

I tapped out a reply straight away. 'Cool. Will do. See you straight after work?'

'Okay yeah.'

'Work' was a word we used for school. Gaby had this thing about how going to school was our job. Seemed ironic since she didn't come that much. But still, the shadowy patch in my mood was definitely brightening. I could endure the lunchtime litter pick now, knowing I had at least one half-friend in the universe, even if she was sticking by this stupid idea that we mustn't be seen as mates in school.

But then I realised she hadn't said *anything* to suggest she wasn't still going to be mad at me. Had she? Maybe she had. I'm so bad at this. I could convince myself everything was okay, then convince myself it wasn't, just as quick.

The other two of Kleener's morning victims had the guts not to show for the litter pick too, so there was plenty of time for me to drown in my own, useless company. Plenty of time to feel the eyes of the whole school as I spiked empty Coke cans off the floor and dropped them into a big, yellow bucket. Plenty of time to make sound mixes in my head – repeats of the warning Kleener had given me along with litter tongs: 'You'll be doing this stuff *every* day, minimum wage, for forty years if you mess school up, Luca Lincoln-James.'

And there was plenty of time, too, for me to match that soundtrack in my head with an image. The other thing I couldn't stop dwelling on. There they were, in the background the whole time. Those empty faced spirits from the middle of the night.

* * *

Out on the west of Chapel Shores was Bunkers Beach. It
had some long and winding Welsh name, but to everyone
local it was known as 'Bunkers' because the shoreline was
dotted with rotting concrete from the Second World War.
Like the set of *Call of Duty*, there were these huge, square,
lookout turrets wedged into the dunes from when Wales
used to fear invasion from Germany. The ocean and tide
had pulled them all over now, so they were dangerous and
smelly, covered with graffiti and algae. Some of the kids
my age – or at least the ones who went outdoors instead
of playing *Call of Duty* all day – loved them. We often hid
away here, me and Gaby, so I knew this was where she'd
meant by that text.

There was a little bit of fog, really cold, down by the
beach and a sharp wind to blow it sideways along the wet
sand. The windows of the derelict shop and pubs on the
sea-front were thick with the salt left behind.

I loved the way this town was slowly falling apart in
the sea air. I remember my History teacher, Mr Lloyd,
explaining to us on a field trip to the bunkers once about
the army stuff that got built here. The factories that came
after it, plus the shipping lanes and industrial waste meant
Chapel Shores was ignored when they set up the holiday
resorts. No one had bothered removing the bunkers, he
explained, because the beach wasn't ever going to need it.

Yes, it was official. We were growing up in the only beach
town in Wales that hadn't escaped looking and feeling like
a ghetto. There were a few posh streets on the one little hill,
and Gaby lived just on the edge of that area. On the east of
that hill were the ropey houses and my street, and then on
the other side was the old road out to Bunkers. Apart from

that, the only other thing the Shores was famous for was being surrounded by miles of boring, flat land that was full of warehouses, supermarkets, DIY shops and empty offices. Chapel Marshes had a sign that claimed it was the 'Heart of Coastal Commerce', but not even my dad believed that. It was always getting flooded too, being something silly like a third of a foot below sea level.

Anyway, while most of the kids in this town moaned that they lived in a dive – and couldn't wait to get on with some far-fetched, dream career which would let them leave, like footballer, Wolf of Wall Street, fashion model or fighter pilot – me and Gaby decided years ago that this set-up suited us fine. It was always quiet and desolate here, even in summer. The whole town seemed like a place to hide.

Gaby was sitting on top of the furthest bunker. I could see her outline through a little patch of mist – that short hair wrapped inside a fluffy head band that went over her ears. I ran towards her, slowing once I got near so that I wouldn't seem too anxious to see her.

'Alright?' she said. Her feet were dangling over the side and she was scratching the surface of the concrete with a sharp stone she must have found at the high-tide mark.

'Yeh. You?' I climbed up and stood on a little platform in the cement just below her. I could see what she was sketching. It was the outline of her own hand, and she'd added claws to the fingertips.

'You got my message then?' she said.

'Yeah.'

'Well?'

'Well what?'

She rolled her eyes, so I asked her if she was okay again.

'I probably would be if you'd said the right thing just now,' she said.

My mind grabbed at her words, but found nothing.

'Er…' I mumbled. I was drawing a blank.

'That you're *sorry*?' she suggested. 'Sorry for humiliating me yesterday?'

That was easy enough for me to say, but was that really what I'd done.

'Just trying to help,' I said.

'Is *that* what were you thinking?' she asked, staring straight at me.

'I was… I was *worried*.'

'Well don't be,' she said, frowning. 'D'you really think I need it? *Your* worry?'

I didn't answer.

'Anyway, we've spoken about this before,' she added. 'We don't really go round together *in school*. I get stressed about it.'

'I know, but…'

'And especially when we end up in the same class for an hour!'

I wanted to tell her this was a stupid rule, but she'd insisted on it from the day we became friends and I could sort of see the logic behind it. For her, anyway.

'We can hang around *outside* of school because that's real life,' she explained. '*In* school, though, it's not real life, and it suits both of us to keep apart.'

I shouldn't really have been expecting her to say anything else. I knew how it went, now, anyway. Once she finished reminding me of these 'rules', she'd be okay again and we could probably be almost normal.

When I told her about Joseph Poundes tripping me up she said it was proof that she was right.

'See what I mean? You watch. You're only going to learn this the hard way,' she told me. 'They'll go for you if you associate with me too much. Trust me.'

30

'I don't really care, though,' I told her.

'Yeah you do. You think you don't but you do. Your calling, Luca, in life, is *normality*! Don't you get it?'

'No.'

'We're going in opposite directions, see.'

'What d'you mean?'

'You're coming *into* the world of normal people from outside of it. I'm going the other way. That's why we get on. We're passing each other on route to swapping places.'

'Eh?'

I knew what she meant, though. I think.

'It's all about how things *look* in school,' she added. 'We need to play the game there. We can compare notes afterwards, in places like this.'

'But what about if I see you get so upset in class like that?'

She stopped scratching the stone in her hand and looked up.

'I was fine.'

'Really?'

'Yes. Really. If you ask me about that again then I *will* kick off on you.'

'Fine.'

There was a little pool of water in front of this bunker, where the sea had dragged sand away as it bounced off the concrete. On high tides waves could smack into this and bounce white foam up in the air. The fog was sticking closely to the shoreline, grey layers of vapour drifting heavily in the wind.

Gaby flicked the stone she'd been using to scratch her handprint on the bunker. A perfect spin took it across the pool in three neat rings of water, before it caught up with itself and sunk.

'Come on then,' she said, lowering herself off the opposite edge and dropping to the sand. 'Let's do a trawl. I need you to help, LLJ. You can be my second pair of eyes.'

This was chiefly why we came here. With the vast range of amazing waste people had left in the sea, Bunkers Beach was the best place in the universe for collecting odd objects. Gaby liked to call it 'sculpture work', and stuck together the items we found in odd ways. Back in her house she'd saw things and bend stuff to make these beach statues that represented some kind of meaning.

'Check it out! This has to be from a dead person!' She was holding up a plastic picture frame, the glass long ago cracked out of it and probably turned to sand. 'Yes!' she said. 'This is gonna be so *meaningful*! I should soak some photo – maybe black and white – in it, then drop little bits of colour on once it looks faded enough. What d'you reckon, Luca?'

When we used to trawl the beach near my house Gaby would stash things she found in my garage – then we'd either get my dad to run it over to her house closer to the west side of town, or she and I would both carry them together. We walked a rusted trampoline over to her place once, stopping for rests along the way. Her folks never came down to my street, though.

'Hey, I'm really liking this frame idea,' she said, still looking at the places where the sea had taken the colour out of the plastic. 'Reckon this would bend? Have you noticed how salt water makes plastic all flimsy and ready to crack?' She went to bend the object slightly with her hands.

'Ooh. Don't want to risk it,' she said. 'I'll spray this with lacquer once I've made my piece with it.'

Our Art teacher, Mrs Rogoff, thought Gaby was the brightest talent she'd ever had in her class. Gaby was allowed to do whatever she wanted for her GCSE coursework, while the rest of us got forced to do some sort of copycat project on sculptures and paintings Mrs Rogoff had photographed on a trip to this arts city in Colombia, called Cartagena. Some teacher team had been with her there on a trip to prepare artwork and Mrs Rogoff never shut up about it. We had lessons that felt like Geography thrown at us, all about that Cartagena place and its buildings, and Gaby was the only one allowed to follow something else for her main project.

But still Gaby refused to use this stuff from the beaches in Chapel Shores, ever. When I asked her why, she always said the same thing. 'Coz GCSE Art's not real life and this is!' In school she painted fruit bowls or still lifes of her own hand. And still they lapped it up.

'Luca! Come on. What d'you think? You know I need you to call it for me. You're my *muse* – you tell me what flies and what won't.'

She was still staring into the frame. 'What d'you reckon then? What do we need to put in this picture frame,' she asked. 'Or *who*? Shouldn't be an alive person or anyone too real! Howabout I sketch someone?'

'Could work,' I said, and then after a moment's thought, 'Maybe I could...'

The idea hit my chest and head so hard on the way out that it stayed put.

'Could what?' said Gaby.

'Ah, nah. It wouldn't work.'

'What wouldn't?'

'Nothing.'

'Come on. What's your idea?'

'I dunno. Just, like, maybe... Maybe imagine some people on the sand somewhere. You know... Like, shadows or... What d'you call them...'

'Silhouettes!' she said.

'Uh, yeah. I think.'

'Like those Jack Vetriano paintings Rogoff loves?'

'I dunno. Maybe,' I said, going off the idea already and super reluctant to tell her any more.

'Like what then? I know. I could colour one silhouette while the others were just shapes. Maybe I could find some cloth or something down here, to paint them on, like? Something the sea's bleached.'

She fell to rummaging in the shoreline, and my moment to say any more about figures, silhouettes, alive people, dead people or strange shapes of any kind on the sand had passed.

'Ooh!' she yelled, yanking a ball of rope out of the ground to see if it was attached to anything else. 'Come on. We're gonna find something to use. I can feel it!'

As for me, I could feel the first hints of a bit of rain. That wasn't going to stop her, though.

'Come *on* LLJ. Two can trawl this beach quicker than one.'

'Fine,' I said. 'I'll take the lower tide mark.' And off I walked, to help someone else make something better out of the stuff that was in my head.

*　　*　　*

It was raining hard by the time we got off the beach, and we ran for shelter under the old electricity box they sometimes used as a lifeguard station on the summer days, when there were more than five people here.

Gaby had found some flat wood that she thought might fit in the frame, but apart from that the fog, the cold and the wet had made it hard to get really into the trawl. We could come back, though.

Our pace going up the broken road from Bunkers to the outskirts of town was quick and we were getting wet. It was getting dark early, too, and the few places that were open on the sea front – some offices, a community centre and a big, rundown pub – were closed.

'See you again, LLJ,' Gaby said, as she turned off the main road and headed uphill towards her house. A few steps off, she turned and added, 'Oh, forget about the school thing. I won't be in tomorrow anyway. Not in the mood. Dunno why. Can't say.'

'Yeah, okay. Nice one. T'ra.'

And then I was alone again. I started running as the rain thickened. I reached the first of the roundabouts where cars could turn to drive out across the Marshes. Staying on the sea-front, I kept going, feeling my heart and lungs rising to the task of jogging as my clothes got wetter. A few minutes later I was past the pile of barnacle-covered rocks that broke the town's beaches in half, and had arrived on the eastern end of the Shores. The lamps of my street stuck out at the far end, disappearing around the back of the biggest dune, and after that the only specks of light were fishing boats out to sea.

Dad had finally sold some of the Reeboks and I got home to find him frantically boxing stuff up to post.

'Alright Lukee Boy!' he said. 'You're lookin a bit wet. Why didn't you ring for a lift?'

'I'm alright,' I said. 'Made a sale?'

'Too right I have! Sold half the batch.'

'Don't ask him the prices he got,' said Mum.

I wasn't going to.

'They're fine!' he argued back. 'It's all about *turnover*, Hannah. Keep the cash flowing. All of em settled up with PayPal right away. I can ring Jeff Rafferty now and look for some more stock.'

I made for the stairs.

'Off up quickly?' said Dad.

'Yeah. Got to get dry. You just said.'

'No I never. I said you look wet, but not that you have to storm straight off when we ain't seen you yet today.'

'Get up earlier, then,' I told him.

My mum cut in again:

'Luca's done really well with waking up, hasn't he. Attendance, attendance, attendance! You're on it now. The Comp will be off your back in no time. Where you been anyway?'

'Looking for bits on the beach.'

'With Gaby?'

'Yeah.'

'Sounds fun,' said my mum. 'Don't you think, Steve?'

My dad looked up from his reel of box-tape.

'Eh?'

'Been on the beach with that Gaby girl, he has,' said Mum.

'Wahey,' said my Dad.

Now I *was* going up.

'Ah don't be like that Lukee Boy! She's alright, she is!'

'He knows that, Steve,' said my mum. 'Luca knows exactly what he's doing.'

'What's that supposed to mean?' said my dad.

'That you can leave off *wahey*-ing him about teenage girls.'

'He doesn't mind it!'

'Have you asked him?'

Once I got out of earshot, I could hear them talking a bit more, and then laughter. Not long later my mum called up the stairs to tell me to make sure my school clothes were drying.

'Wouldn't want hanging out in the rain with Gaby to cost you your education would we! Or your attendance figure!'

'Fine,' I said. 'It won't.'

*   *   *

There's another reason behind Dr Wentloog's idea, I've realised now. The guy might say he needs *me* to understand how I got into this mess which isn't really a mess. Really, though, he needs to understand a bit more for himself, because I haven't really given much away.

But that's fine. Once I'm finished doing this, I'll do a different one for him, maybe. It can be all watered down and tamed, and he can puzzle over it and say something deep. Then he'll get paid, and I'll get to go and finish my GCSEs – with the aid of some horrid cover note telling the exam board about how I have to have my pencil case opened for me, and have extra marks and extra help and then pass even if I fail, or else I might do something bad again.

Again?

Apparently, I can't admit there was any problem with what I did. That's a tough one – since I don't really think there was. Nobody got hurt, did they? Still, though, might have to just swallow my pride soon and say there was something wrong with it, just to get out of here. Out of this place of pillows and disinfectant that's meant to make someone like me 'better' but only really makes things worse.

'Seeing things,' says Dr Wentloog, 'can be very frightening if you don't understand why or how it's happening. That's why it's so important to share what's going on in your version of the world.'

Fine. You believe that if you want, Doctor.

I'll believe my eyes if you don't mind.

Chapter 5

With her stay-at-home plan, Gaby was onto a winner as far as school went. There was me, racing again towards that gate with only two options – be on time and have to sit through Reg, or be late and get into trouble – while she just stayed away whenever things weren't quite right for her.

It was two more days before she showed back in school, and by then she only had to get through Friday. I was getting my stuff out in History when I saw her walk through the corridor.

We were doing the Vietnam war and Mr Lloyd was playing with my initials again, which I didn't like since it drew too much attention – especially in the light of what I'd been putting up with this week. Instead of 'LLJ', which *was* the correct letters for me and something I didn't mind people using sometimes, he'd been calling me 'L*B*J'. To make people learn, he claimed.

'LBJ was the president who took America into Vietnam,' he kept saying. 'Lyndon B Johnson! Luca's initials are close enough for us to remember it by.'

Then he'd look at me and say, looking too pleased with himself each time, as if it was his first mention:

'And anyway, Luca, you've got another US President in your name too. Lincoln! The guy who founded the whole America *project*! That's a lucky surname to have. I have to make do with one half of the only Welshman to become prime minster – Lloyd-George. *David* Lloyd-George. Wanna swap?'

I never, ever replied with words.

And this never, ever stopped him.

'DLG... Not got the same ring to it as LBJ eh?'

Especially when they're not even either of our names, I wanted to tell him – except that would surely attract more interest than anyone should ever take in me.

I'd started sleeping okay again since my bad day with the Gaby and the Joe Poundes thing. My sleep patterns had been something that made my parents worry a lot – especially since the *even worse* days from like a year ago or so. So whenever I slept bad now the most important thing to do was not let them find out about it. Whenever I got slammed by the thinkies at night, I had to use the private option of earphones and good music to get through – and *not* anything that might let them get scared about me again.

That was why I figured it would be best to hold off until the weekend to next look at the shoreline by night. That way I could lie-in both the morning before and after going. As always, on Sunday there would be no consequences of being up so late. If I looked tired one morning in the week, it might lead to tough questions, especially from my mum. My dad wouldn't notice whatever state I was in.

Still, best to play this one safe.

Saturday night it was, then. The night when my mum and dad always locked themselves into the front room and watched terrible films from the eighties or nineties with a bottle of rum – so they'd never notice what I did then anyway.

I went up early and dressed myself in black jeans and a dark blue hoodie. I pulled a brown hat over my head and even thought about whether to try and smear my face with something, too. This was the best I could do for some form of night-mode camouflage. If ghosts could see at all, then they'd have to strain their eyes to catch a glimpse of this kid.

My mum was coughing as she hobbled up to bed about one-ish, and then I could hear Dad snoring and swearing in his sleep from the couch below. The door to the living room was open, and he'd probably follow up soon. I waited a bit more, drifting in and out of super relaxation. I was pumped about where I was going, but chilled enough not to be in a rush. I'd go when it was right.

She must have dropped the heating before heading up, because I could feel the air in the house starting to freshen, the old radiators clicking in the dark as the metal changed size and shape in the cooling night. Outdoors, I heard a car roll in and out of our street, its door opening and slamming shut again. Two a.m.

I gave it another half hour and still my dad wasn't budging, so I slipped down the stairs and past him. That was the sketchiest bit – every step had to take my weight gradually so it didn't creak. There was stale smoke settling in the living room from his roll-ups, and their bottle of rum was two thirds drunk. He had a leg hanging off the sofa and had pulled the throw my mum got from India off from the back cushions and down over himself.

I looked at him for a little while and watched. Best he'd ever look. He wasn't thinking of anything – you could see it in his face – and whatever dreams had made him curse were gone too. I wondered if he'd last the night or get cold and head upstairs.

Even if he did, he wouldn't check on me, anyway.

I slipped out, dropping the key into my hood pocket and threading it through this little piece of elastic that was attached to the inner lining.

Everything was empty. The streets were doing nothing but waiting for morning. The air was tight and cold, and the ground felt hard as I jogged gently towards the bottom of my street and slipped under the canopy of bare branches that formed the path to the shore.

It had been dry all week, and there was only a slight breeze. Patches of swollen, round cloud were lit side-on by the moon, now only half as bright as it had been when I came down here on Monday night. The shore was exactly the same distance as before, even though it was now the other side of the tide. Incoming, instead of dropping back.

I slowed my steps as I got near the beach and the steam coming from my mouth was allowed to catch me up. There was the same even rhythm of the sea licking the shore. In the darkness it was amplified, so you could hear the little round boulders popping and clapping together as they were dragged in and out of the tripping shorebreak. Each time, the grumbling stones were drowned out by the fizz of the water mixing sand on sand, as it sloshed up to the rocks beneath my feet.

I looked to the moon, further across the sky than before, and then gazed down and tracked its glinting pads of light across the dark surface. A billow of cloud slipped gently across, turning the ocean glimmer off, before gently twisting the dial back up again as the shining crescent emerged again the other side. With the breeze scratching the surface, the moon's half-light was skipping and shaking softly, a column of silver stretching across the ocean to the blackness beyond its horizon.

I didn't have to wait very long. Ten minutes, or maybe fifteen, but that was all. The first head broke the surface right in the middle of that column of moonlight. Just like it had done last time.

It was travelling the same pace as before. Again, I noticed a gentle current forming on the surface, which turned darker as more water started running off the object that was causing it. The head came up slowly enough for there to be a little bit of time when I wasn't quite sure if this was really happening again. As if there was an extra finger of rock, or a forgotten mooring post beneath the high tide line, all I could see were moonlit rings of broken water. It took a little bit of time for the black in the middle to form enough of an outline for me to make out its movement, but then there it was, no doubt about it, rising steadily outwards and towards land.

His shoulders were up and out of the water, and then I could make out the clothes again. Like before, his hat was totally unmoved by the water draining off, and the jacket kept its shape too. The white outline of his shirt beneath let me see his waistline as that also came up out of the sea. The wake he'd left in the water was tracking outwards, a mini pulse of diagonal lines growing away from him as he walked – and then, straight behind, in the same place exactly, was the darkening spot as the second head started to push up from below.

The intervals were perfect. This time, I was already sat back against the same cold rock as before, and I'd reminded myself of things to look out for and learn. I wanted to count it all up. Check there was the same number, check the distances between them and the times.

The lead figure had his first footsteps on dry land now, while the one behind him was a head and shoulders shuffling forward. The incline of the beach here was super shallow and it must have been a gap of ten or fifteen metres between them. I watched the water running off the trousers, which were tucked into high socks, like last time. There were little pieces of seaweed – a dark green confetti stuck to his shirt and face – and a small patch of silt running with the water out of his jacket pocket, as if he might have filled it with sand which the ocean had now partly lifted back out.

His expression was the same, too. It was blank beyond blank, and yet I could see the focus of his eyes, trained perfectly ahead to where he was walking. His stare was on the land ahead, exactly as your eyesight would catch it if you were looking forward, and he seemed to have no need to watch for obstacles underfoot. His steps were so slow, so steady. As he passed me I watched his feet, somewhere inside those softened, soaking boots of his, carefully feel out what was under them before padding firmly downwards, pressing the ground away with each stride forward.

One… two… three… four… five… I started counting in my head from the exact moment he was level with me, as close to even seconds as my memory would allow. Nine… ten… eleven… twelve. I made no noise, but just gently nodded my shadowed chin forwards with each tick-tock in my mind. Twenty… twenty-one… twenty-two… He was nearing the middle of the dune behind as the second figure followed across the sand. Keeping the count, I looked back out to sea where the third one was now rising, shoulders and armpits up and out of the nightime oil.

It was thirty-two seconds. Each was exactly that time-lag apart. I tried it over and over. This made the whole procession well over ten minutes long – from the first showing of the first, beret-capped head, to the moment when the nineteenth man's heels carried him over the dunes and towards the streets behind.

I'd promised myself I'd do this, and now was the time. I wanted to try and find out where they were going, so as soon as the last one had gone from sight I ran, with the softest steps I could, after them, hunching low so that they couldn't see me. Not that they were likely to look back, mind.

I made my way to the top of the first dune and stopped right where I was. I didn't need to go any further.

Down, below me, in a deep trough of sand, they were moving, and I saw exactly where they were going. There were three left, and one of them was half gone from sight.

The moonlight was shimmering across the flats of sand in the middle of this dune with nearly the energy that it had been jumping on the sea surface. Right on the edge of the most silver patch of ground, a steep cliff of sand-bank rose out of the dune, well over head-height. Its top was lined with dangerously balanced grass, with roots dangling off the ledge and leaking soft sand back down. The men were walking *into* the dune, disappearing face-first into the wall of sand.

Two left.

I lay and studied them. The last but one kept his pace – exactly the same strides as on his way over here. As he neared the rise of sand before the ledge his legs started to sink into the ground as if something were gently pulling at his heels. Then, without changing speed or movements in any way, he stepped on and through the wall of cold, hard sand as if he were walking through a waterfall. Then he was gone.

The last went by, and for a nano-second something in me – maybe even something confident enough to have a voice – said, *Follow them! Do it! NOW!*

But I didn't listen. I mean, you can't *wade* into a dune of packed sand and mud, and roots and sharp grass, can you? Not if you're normal. Not if you follow the rules we live by.

So I did the next best thing, and retreated back to the sea.

Watching it, settled back to its normal movement, I waited as the shimmering reflection from the moon evened out. Gaps in the cloud were letting a few stars pop up to shake weakly in the black over my head. One was much brighter, but it never seemed to stay out for long. Just keep looking, I thought. Try to understand it more tomorrow, or on Monday, during daylight when the impact of this stuff would be nowhere near.

Anyway, did I have the courage to wait more, to see if they'd return to the ocean before dawn?

* * *

There was no sound but the sea, and I let my thoughts float with it. Keeping totally still apart from breathing, I closed my eyes for two waves at a time, and then opened them for two. When closed, I'd listen to the noises the shingle pebbles made getting crunched around by the water, and I'd try to make out single stones. I kept guessing at their direction, where the tide was taking them on their journey. I wondered how long it took them to get broken down to sand. How small a grain had to get before it stopped getting worn down, stopped getting any smaller. It seemed as if each stone had a musical note it could make. During the spells when my eyes were open, I'd try to make out a little pebble through the dark, and see if I could match its movement to a noise. After a while, eyes closed again, I started being able to hear when one stone rolled along, knocking others out of its way – and then when it came into contact with a bigger one itself, and had its own note drowned out.

The first noise to break this was a stirring in the dune grass, off to the east – the other side of me to where the men had gone. A fox stepped out onto the shoreline, and fixed its gaze on me. It recognised life, but knew right away I was too big. There were several foxes living in the marshes around town, I knew that. Maybe they only headed towards streets in the night. He probably saw the same things down here as me – the freedom, the safety from bigger, badder humans. Now, here I was messing up his plan. He looked at me for five repetitions of the dredging shore-pound, and then – a little boulder coming into contact with a bigger one – he shot away.

The sounds of the night filled back in – the emptiness, the swishing, smashing of the sea filling my ears in the absence of enough light. The men came back about twenty minutes later, just as the first bits of birdsong hinted sunrise was around the corner.

I couldn't tell you which one was in the lead, but it wasn't the one who'd been first *up* the beach when they were going the other way. Him I would make out every time, because I'd got to study him closely, twice, now. It had been the same man coming out of the water first both times – but now, heading back, the steady procession was led by one of the others.

Had they come from the dune-ledge? Had they strolled out the ground like they had from the sea? I didn't want to move along the line to try and find out – even though it was almost certain they'd seen me by now. They had to have done. My pathetic cammo outfit, realistically, was only to hide from adults, crimms or tramps and to *feel* less visible, anyway.

Still, I tried to stay as concealed as I could.

I took a close look again at each set of feet. They were stepping on ground they seemed to know off by heart. The boots were drier now, but still looked soft, like the seawater had turned them into soggy socks or worn slippers. Their eyes were gazing straight out to sea, so they were making no attempt to watch their steps. It was as if the feet were feeling out where to tread but without pausing, apart from to push up, away from the ground again with the right sized stride to make everything constantly move at one speed only.

The men were still perfectly in line, too. Same interval, same speed.

I watched the new one who was in the lead. His steps seemed to become even more uniform once he was on the sand, counting down the footprints left until the shore licked at his toes. Now his movements became slightly more laboured under the weight of the water pushing into him. Once his knees were under, the strides suddenly looked oddly small – all I could see were thighs pushing through the surface, until his waist was under. Soon the sense that he was stepping at all was lost for good. Now only his torso moved with a perfect, even slide, further beneath the dark liquid. His jacket tails floated for a moment before getting pulled under by the body they were attached to. His hair, curling down past his ears, washed itself straight, as the ocean came around his face. Then, beret hat still attached, his head sunk and left only that little plume of disturbed water – the same mark on the surface that had told me when they were about to emerge earlier.

Following him, the rest of the group rolled by, each set of feet entering the ocean just as the head of the one before was about to go under. And again, I counted them. Thirty-two seconds apart. Sixteen men, then seventeen, then eighteen. I didn't want to lean up over the rock and turn my head to watch them coming over the dune, so it was only a guess how many would pass. Eighteen, and then a gap.

I froze, pinned back to the rock I had leaned on. Dawn had started bleaching the sky out to the east. There was birdsong in the dunes. It was still dark for a bit longer, but the moon, low on the other horizon, was only a pale yellow. It was losing its power as a different source of light started to spread.

Nineteen.

The last one was the leader from the other times. I recognised him sure as you could ever be of anything. But, for some reason, he was more than a minute behind.

My breath almost stopped, I was trying so hard to keep quiet as he passed.

It did no good, anyway.

Just before his feet hit the high-tide mark, and he reconnected with the slowly brightening sea, he turned. That face, which I'd only ever seen looking blankly ahead, changed slightly.

The eyes shifted slowly, and picked me out.

His feet kept pointing forward as he leant his body gradually around, head tilting and hair slipping across his cheek. Those white, motionless eyes held mine, and his arm went up. Using his whole hand, cupped and bent at the wrist, he beckoned. He was scooping the last of the night air towards him, repeating the gentle raising of his palm upwards. Like every other movement that each of them had made, it was careful, steady and repetitive. It was clear too. He was beckoning as if he wanted to be followed.

But I stayed put. All I could do was watch.

He held his position for a few lappings of the shoreline, then started moving out to sea. As he sunk from sight, the hand kept rocking gently up and down, as if trying to haul the air, as well as me, in his direction. Only once his arm was under to the shoulder did he turn square to the horizon once more, and take the last few steps under the ocean and away to wherever he had come from.

The sky had two different ends, now. Off to the east the black had washed into yellowy grey, with streaks of red lining the strips of low cloud. Only one of the stars above was still out – a thick, violent one that had been flashing overhead all night whenever the clouds weren't in its way. Night was still strong in the west, but it was going to lose out soon.

The surface of the ocean was gaining its colour. The patch where the moonlight had been, where the men's heads had finally sunk from view, had lost its importance. As the east end of Chapel Shores crept into view, the sounds of the sea seemed to grow dull in my ears. Any time now would come motors and people and daytime.

The tide was pulling. More of the sand out front was appearing, wet and dark, with each wave that drew away. Sunrise was seconds away. A seagull bleated hard, and I headed for home.

Chapter 6

'Doing the boot sale, in't I! You coming?'

Crap! I'd managed to get back into the house with the stealth of an elephant. I spotted the lights in the kitchen and slipped in quiet, but he saw me in seconds. When I got in, my dad wasn't only off the couch, but awake, showered, dressed and getting ready to go out.

No bollocking though – not a single word about it. I'm serious. Gaby's dad would kill her, ban her from having certain friends, stop her going out for months if she came in like an hour late. Me, though? I could come through the front door at six-thirty a.m. and he'd barely notice.

'Market is on, up in the Marshes,' he went on. 'They're gonna be busy today, too.' He'd stacked about forty pairs of trainers, in their boxes, against the back door. I yawned, deliberate and long, and made like I was going to speak.

'You might as well come, if you're awake, Luca.' Then he paused, like he'd only just realised. 'Why *are* you up, anyway?'

'Homework,' I told him. 'Got to measure the time the sun takes to rise.'

He laughed. 'And you're bothering? You can look that stuff up online, buddy!'

'I wanted to do it, anyway.'

'Okay. Fine. Don't tell your mum, though. She'll just think you're not sleeping again.'

'I won't tell her, don't worry.' She'd also probably have the brainpower to realise no teacher in Chapel Shores Community Comprehensive School would *ever* show enough imagination to suggest kids watch a sunrise for homework.

'So you coming, then?' he asked, again.

'No.'

'Aw, come on. I'll pay you *commish*.'

'You won't sell anything to give me commission from,' I said, immediately wishing I hadn't. He looked, just for a second, like his mind had stopped whirring, as if it needed to be reset. The usual look came back in no time, though – my mum called it his 'invincible smile'.

'Fine,' he said. 'I'll manage, anyway. You can still help me load up, though.'

And so I was roped in for this bit of his plan at least. I lifted his tatty 'Licence to Sell Goods at Chapel Marshes Open Air Trade-a-thon' off the top of the shoe stack, and started moving boxes to the boot of his Fiat van. Like all his other routines, I knew the pattern. I'd been through it before, too many times. On a sunny day there would be loads of people who'd take the short little drive off the motorway to the Marshes to pick and sneer at the stuff being sold by people like my dad, people from a town twenty years behind the rest of Wales. The only guys who'd shift anything, though, even in good weather, were the pros who came in from Cardiff, Swansea, Bridgend, Bristol and other places to sell the stuff that genuinely needed a bit of brains to choose. Mobile phones, computer games, clothes, sunglasses, onesies.

However, like all the other people we knew from Chapel Shores, my dad would go up there with no plan other than to make a fool of himself begging city slickers or motorway breakers to buy things they didn't want or need.

It was only me and Mum who could see it, too. So here he was, not put off in any way, and loading all the crap I'd seen him fail to sell in the past few weeks – into the boot of a van that got clamped by the local courts about once every six months when he forgot to pay one of its bills.

In it all went, carefully pushed in until there was no room for anything else. After the shoes – which, like my mum had said, were all the massive sizes that only NBA basketball players might want – came the rest: Diving flippers and water-proof wading trousers for river fishing. Plated guitar strings and ink cartridges that were the one colour which never ran out. Faulty selfie-sticks and fifty of something called a 'julienne' for peeling vegetables really thin. Plus there was the ten-year old metal detector he'd tried to make me sell Gaby last month.

'You got all that buried war stuff, plus silver from shipwrecks on the low-tide mark and lost coins in all the mud-flats! Someone will buy that thing off us in a week.' That week could easily turn to years knowing him though.

The swelling clouds I'd seen blocking out the stars overnight were spreading in thick. As he fired up the engine to reverse off the drive, the day was well on its way to being properly gloomy. It was definitely Chapel Marshes Trade-a-thon weather at its finest. He must be getting desperate.

I went upstairs, trying to make as little noise as possible, and tugged on my door to make sure the latch had clicked. Then I shut the curtains. The grey-white of daylight was only getting in through a little crack in the middle, and my head started swimming down into my pillow. Sometime between sleep and deep sleep I might have heard my mum getting up, but it didn't put me off being properly zonked out for the count.

I closed my eyes and saw the only thing that really had

my interest right then. There he was, in the blackness of my eyelids. That man, the figure. The first one up the beach and the last one off it. Their leader, their guide – or *spirit*, even – the one who'd lagged a minute behind the others before stopping and beckoning to me directly.

There was his hand, coaxing me off the rock, towards the shoreline – towards *his* shoreline. I saw the frozen stillness in his eyes, the way they slid, slowly, towards whatever they were looking at next. My duvet was getting warmer and the room felt darker. As my heart slowed and my breath smoothed, I saw his pupils fix on me. Still, the hand kept beckoning. The sounds of the sea were replaced by my own breathing. Air coming heavily through my nose, I fell further away from the world.

It was nearly tea-time when I woke up.

*   *   *

Still tired, for some reason, I headed downstairs, to where voices, loud and excited, were carrying themselves over thick layers of ska music. I opened the door to the living room, and it was like turning a volume meter. Up everything went, decibel after decibel, and the attention was shifted right onto *me*.

'Here he is!'

'Lukeeee!'

It was my mum's two best friends, Rachel and Amy – the pair who claimed to have set her up with my dad, and loved telling the story all the time, seventeen years later. 'Only thing we did right on that whole trip,' Rachel would joke. 'Apart from that, the *whole* of India was a *disaster* for all three of us!'

The rum bottle was out again, but with the lid on, still waiting for some love. A bottle of that creamy stuff they liked to drink had been opened in its place, though, and they each had a nearly empty glass.

Dad never seemed especially grateful for whatever favour they claimed to have done him in India, either, because he was almost always out when these two came around. I walked to the window and looked at the drive. The van was missing, sure enough.

'How's life then, Lukee?' Rachel asked, and I looked at her in a way that said, 'As if I'd tell *you*'.

'Ah, don't be rude to them now,' said my mum, semi-sternly, before turning to reply on my behalf. 'He's doing just fine, girls. Sleeping better than ever, and he's been to school every day this term.'

'Ooh, nice work,' said Amy, swigging from her glass of what looked like gone-off milk. I'd tried red wine, vodka and beer a few times with Gaby, but anything either of my parents or their mates liked to drink was forever going to seem rank to me, and I wouldn't even need a sip to know it.

'Want a slice of pizza?' Amy added, lifting the lid on their Domino's box.

'Nah, I'm alright.'

'Oh, come on! We're not going to have any more ourselves. You've got to eat! Growing boy an' all…'

I moved over to the couch and picked one of the cold slabs of pizza up.

'That's it! Get it down you. So how are you doing then, Lukee? Haven't seen you in a while?'

It's not as if they were going to get much anyway, but before I could even begin to formulate replies, my mum was answering for me:

'He's doing brilliant!' she said. 'GCSEs well under way. He's good at them all. Got Bs for effort in every subject.'

'Good…er… effort,' said Rachel, before all three started laughing. I looked across the room.

'And he's got a really nice "friend" now, too,' my mum went on. 'Gabri*elle*.'

My gaze flashed at her, and I tried to sharpen a blazing squint, but it was too late.

'Ooooh,' said Amy. 'Is she *fit*?'

My mum laughed. 'They're just friends. He wants it to be more, though.'

'No I *don't*!'

'It's cool, Luca,' said my mum, her hands making a calming gesture. 'That's perfectly normal, anyway. Yes, Aim, she is *gorgeous*. Gabrielle's a *stunner*. She's really, really bright too. She's the daughter of... You know, that family that owns the Carranero hotel. You know, the one with the gym and the spa – on the motorway junction... Out by the Marshes?'

'I thought that was owned by some businessman with those tall headquarters in Swansea?'

'Yes, same people! Her mum runs it all while he's away looking to their other places. Well, "runs" on the treadmills, anyway, while some manager looks after all the work for hardly any money. That's what I heard. Anyway, their daughter – she's the youngest, I think – goes to Chapel Shores Comp. Her and Luca are *always* down the beach. You should see her artwork, too! Collects all these bits of flotsam and jetsam off the beach, the girl does.'

Amy thought for a moment, and then asked, 'Hey isn't that the girl who got...'

Immediately Rachel elbowed her, and hard. Leaning back in the sofa, I kept my head still but turned my eyes to look at the pair of them. Go on, Amy, I thought – the girl who got *what*?

'Shut up,' whispered Rachel, about twenty decibels loud enough for me to hear.

'Why?' said Amy. 'It's true though, isn't it? Come on. As if a family like that can be allowed a secret. Didn't they take her...'

Rachel hit her again.

'OUCH!' laughed Amy. 'He'll probably know all about it anyway. It was her, wasn't it! They thought she was...' and then, rolling her eyes, Amy spun her index finder around her temple in a circle, as if to say *mental*.

Before I could do or say anything, though, my mum claimed the conversation back.

'Dunno what you two are bitching about,' she said. 'Gabrielle is lovely. Like I said, she's gifted. Makes these little sculptures and collages with the stuff her and Lukee find on the beaches. Really, really talented young lady.'

Amy and Rachel both took another drink, while I went for a second slice of pizza because there was nowhere else to go. Amy looked like she was hiding a laugh.

Then my mum put her hand sideways across her face, palm facing out as if that would suddenly stop me hearing, and whispered loudly to them: *'She's probably not that interested back, but he can try, can't he?'*

Rachel and Amy both looked at me with this horrid mixture of both pride and pity. They both didn't have kids themselves and changed boyfriends three times a year. Did I really need to be taking any advice from a pair of party girls my mother's age?

It would come, though, anyway. You could be sure of that.

'Buy her a present, Luca,' said Amy before Rachel blasted in and shut her up for me:

'Oi, how's he gonna buy a *present* for the girl whose folks own Carraneros?'

'Dunno. Maybe he could score her some Prozac,' Amy giggled, before Rachel hit her again, the hardest yet. 'OW! Leave it out!'

'You are a nasty piece of work,' Rachel said, smiling.

My mum stood up and walked to the freezer for more ice.

'Just keep going the way you are, Luca,' she said. 'They'll be falling for you all over the place. Don't you worry.'

The other two laughed.

'And anyway, you've got bigger, more important stuff to sort out first. He's got to get to school on time tomorrow.' She turned to both her friends and raised her eyebrows. 'No more late marks for the rest of the spring is our target, isn't it? They phoned on Tuesday.'

'Who was that then?' asked Rachel.

'Kleener,' said my mum.

'No way! He was there when we went! He must be *ancient* by now! Luca? Is he… ancient?'

'Dunno,' I said.

'He was younger than we thought,' said my mum.

'Now *he* was fit,' said Amy. 'Well, in a sort of… teacher way, at least.'

They laughed again, and my mum dropped more ice into their drinks.

'He's gonna be fine for being on time, as long as he keeps sleeping well,' she said, her tone a little more serious again.

'Give him a glass of Baileys then' said Amy. 'That'll knock him out!'

'And it will impress GABRIELLE,' added Rachel.

She leaned over the coffee table and chinked her glass against Amy's, which had been set down while Amy and my Mum flicked through a stack of CDs.

'Oh my GOD!' shouted Amy, arriving on one she liked the look of. 'You've got *this*! The Bodysnatchers! This needs to be on, *now*, and LOUD!'

Amy choosing music and trying to make my mum and Rachel dance with her in my living room meant things could only get worse from here. I'd seen this before enough times and it wasn't going to be my idea of how to spend the next hour. I had two options to distract myself. Take another slice of pizza, or leave the room. I went for both.

The ska shifted into some sort of hideous electronica as darkness fell outside and the evening grew cold. So I pulled out my headphones and went chasing after my own version of the world. Sitting back on my bed, I thumbed my iTunes looking for the release. Bunny Wailer was loaded and paused, ready for tomorrow, just where I needed him. Whatever went on downstairs, he'd get me through that gate okay in the morning. Storing *Cool Runnings* and Toots's *45-56* as my backups, I flicked back through my other favourites, slipped the repeat mode on and went for my evening track instead. Next album along. Bunny again. Song number five: *Dreamland*. In kicked the off-beat and my little Luca head succumbed straight away to the wiggling, whistling patterns of soothing noise. Out went the anger, before it even knew it was there.

I lay back and looked at the ceiling. My chest sunk back, and my shoulders loosened. Awake less than two hours today, but that would do. There was a whole night to catch up on anyway. I closed my eyes, and rolled them in the top of my head, as the music made its way through the gap between my ears and met somewhere in the middle. Where it did, there was this warming, tingling buzz that began to trickle down my spine until it made its way out to my fingers and toes. I slipped and floated around in Bunny's harmonies as his voice told me, and all the millions like me who were out there somewhere, about that place in his head, where food came from the trees and water was warm and life was easy and where nobody ever, ever died.

And d'you know what? As long as I kept that message on repeat... As long as it was on loud enough and was all my ears could pick up… then… then that place of his existed. Who needed to worry about how to go there one day? *I* was there *right now*, and could stay as long as I wanted.

Which was, of course, forever.

Chapter 7

Forever never comes, moans some ancient singer in the title and chorus of one of my mum's favourite songs – unless, of course, you go to Chapel Shores Comp and your alarm clock marks Mondays.

Not even Toots can save you from those facts, but with my little bit of musical assistance I was up and out and keen to avoid the Kleen. Dad had come back some time after I turned in for the night. He'd been to the pub with Jeff, the same idiot who'd been trying to tune him to part with some cash in a jewellery deal. He'd fallen asleep on the couch again, and under orders from my mum was downing his breakfast of Sugar Puffs and offering me a lift.

During the tiny distance to the school entrance, now made even quicker by Dad's Fiat-powered van, I was desperately trying to adjust my timings on the Bunny song so that I could still pass the gates as he sung the 'dawning' line like always. Dad, meanwhile, was trying to tune me into coming to the market with him when they went, later in the week.

'Jeff's offering to take us both Thursday. I reckon it would be good for you, Luca. There's so much money in jewels. Having experience from such a young age could set you up better than any of those exams they're gonna put you in for.'

'Mum won't go for it,' I was saying, thinking A) that was true, she wouldn't; and B) even though I'd love an excuse to miss school, it was stupid beyond belief to think that knowing your way to a jewellery market with Jeff Rafferty would stand someone in better stead than passing your GCSEs.

'She'll go for it,' said Dad. 'She worries about you. If she thinks you're into something she'll support you.'

Into something? No she wouldn't.

'She'd be happy to think we were one day gonna have a family business,' my dad added.

'You really believe that?'

'Yeah. Why? Don't you?'

I couldn't be bothered to tell him. Even though I found the idea of what to do when I grew up terrifying – and it could easily get me into one of my episodes – the one thing I *didn't* want was join him in the world of loser, small-time conmen and failed Ebay traders. Even if him and his mates had the biggest diamond in the universe, they'd still manage to screw it up. We'd been reading this book in English about a pearl diver who did that – found the most beautiful pearl ever made – but he didn't have enough game to do anything with it and just ended up a sitting duck for all the clever people and the powerful types who came knocking on his door. It was by the same guy who wrote *Of Mice and Men*, so you can imagine what kind of ending that one had.

And anyway. We weren't talking perfect pearls here either, were we. I wondered if they sold oversized Reeboks at Jeff's favourite jewel mart.

'Family business,' my dad repeated. 'If I can turn around two grand on buying cheap gold, it'll more than double. The kind of money that deal could bring in would mean focussing on only the one line of trade, then. No more Chapel Marshes or eBay. We could wholesale! You'd have a job to go into then, however you do in school.'

Saved by the bell – or the threat of it, at least. I pointed the time to him and jumped out of the car. I'd multi tasked good, too – listening to Dad and DJing at the same time. The Bunny track was only eight seconds out, and I could slow for the right moment and still make Reg on time.

The same supply teacher was still babysitting our form, so I hid one earphone and left Bunny to sing in my other ear while she tried to explain to us about a careers fair that was coming to Chapel Shores soon. Then she told us that, because there would be 'experts' there that could go over all the important stuff on jobs and college options, our actual careers *lesson* was going to turn into PSE, again. Great. Two consecutive Mondays of it. Normally they went with every other week for both careers and PSE, but maybe Miss preferred trying to make Joseph Poundes do worksheets on where cocoa came from than forcing us to think about what we had to do next year once our exams were either passed or failed. Actually, thinking about it, I didn't blame her.

Gaby was in, too, so this was like a full blown repeat of everything that had happened last week. She frowned at me for a second then stuck her head into the worksheet. Poundes came late, got sent to the *back*, which was exactly where he'd want to sit anyway, and just spent the whole time throwing broken bits of a novelty rubber at me or anyone else who didn't deserve it. A slow hour passed of feeling like crap, and doing nothing with any point to it – just how we'd all like to start a week in school, eh?

But I'd ignored Gaby correctly this time. That was the important bit.

The low mood thing still hung around me most of the morning, though. The trials of last week were there, lurking in the background the whole time, and I spent the rest of the morning thinking about why Gaby didn't want to be seen being friendly in school, and about what my mum and her mates had been saying when they were ribbing me about this last night.

She's probably not that interested back, but he can try, can't he?

'Try what?' I wanted to ask. It wasn't like that... Honestly. It wasn't.

*   *   *

To say Gaby could be a bit 'complicated' in school was an understatement. She'd *tell* you all the time about how being popular and having loads of friends and influence wasn't important to her. She'd use words that sounded stolen from teachers like 'irrelevant'. 'Whether people like you is *irrelevant*,' she'd say.

But what she said, and what she did... were often not the same thing.

One kid from my Reg group who I was sort of friendly with, Jaime King, had given me his big theories on her once, after he'd tried to go out with her for about a week. I remembered getting really pissed off with him for telling me and not really wanting to sit near him in Reg after that. Couldn't show it, though. He didn't really know that me and her were friends.

'That girl,' Jaime had told me, 'chooses friendship groups and allies so carefully you'd think she could go into *business*.'

Maybe he'd said it because we'd just started a Business Studies course, or maybe he understood the deal better than me. Who knows. Two weeks later we were learning about how companies get investors to put different amounts of money in by giving them packages with different names – creating different 'tiers' of contributor, according to Ms Vieira, our tutor.

'Look at this example,' she then said. 'You can buy gold, silver and bronze memberships to a banking scheme. What's the *implication* of this?'

As some other kid answered, Jaime had whispered in my ear 'Just like the whole *Gabo*, *Gaby* and *Gabe* thing, really, int it? That's basically gold, silver and bronze, too.'

I'd decided he was just bitter because he'd probably tried too hard and she'd dumped him. I knew the other version of the story too, and it went that he'd put 'pressure' on her, if you get what I mean. 'Pressure' and Gaby would *not* go together well.

Still, though, he'd left me thinking. It was clever how quickly she could work into someone's favour if she wanted, and yet not really get close enough to let them down or to cross anyone. Apart from me obviously, who she crossed any time she liked, but that's because she knew I'd never ditch her.

I thought about the handful of times I'd been in lessons with Gaby other than PSE – not counting Art where she worked really, really hard. Jaime was right when he said in class she'd line up with the most successful people; kids either too nice or too sure of themselves to bother having a problem with it. Since Gaby was super sharp it would normally work both ways anyway.

'What was that word from biology?' Jaime had said. 'A *symbiotic relationship*. Yeah, that's it. Something that suits both parties.'

In breaks, meanwhile, she'd try really hard to make it look as if she liked being by herself. Really, though, she spent her time outside of lessons with a couple of really gnarly girls who were about thirty years old already in the way they behaved. Whenever I saw them together they reminded me of Rachel and Amy. Which was why not having so much to do with Gaby during the 'working day' wasn't that much of a bother to me, most of the time.

And then the school day would end. The bit she called the 'fake' half of the day, or 'our jobs' – she still called it that despite not being in a quarter of the time – would be done, and she'd switch off. That was when she became the amazingly interesting, kind person with big ideas and interests and plans to work out what was wrong with the world and, if she couldn't do anything about it, at least make everything better by laughing.

Very occasionally, there was a glimpse of that warm and nice Gaby during the school day, but it was rare. Usually it would be something indirect, just like what happened in BTEC Science later that Monday, when a revolving seating plan put me right next to one of those thirty-type girls from my year that knew the daytime version of Gaby.

Ella Bowen, rapping her long, light green fingernails on the desk and swishing her hair that was blonde as a light bulb, started ribbing me right away about what had happened in PSE last week. As you can imagine, that wasn't ideal. Just as I could feel my chest going to tighten, though, she seemed to relax a bit.

'It was kind of funny anyway,' Ella said, raising her eyelashes like a stage curtain. 'Gabe (because Ella got to use that *Gold*-friendship name) found it sweet.'

'Really?'

'Yeah, she told me. Said you could fight Joe Poundes for her too.'

I sighed. Very funny, Ella.

'Sorry. Nah, she didn't really say that last bit. She did think it was sweet, though. She's in Product Design now. Bet she'll laugh when she knows we're sat together.'

Ella whipped out an iPhone in some cheesy white, diamante cover and her fingernails skidded across the keypad to unlock it.

'Sittin' by your nite in shining armour in BTEC,' ran the message.

Great. Now I was done for.

Ella slid the phone back under her handbag and we both pretended to concentrate on the PowerPoint. Then her phone buzzed with a reply, and she waited for a chance to grab it when no one was looking.

'Reply from Gabe: "AW. He's nice INT he. Tell him im going bunkers after we leave the office?"'

Ella showed me the message. 'Mean anything to you?'

'Er, yeah. Er, thanks.'

'You're welcome, LL Cool J.'

I loved getting people wrong. Ella was nothing like Amy or Rachel. We whizzed through our worksheet after that, and got told we could sit together again in lessons.

And anyway, my head was on its way to the beach already. I had something to speed the day up, something to look forward to.

'Why don't you come as well?' I asked Ella.

'Nah. Not my thing,' she said. 'Plus, I have to go to real work. Glass collecting in the pub tonight. Not allowed to pull a pint, see. Under eighteen, so Dad's got me off the books. Child labour, with a load of blokes perving on me and pretending to be kind. Gotta love it, eh?'

Chapter 8

'How are we *doing,* Luca Lincoln-James?'

'Fine.'

Dr Wentloog always talks about *we*. He was super nice when he interrupted me just then, which makes me super sure he's up to something.

Mind you, though; apparently he was impressed by how into this stuff I was getting yesterday and today. The 'diary'. He thinks he'll get to see it one day soon, so he can bust open my case and stick me in one of his books or talk to loads of Americans in posh clothes about me.

Well, I reckon good luck to him. I've started his version now, too. In the little book he gave me. It's so clean you'd laugh at it – and then puke, then probably rip it up and set fire to it. Or just throw it aside bored. I almost did that about every ten minutes while I was doing the first bit, but then I kept reminding myself how important it was to make sure he had something to look at. It's the deal he made for me – in order to stand any chance of being left alone before I'm twenty-one.

Oh – and he also told me this morning that I'm *not* going to have to go to the police station when I leave, either. See! *They* don't think there's a problem, and the cops haven't heard *any* other version of the story apart from what they think they saw.

Anyway – what *I* saw is the bit that matters. Hopefully you can use that as proof I'm not making any of this crap up. Why would I?

*   *   *

It was bright and windy down at Bunkers Beach. The sea was acting like a giant fridge and as I ran across the gravel and broken tarmac of the carpark I could feel the cold cranking up. Patches of sand were swirling in the breeze, and there was the smell of something really thick and man-made from the industrial estate behind the far end of the beach. A patch of reddish brown water was drifting across too, where that little stream from the Marshes ran out to sea.

That was the bit of the beach we had all been told, since we were old enough to speak, to stay away from. So noawadays, of course, it was the bit of beach me and Gaby used to make a point of going to.

I reached the furthest bunker before she did, and had a few minutes to worry if she was going to stand me up. I had a sudden moment of panic in which I imagined Ella Bowen and a load of others, maybe even Poundes himself, stepping out from behind one of the concrete lumps and taking a photo of me looking all lonely and pathetic then sharing it everywhere. Paranoia can do funny things to you. It shouldn't be ignored, either – it keeps you safe.

She showed, though. Like I kind of knew she would.

'Alright Lukee?' she laughed. 'Tough day at the office?'

'Better than it could have been,' I said.

'Ah, yeah. Heard you sat by Ella in BTEC. She's taken a liking to you already. And why shouldn't she.'

'It that a trick question?'

Gaby laughed.

'She's got you as "Gabe", too,' I said. 'Saw it on her phone. What did she do to earn that one?'

'Ha! See, there are a few of them out there. I dunno. It's not like something *I* decide.'

'It isn't?'

'No. It's got to fall naturally, you know what I mean. Like *Tu* and *Vous*...'

'...Or *Ti* and *Chi*.' I finished her sentence.

'Yeah. It's a kind of organic thing, right?'

'Organic?'

'Yeah.'

'I thought that meant food that my mum always wants to buy,' I said, stopping short of adding, 'but my dad won't let us coz it's expensive.'

'Same thing,' she said. 'It means not forced. Something that's allowed to happen the way it wants to.'

'*That's* what organic food means?' I had this vision of a chicken being allowed to walk onto your plate and chopping its own head off.

'Kind of,' she said. 'Anyway, tell your mum to come for dinner at my place. My mum *loves* organic! D'you reckon they'd get on?'

I thought about the way I'd heard my mum, Rachel and Amy speak yesterday, and wondered if Gaby's mum was on a treadmill right now.

'So I could just start calling you "Gabe", then, and that would be organic?' I asked.

'Er, maybe.'

'Okay then, *Gabe*.'

Her face tightened and she stared right at me. Then she smiled and said, 'Didn't feel natural, though, did it.'

She was right. It didn't.

'Maybe I'd get used to it,' I said.

'Yeah, but then that would be forced. It wouldn't be *organic* anymore,' she replied.

'Gaby, d'you believe in ghosts?' I asked her.

'Of course,' she said. 'Why d'you ask?'

'Dunno.'

'Er, okay. Bit of a random question, mind.'

'Yeah. Sorry. It's just…'

'Just what?'

'Never mind.'

*   *   *

We set out walking west, with the tide pretty much high. I tried to work out where the watermark would be right now on the beach near my house compared to where it had been when I saw them the other night. Then I counted the hours ahead, trying to work out when this stage of tide would next occur during darkness, before Gaby distracted me with a few finds.

'A doll's arm! Ew! Creepy as! I'm keeping this. And d'you know what all these little blue, plastic sticks are from?'

'No.'

'Cotton buds,' she said. 'The cotton rots off then the stick washes ashore. These are probably from ships. Imagine that? Sailors on those minging oil tankers that pass towards the Marshes, rubbing these things around their ears!' She waved one in my direction, like a toy sword.

Gaby still had her schoolbag on her shoulders, and lifted it off. That was part of her non-gender stereotype thing – she wore a backpack with both straps, whereas most of the girls used satchels or handbags which never had room for anything big, and it meant they had to keep going to their lockers between every lesson.

She dropped it to the sand and started fumbling around inside her Art stuff. She had a mini plastic, see-through sack in there for bits she collected off the beach, and then her sketchbooks.

'Are you looking for something in particular?' I asked her.

'Just somewhere to put more stuff,' she said, before reminding me of an important fact for about the millionth time: 'Luca, you know I don't use beach stuff for my GCSE?' She tapped her sketchbook.

'You should, though,' I said. She laughed.

'What would *you* know? You've never seen inside my sketchbook, anyway. You only take Art because you had to have ten separate subjects anyway.'

'So.'

'So, how's *your* artwork coming?'

'It's not,' I told her.

'Well it *should*,' she laughed.

'Maybe I'll find something today.'

'If you do, you can give it to me,' and she punched me gently in the ribs, zipped up her bag and moved on, adding, 'Coz Rogoff isn't gonna let *you* sculpt anything and you know it.'

There was driftwood in the shore, and we'd come a good way west of the last bunker, now. The runoff from that feeble little stream that came out of the Marshes was dyeing the ocean the colour of black tea. This was the best place for finding stuff, and before long we had a decent haul of items to wonder over.

I held up the plastic casing from a shotgun cartridge, while Gaby held a toilet seat around her head like a halo.

'What d'you reckon then, Luca? Someone been shot while on the bog?'

'Yeah, in a ship, then all evidence thrown overboard.'

'Nah. That could only happen on a cruise liner. They never pass here. On a cargo ship or a tanker they'd gut you instead of shooting you. Maybe this one happened on a pleasure boat. You know, like a little speedboat from some rich dude in Cardiff or Swansea? Maybe a posh sailing boat. You've seen *them* go by, haven't you?'

'On their way somewhere else, yeah. And you think they're full of people murdering each other as they go to the loo?' I said.

'Ew! I bet there's murder on those kinds of ships all the time,' she grinned. 'There was one in the papers a year back. Hands washed up on the beach, round here somewhere. No rings though, so they're probably in the shoreline somewhere – with the *diamonds* still in 'em!'

She kicked a load of litter and seaweed.

There were bails of rope and fishing lines strewn across the shoreline, and heaps of plastic bottles. In between it all, me and Gaby foraged about for anything else interesting.

She came up a minute later with a bar of old metal.

'Look at this one,' she said. 'The bottom end is probably copper!'

It was about a foot long, and seemed to change colour exactly half way down. As she held it up, I saw that one half was really smooth and almost shiny. The other half, though, was so rusty it almost looked alive. Gaby was holding the smooth end, and waving the whole bar around like a mini sword or club.

'Woah,' she said, stopping it near her face and looking closer at the rusty end.

The bit she was holding had squared edges, still hard enough to make a little dent in her left palm when she moved it to her right. There were beautiful turquoise streaks of what looked like lime-scale running along the flat surfaces of the end she was using as a handle. But the other half had decayed underwater so badly it had swollen into lumps of spongy brown mushrooms, like coral heads of crazy sea-salt rust. That end looked like the stuff you saw in those deep-sea pictures of rotting metal ships. The way the top half of the pole was so different from the second half made it look like some stick of toxic candy floss.

Gaby wielded it gently through the air again.

'Maybe it was a lightsaber,' she suggested, swinging it around her head like the *Star Wars* Kid. 'The copper would carry the charge. The rotten end must have been the handle. So I'm probably holding it back-to-front. Reckon it was a Dark Side one? Can't imagine this thing shining a blue beam.'

I held my hand out. 'Let's have a look?'

She passed it to me, and I realised how heavy it was. Must have been in the sea for decades to get so rusted at that one end.

'Seriously,' I asked, 'what was this thing?'

'I honestly don't know,' she said. 'And we'll never, ever find out either. I could give it to one of the plumbers who work for my dad but they'd just trade it in. They weigh-up used copper, see. Dunno what the other metal would have been. Can't be aluminium.'

'Maybe this was a weapon?' I suggested.

'Nah. I reckon something from a ship's weather vane. Gonna be years old, mind. Good find, eh? Want to borrow it for your Art project?'

'Can I?'

'No!' Gaby laughed and yanked the bar away again, before holding it out to me and saying, 'Unless you ask real nice,' she added a wink.

'Whatever.'

'Ah, don't be like that, Lukee! You know I'll help if you need it.'

'While we're in class?'

'Don't push that Lukee luck.'

She turned and trotted back along the shoreline, heading west again, away from town, and I followed just behind.

'Low tide is much better, though, isn't it?' she said.

'Yeah,' I agreed.

'That's when we'd have the best chance of finding stuff from the legendary shipwrecks.'

Gaby liked to go on about these, and I was never sure which ones were true.

'Must have been such a different place back then,' I said.

'When?'

'You know, like before when the Shores was full of people.'

'It was a landing beach then,' she said. 'Just pirates, wreckers. And Vikings.'

'Wouldn't they all have been just a *little* bit apart in history?' I pointed out. 'Vikings and pirates?'

She play-hit me with the rusted bar, before stopping and opening her backpack to store it away. '*Obviously*. But they all came here once. There must have been Viking stuff and coins from galleons and all sorts on these beaches back before the army moved in. The smugglers probably kept going right up until they filled this place with tanks.'

Our history teachers always loved the fact that both Chapel Shores and Chapel Marshes had been used for war training. The Marshes were filled with irrigation canals that were once fake trenches for soldiers to practice in during World War One. The military town that had sprung up from those days was why this beach then got used to rehearse for D-Day. Teachers were just about the only ones who cared about that today, though. It only concerned me and Gaby because it meant the shoreline was always washing up little bits of metal from guns or tanks.

'If people think it's cool finding stuff from the forties,' said Gaby, 'they should remember that putting all those boats and armoured vehicles on the sand probably trashed all the stuff from the more exciting times.'

'What about the unexploded bombs?' I reminded her.

'Myths.'

'Just like the famous wrecks you go on about then.'

'Not all of them,' she said. 'The one my great-granddad was on was real.'

'Eh? Your great-granddad?'

'Yeah! Haven't I told you that before?'

'No.'

'He was a trader and sailor of some kind, too.'

'You what? Here?'

'Yeah. Where else? You don't believe me, do you.'

'Well, I haven't got a reason not to,' I said. 'But you've never mentioned it before.'

'You've never asked before.'

Why would I go around asking her if there was some remote chance she had an ancient relative on one of these old shipwrecks she used to go on about?

'You normally act all tired and over it when I talk about shipwrecks,' she said. 'Why the difference now? It's as if you've suddenly decided to be into it?'

Yeah, I thought, why *is* that? Was I going to fess up, here and now, to the fact I'd recently seen some out-of-this world stuff that had got me thinking about all this? Was I going to talk to *Gaby*, the girl who could make me almost flip out in school like only a few days before she might invite me to come here with her and then be all nice?

'Er... I... well, no reason,' I said. 'Does it seem that way? As if I'm suddenly interested?'

'Hmm, maybe not,' she said. 'Okay. Anyway, d'you wanna know?'

'Of course.'

'Well, I'm not making anything up. That's exactly what he was. Gianni Carranero. My great, great, great-grandfather. He moved coal and other stuff back and forth to America like more than a hundred years ago, from here – when Chapel Shores was just a dock. My dad's got some leather-bound family history thing that my grandpa had made and it's got all about those days in there. No photos of him. Well, one, but it's crap. So I've drawn it instead.'

'But he was on a wreck?'

'Yeah!'

'As in a shipwreck?'

'Yeah.'

'And here? Out *there*?' I pointed out to sea.

'Yeah!'

There was one big question I needed to know right now. But was I showing too much interest, like she said?

'His boat sunk within sight of Chapel Shores,' said Gaby. 'There are old logs about it.'

'Was he okay?' I asked.

'No.'

'Oh.' I tried to hide the leap my heart and lungs had just made inside my ribs.

'He died,' said Gaby. 'Lost at sea. Never found. My dad reckons he was involved in some dodgy smuggler business too, though, so he might have just pulled a fast one. Hey, maybe he's out there now! He'd be like a hundred and twenty or something. Bet he'd have rings on *his* fingers.'

I laughed and bent down as if to look at the shoreline with my hand. 'They'd have fallen off by now, when he rotted.' I tried to recall the nineteen pairs of hands I'd seen traipsing up the eastern shores, and whether they had any rings or jewels on them.

'Ew! Thanks for that, LLJ!'

'But you're not joking?'

'No. I'm dead serious. Honest. Ha. Get it? *Dead* serious?'

'Good one.' I pushed to hear it again, for sure: 'So you had a great-granddad who died in a boat tragedy out here?

And I'm only hearing about it now?'

'Like I said, why would you care?'

'What was its name?' I said, not worrying anymore about seeming too keen. 'The ship.'

'The *Pictor*,' she said, straight away, no time needed to think.

'I've never heard of it.'

'Just one of hundreds,' she said.

'What were they all wearing?'

She gave me a look as if I had three heads or something. 'Wearing? What kind of a question is that?'

'Er... Sorry. Dunno what...'

'LLJ, you're so weird you don't even know you're weird,' she laughed. 'I love it.'

'Sorry.'

'Nah, don't be.'

'I just thought... you know...'

She didn't know.

Neither did I.

I wanted really badly to say something right now, anything, to tell her about what I'd seen the other night. But, each time I thought seriously about it, that hot feeling would hit the sides of my head and my chest would squeeze again, just like when Poundes tripped me.

Maybe I should have, though. I can't even imagine where we'd be right now if I had. Anyway, no point thinking about that. It's too late, isn't it?

'Hey, I'll tell you what, Luca,' said Gaby, moving us on and closing that tiny window once and for all. 'Thing is, we don't know much about Gigi Carranero and how it happened. It's a fun story though, isn't it! The one mystery in my family history. Everyone has to have a question hanging over them like that.'

'Yeah.'

'Anyway. What about *your* great-granddads? You probably had eight, just like everyone else.'

'Four,' I corrected her.

'Same difference. Four. Howabout yours, anyway? They ever got up to anything dodgy?'

'Er, on my dad's side probably. They were all posh until he let the whole thing crumble,' I said. Then, feeling bad for drawing attention to it, I apologised again: 'Sorry. I shouldn't mug him off to someone like you in that way.'

'Why not?'

'Well, he does his best,' I lied.

'*I* like him,' she said. 'He's on the edge. It would have taken guts to just blow off what your family expected from you. He did that, didn't he?'

'What, dropping out of college and running away to India with a load of freaks?'

She rolled her eyes. 'My god, man! Don't you realise how cool that is? Hippy parents must be so awesome. I'd *love* parents like that. Just give him a break!'

'Whatever.'

We were slowly strolling back eastwards now, and it had been a little while since either of us looked at the shoreline. With the wind behind us, it wasn't long before we reached the bunkers again. She stopped and climbed up onto the one we usually chose. Her handprint, scratched by the stone, was still on the top of it, just starting to fade in the salt air. She placed her palm down and looked up at me.

I watched her short, cropped hair trying to blow into her eyes but not quite having the length. I climbed up after her and she offered another gentle punch at my left arm. Wriggling her backpack off clumsily, she put it down firmly between us.

'Hey,' she said. 'Luca… Wanna get closer?'

'Sorry? What?'

'You heard.'

'Er, not sure. What d'you mean?'

'Here. Maybe I will let you look in my sketchbook,' she said, fluttering her eyelids. 'Just once. If you want, of course?'

'Why would you do that?'

'Come on,' she said, shuffling over to me. 'This is an offer you can't refuse.'

'I can look in Art,' I said, trying to be funny but failing. 'Mrs Rogoff keeps good work in a booklet to share with us re-treads for copying. Bet you're in there plenty of times.'

'She won't have this though,' Gaby said, leaning back away and putting her hands on her backpack.

She opened it up and pulled out a heavy book which she'd loosely covered in thick, red wallpaper. It was a different one from the Chapel Shores Comp drawing pad she used for GCSE, and I could see from how the sides of some of the pages were ragged and some really clean that is was almost exactly half-used.

'This is my private sketchbook,' she said, and began flicking through it. 'You probably are gonna be in *Gabe* territory once you see this. I've shown it to no one. Ever.'

She settled on a page, which she looked at hard for a moment before making her mind up to go ahead.

'Here you go,' she said. 'The only picture of Gianni Carranero doing what he did best. In his smuggling gear, about to set to sea. I've imagined it, so that's how he *has* to look from now on.'

She flipped the book round to show me, and the air dropped out of my lungs.

Worse still, she picked up on it straight away.

'I knew it!' she said. 'Something's got you, hasn't it!'

I tried to hold my cool, as three fast heartbeats seemed to pump air out of my mouth and ears.

'That's awe… some,' I said, slowing my voice and trying to make it look like the actual artwork was what had spiked my interest, rather than her choice of what to draw. Don't get me wrong, either – her style was pretty good. She'd sort of scraped against the page with some kind of pastel, knocking these straight, up-and-down strokes into the form of a person – a figure – before shading it with what looked like a grey water colour or acrylic. There were traces of her thumb print left where she'd smeared tone into his face. Or was it shadow?

It was how similar he looked, though, growing on me one second at a time, that was holding my next breath out there somewhere across the cold bunkers.

His hat was nearly exactly the same, except it was tipped towards the back of his head. He had a stupid musket of some kind in his hand. Or was it some other sort of weapon? The way Gaby had deliberately blurred it all – besides being super-clever – kind of left you to make up your own mind. I wondered for a second if the thing he was holding was the useless, half-iron, half-copper bar in her bag. There were so many similarities. *Too* many similarities. The shape of his stride. The length and shape of his hair. The heavy look as the pastel ran off him with the weight of nightime water.

'You should show this to your folks,' I said to Gaby, as I carried on staring.

'Why?' she asked.

'Dunno. He's kind of… *real*, when you look at this, in't he…'

She didn't say anything, but just watched me – as I watched the pastel Gianni, wondering what he'd look like wading up out of the deep under a half moonlit night.

He had the jacket too, and the light tunic- or shirt-type thing on underneath. She'd given him trousers that went all the way to his ankles and over his feet. That bit wasn't right.

But the way they were baggy, and the way the shaky charcoal made it look like he was moving… It was still too similar. Too much of a coincidence. His face she'd pretty much left without any smears or blurs, and it had exactly the blank expression. And the eyes? They were the spookiest bit.

'You've left them empty?' I said, pointing without touching. 'No pupils or irises?'

'Yeah. Cool, innit. His photo – the only one my dad has – it makes his eyes look super white, like there's nothing in them. D'you like it?'

I looked for words, but everything I thought of saying seemed like the wrong decision.

'I know him,' she said. 'Well, I *feel* like I do anyway. This is him from now on. I mean it. Maybe I'll find out more about the guy one day. Maybe I should write his book. Or maybe you can. I'll be the illustrator. How d'you like that idea?'

'Er, why not,' I said. It was getting hard to match her enthusiasm while my head was reeling like this.

'What's up with you *now*?' Gaby asked. 'You seen a ghost or something?'

I laughed, softly and forced.

She fake thumped me on the arm again.

'That's it! I knew you were a creep,' she laughed. 'Ella reckons you're gonna try it on with me one day, but I know your real secret. You were just waiting till I'd opened up to you, got my sketchbook out, like. And now you've seen my private doodles you're gonna nick 'em and leave me on the beach all mugged and half dead.'

'Yeah. You've got me,' I said, voice as flat as I could make it.

'Well I'd smash you first, anyway.'

She went to turn the page of her book, and suddenly I wanted to do anything to prevent it.

'Hey. Don't do that,' I said. 'It's fine. Look, it's an awesome pic, but you don't need to start showing me more. I mean it. Keep them to yourself.'

She looked at me hard, and squinted, like she didn't quite trust what I was saying.

'Okay. Fine. If you want,' she said. 'But it wouldn't matter. I left the next page blank, anyway. That's what I was gonna show you. It's blank in case anything else needs to go there in an emergency.'

'We should be getting back,' I said. 'I'm hungry.'

'If you insist.'

'Come on.' I jumped off the bunker and onto the sand below.

Gaby put her sketchbook away, and pulled out the rusted bar again. 'I'll keep this out on the way back,' she said.

'Whatever.'

'Protection,' she said. Then, just as I was about to take offence, added, 'For both of us. I heard some of the druggies they kicked out of the sixth form last month were coming up here tonight. Ella told me coz they invited her.'

'She's working tonight,' I said.

'Ooh look at you suddenly her best friend.'

I scowled at Gaby, and she flexed the bar at me.

'Bet you two were talking about me, weren't you.'

'Not much,' I said.

'Bet you were, though.'

'Only a little.'

'Go on, then. What did she say?'

'Nothing serious.'

'Bull. Bet you did. Bet you were both having a full-on gossip about me.'

My breath jumped off another heartbeat, and I blurted, 'Only one thing,' and as soon as it was out, I caught this hot rush of regret.

'What? I knew it. Come on, tell me.'

'Well, she mentioned your art, and it was clear she didn't know you did driftwood and that you collected stuff from the beaches. Why doesn't she know? If she's like your best mate?'

'Coz I don't use that stuff in school,' Gaby said, again, not needing a moment to think. 'You *know* that!'

'Yeah. But not telling a friend about it?'

'Why should I?'

'I dunno. Seems a pretty big part of you, to me.'

'Pretty big part of *this* me,' Gaby said, stopping in her tracks and tapping her head with the bar.

'Yeah, I know you say that. But I don't get it.'

'You don't have to,' she said. 'I've said it before. There's real life and there's fake life. School and Art classes are fake life. Why would I want to waste real stuff on my fake life?'

'How do I know *this* is your real life then?' I asked.

'You don't. But it has to be, for you, doesn't it? It's the bit where you exist.'

'That's harsh, Gaby.'

'No it's not. It's beautiful.'

I didn't say anything more. The carpark was a few steps away now.

'Plus,' she added. 'I'm gonna make money from my beach art. You watch. Don't want Mrs Rogoff or anyone else to have a legal share in it, do I! You can have a cut, though, if you stay my friend long enough.'

She was slipping the bar away into her backpack again.

'Just you watch,' she said. 'It'll all be worth a fortune one day. I promise you it will.'

'You sound like my dad,' I said.

Chapter 9

I suppose (and this is *not* something to admit to Dr Wentloog, ever) that being harsh on my dad is something I started doing for survival.

That might sound a bit funny, but it's the truth. There you have it. Being as honest as I can, there. I basically got so much crap from other kids about him, that eventually I realised it was better to just take control of the whole situation, and my way of doing that was by making sure no one could slag him off more than I did.

Didn't really work though, of course. I just ended up nearly in fights, or getting put down by kids so badly that I wanted to simply stop *being* anyone, anywhere, ever. So then I became his main defender. Then I went back to being his worst critic, until one day this middle ground kind of found me.

He's never made it any easier for me, either.

What happened pretty soon after I started ragging on him myself to other kids was that I'd feel really bad about it. I used to call him a loser or say I hated the fact he used to be posh. That all seemed fair game, but when kids then started saying the same stuff back to me, or even worse stuff to each other in front of me, I got angry quick. Seemed I couldn't *hear* the same things I was saying. It was like I owned the rights to it. Which is *not* how things work in Chapel Shores Comp.

Once a few of the nasty ones worked the situation out, I was done for. It's funny how those types do somehow suss stuff first, isn't it? It's like they have some sort of sixth sense for what's going on in timid kids' heads. Two of the whinier ones in Joe Poundes's crew seemed to know my thoughts, and how to play me, even before I did.

That was what caused the first of the little incidents that got my folks worrying about me. Or my mum, at least – Dad hasn't ever really worried about anything. Maybe it's the leftover posh in him. Ouch, there I go already.

Anyway, what happened was that this kid, who operated under some kind of protective umbrella that came with being in the Poundes gang, got right on my case about my dad and I lost my rag with him. The kid was called Sylvester George, but they nicknamed him 'Skunk' and he properly lived up to it. He got the name from having some sort of stripe in his hair when he was a bit younger, but I reckoned it suited him better because of the way he went round firing these stinking jets of spoken poison at people he didn't like. Or worse still, at people he thought it would impress others not to like.

In History one day Mr Lloyd was running through his 'LLJ-LBJ-Lincoln-etcetera' routine, and then making it all about himself with the 'David Lloyd George' thing, before noticing Sylvester and going 'Hey! I didn't even notice that. Sylvester *George*. Well I never! With you and me there's a Lloyd *and* a George in here. And also a David!' He pointed at some silent girl in the back who's surname was indeed David.

'Brilliant!' he went on. 'We've got them all. Just need an Abraham now and we can make at least two full president names or initials in this classroom.'

'Luca doesn't count though, Sir,' said Skunk.

Mr Lloyd, fully missing the point, just thought there was a gap in the history knowledge and went to correct: 'No, it's not the Luca bit, Sylvester, that we need. It's "Lincoln". Abraham *Lincoln* was a US president.'

Then he turned to me, finally shredding any hope I had that he might drop this embarrassing thing of his and run back into whatever his lesson was gonna be about.

'Anyway, Luca,' said Mr Lloyd. 'Is that part of your name on your Dad's side or your mother's side?'

'Eh?'

'Who's Lincoln and who's James?'

'Dunno, Sir.'

He looked at me, exasperated. 'You *don't know* which of those surnames was your mum's and which was your dad's...'

'Oh, er, yeah. I do.'

'So come on then. Which was it?'

'Which was what, Sir?' There was one of those horrible rumbling chuckles, when the class are laughing *at* you rather than with you. They never laughed with me. That was a privilege only really kept for people like Skunk George or Joseph Poundes.

Mr Lloyd sighed again.

'Luca,' he said. 'What I mean is,' and he paused again to show his exasperation, 'which surname in your *second* name – "Lincoln-James" – comes from which parent? More important for *us* here, in what is meant to be a History lesson of some kind, is whether "Lincoln" is your dad's name or your mum's.'

'Oh, er... it was my dad's,' I said.

'Good. So your *dad* is Mr Lincoln?'

'Yeah.'

'Ideal. Now, we've got there, at last. Thanks Luca.'

He turned to the class then said:

'So Luca's father is clearly the one with presidential characteristics, then.'

Which was when Skunk laughed.

Mr Lloyd didn't get it at all, and added. 'I know. It's a funny thought, isn't it? Glad you like that, Sylvester.'

Skunk stopped laughing and looked at me.

'It ain't that at all, Sir. It's just, have you *seen* Luca's old man? He's like the least presidential person in the world, Sir. He's like one of those charity sellers with a yellow jacket that my mum always refuses to come to the door for.'

Then Skunk sat back, pleased with himself and waited for the class-wide laughter that this life owed to him whenever he spoke up. *Huh-huh-huh-huh-huh*. A class of kids laughing with him, and at me. Again. Before Mr Lloyd could do anything to stop it, there it came. *Huh-huh-huh-huh-huh*.

I think it was the first time I properly got the feeling – the moment this wriggling, clawed creature first woke up in my belly and chest. My head went hot and tight at the back, and then I started breathing super hard because it felt like I was going to be sick. As the cramps ran from my stomach up, I breathed harder and then realised the deep gasps were in order to stop tears instead. That was when the anger started to run at me, and I closed my eyes. All I cared about was that there were loads of people seeing me, and that I had to make sure I didn't do something embarrassing that I'd never recover from. It felt like anything could happen – I could have been about to wet myself as easily as I could have been about to cry. I closed my eyes, breathed deep one more time and then lost a moment. Or it could have been several.

There was a loud bang, and when I opened them again everyone had gone silent. I could feel the pain in my knuckles and then I saw the blood. In front of me was the victim of my only, pathetic little way of coping: a metal pencil case my mum had bought me with 'Reggae Festa' written on it in green and orange letters. It had caved in under my fist, and the now jagged rim had cut into my little finger and back of my hand during the blow. The girl next to me in the seating plan, whose name I since deliberately forgot, looked like she wanted to cry now instead, while Skunk just looked annoyed his laughter had died.

I rammed my hand under the desk before Mr Lloyd could see it.

'What was that?' he asked. I looked straight ahead, trying to keep a blank expression as if someone else could have possibly made the noise.

Mr Lloyd dropped back onto his lesson plan. Only five minutes too late to save the rest of my life.

'Today all of you are going to...'

Who cared what we'd all do. Something had come out of me that day, and it was something Sylvester George was certain to have the intelligence to exploit.

As the lesson drifted on, the pain started to feel good. Feel amazing, in fact. You could focus on it, and I kept telling my brain that it was only some sort of quirk of biology telling it this feeling was meant to be bad. *Enjoy the pain*, said my heart to my nerves. And that's what I did. I was in control, too. As the rising, swirling sadness – which would always follow these moments of panic from now on – set in, I could thankfully focus on something else: the acute buzzing in my hand. The trickle of blood going cold and drying in the folds between my fingers came with the thought I'd chosen that feeling, to prevent whatever had been about to happen in my head. It made me want to yell with joy.

I couldn't of course, and instead I had to spend the rest of the day ignoring Skunk as he tried to rib me about being the 'president's son' and kept saying his parents would offer my dad a job if he ever wanted one. In a way I knew I deserved it, for not managing to let his crap wash over me in the first place.

It was only when I got to the bunkers at the end of the day, on my own, to think and watch the sea, that the real low started to come at me from within. The first wave of it had been a little tremor. This second blast was a feeling that ate you straight up and didn't even stop when there was none of you left to eat. And nothing, not old-school reggae, not food, not even pain could hold it back. This is what it's like, I realised. This is what it's like to envy those who don't exist.

There were plenty of people who didn't exist in school, of course, metaphorically speaking. Kids like the girl next to me in History, the boy whose face was covered with rash and who came to school in pressed trousers every day or the other girl whose surname Mr Lloyd had only recalled when it reminded him of his own. My place had been with them until that day, but then, out of the blue and by my own doing, I'd made myself exist too much to ever be comfy with it.

But then there was not existing, and there was *not existing*. Those kids must have still had tastes and likes, dislikes, hopes and fears, ideas. I pressed my back against the concrete of the bunkers. No blood pumping through them. No short breath, or feelings, or insecurities. How cool to just be a bunker instead, I thought, made of hard stuff and gathering algae. *They* didn't have to think.

Maybe I could wish hard enough and turn into stone, I thought.

Yeah, I wished. Never going to happen though, was it.

Instead, and because I wasn't brave enough to do anything to change the situation, I'd be in school the next morning. Again. The first day of a whole lifetime of being on the radar of kids like Skunk any time they couldn't find a better joke elsewhere.

The time between now and then would involve waiting. Waiting to exist in their eyes while you wished you didn't have to exist in your own. One step closer to the stone pillar I'd wanted to become that first afternoon in History. Or could that be one step further away?

It was only a day before my mother noticed the marks on my knuckles.

As if suddenly deciding to care about what was going on in my life, she quizzed the hell out of me about it. Not long later the sleeping trouble started, and she caught onto that, too. She was checking on me by stealth in the middle of the nights, because to her not sleeping was something to get really worried about. I didn't want to tell her I'd always woken up in the dark to strange sights or wonderful noises, that figures had flitted through my room, that sometimes creatures spoke in the dark, that objects flew and flashed in the skies outside my window. I didn't want to have to tell her that stuff was normal for me – nothing out of the ordinary – that it had been the case since I was four and she'd never bothered to find out then. She would have gone off on one, like she did when the school first phoned to say they were worried I was looking distracted and 'lethargic'. Their word. What on earth did that mean? *Lethargic*?

Just like the teachers, Mum's solution was to nag me so hard the problems felt even worse.

I stopped talking about either my mum or my dad, positive or negative, to anyone but Gaby, after that – and only if she brought it up. That was because she, for some mad reason, kept claiming to admire the guys. Also, since we only really chatted outside of school, it kept a nice, safe wall around the subject during the 'working day'.

But the other stuff? The loosening of my head and the waking in the night? The pounding chest and sore shoulders? That had to stay with me and me alone. No one would understand that, anyway. The easiest thing was to let Mum think all was hunky dory, and to let Gaby think I had a bit of a problem with my old man. Apart from that, the other stuff would go away some day, I reckoned. Like it did for the YouTubers who boasted about it to get subscribers, but who were really these super confident hipsters with no such problems in real life.

'Chill out, Luca,' Gaby insisted, time and time again whenever I failed to prevent Mum or Dad bumping into her, or coming up in conversation. 'Your folks are so cool you don't even know it. You'll realise it one day, though. I bet you do. Trust me.'

That one day, I wanted to tell her, was nowhere near. I'd turn to stone first. I was determined.

Chapter 10

Dad was wearing his charity salesman-style yellow jacket when he came to fetch me at break time for our adventure to Jeff's jewellery den.

'I'm not crazy about this idea,' Mum had said the night before. 'But if it's got to happen then Luca Lincoln-James is attending school first. Needs to get his mark. I've promised Mr Kleener.'

'Aw, come on,' said Dad. 'He should have his mind on the *experience*. Plus he can sleep on for an extra hour then.'

'He's sleeping the right times for school and it's staying that way,' my mum insisted. 'Another promise I made Kleener. Luca has to learn to get up five days a week. And if you're not going till eleven, and Luca's up anyway, then he's going to go in and get his mark.'

'Fine. He can walk, though.'

'He usually does,' said my mum. 'You only drop him in like once a week anyway.'

'It's more than that.'

'No it ain't!'

So that was that. With no real role in the decision myself, as per usual, I was sent strolling at the gates, Bunny wailing in my ear. This time though, I was armed with a note to excuse me for the rest of the day after break because I was apparently going to get interviewed 'for an apprenticeship next year'.

The excuse would have been funny if it wasn't for the fact Dad half believed there was some truth in it. 'It's as good as an apprenticeship, going to places like this, and making the sorts of contacts you'll find there,' he said.

We still had the supply in for Reg, the same woman who'd mishandled Gaby's antics in PSE and who we were all in a standoff with over names. She wouldn't learn ours, so we wouldn't find out or notice hers.

'Er, Miss, I got a note from my mum... about this afternoon,' I told her. 'Can you read it and give me a mark?'

The reply was slow and sceptical, after sniffing through the letter in exactly the same manner:

'Hmm... Aren't these supposed to get signed off by Mr Kleener himself?'

I wanted to reply 'How would I know, since it's your job', but didn't.

'Not sure, Miss,' I said.

'Well, Mr Kleener's at a conference today, anyway. Plus I've only got the rest of the week left before your form teacher has to come back. So fine. What does it matter? I'll authorise.'

And so it was that I walked clear of the gate and the gate-keeper, and Skunk, and Joe Poundes and Art teachers wanting projects and Kleener wanting attendance stats and Gaby wanting to ignore me.

Only to jump into the middle seat in the cockpit of Dad's Fiat, sandwiched between him and Jeff for the long journey across the Marshes, onto the motorway and over to Birmingham – where nothing like an apprenticeship interview was going to happen at all.

Jeff was wearing a jacket and a tie, and my dad had done his best, too. He'd put on a light blue shirt which I didn't know he had, and tucked it inside his best jeans. He didn't have a belt on, so the bottom of the shirt looked scrunched above his flies, and his pointy black shoes were dirty and worn. I'd met one or two of his old posh friends from the past – they usually showed up whenever he hinted at buying something no one else wanted – and they could pull this look off okay. The 'I dress down coz I'm so powerful look'. Trouble was, you had to be powerful to try it.

The conmen at the jewel market would have less chance seeing him coming than Jeff, though, I thought. Jeff looked like he was trying unbelievably hard to be someone he wasn't. Which was exactly the case. His tie looked old, wide and cheap, his shirt was dirty and his jacket and trousers neither fitted nor matched – plus he'd still forgotten to comb the short mop of weedy brown hair that seemed to spin around on his head from day to day.

And *this* was supposed to be our expert guide to the jewellery trade.

'Get rid of your school jumper, Luca,' my dad ordered. 'You'll be alright with the trou and shirt combo, then. It'll pass for office wear or sales floor. Hang on… Let's have a look at your shoes. Fine. Not ideal. They'll do though.'

Jeff pulled a pair of shades on.

'So here's the plan,' said my dad. 'We're gonna arrive and wander around for about an hour. Then Jeff's arranged for us to meet with this contact of his at four. And that's when we need to come across as proper pros.'

I wanted to say that we were nothing of the sort, but Jeff's smile made me feel too angry.

'There's gonna be plenty to look at in the meantime,' my dad went on. 'Diamonds, silver, sapphire, black pearls, emeralds, ordinary pearls. Everything.'

'Black pearls?'

'Better than ordinary ones,' said Jeff. 'For selling. Easier to spot fakes. Plus they're rarer. From Tahiti normally. Tahitians are easier to trust.'

'Is it Tahitians selling them then?' asked my dad.

'Er…'

As if Jeff would know.

*　　*　　*

It was a long way to Birmingham, and there was plenty of silence for me to enjoy and for Dad and Jeff to try and break with various nonsense conversations about the meaning of life, the keys to success and the money they were going to make once they could do a few jewel deals. There was just enough distraction here for me to not be able to think about anything else, and then my phone went off with a text.

Gaby.

Not like her to bother with me in office hours, but she had done.

It read: 'Not in work? Where are u?'

Ah, the power you get to hammer out the real you behind the safety net of an iMessage. I replied:

'Office hours. Why should you care?'

There was a Gaby-is-typing sign, then it went away. Then it started up again, and a another message dropped in from her:

'Not in school aren't you. Therefore you EXIST…'

I ran through the various swear words I could fire back at her, or maybe at Dad and Jeff instead. They all seemed lame though compared to shoving the phone back in my pocket, which my head was telling me to do right away. My arm wasn't listening though.

Until my dad spoke up and told me himself.

'On your bloody phone already? Come on, man! Luca. It's rude. Put that thing away.'

Then he turned to Jeff. 'Youth of the day eh! Stuck to their phones aren't they? They wouldn't know how to breathe if the phone didn't tell them. Mind you, his mum's just as bad. Don't you reckon, Luca? Is that where you get it from?'

I stayed quiet but stashed the phone. Gaby didn't deserve a reply right now anyway.

My dad would be the wisest man in the world if he stuck to the things he said and thought. You'd almost think he meant that crap about using phones too much, but then Jeff was texting away to his heart's content seconds later and that went unnoticed. Dad's own phone was too old and cheap to text without having to tap each key about three times per-letter, otherwise he'd have probably be on it as well, while he drove.

Another thing Gaby thought was cool – Dad's old phone.

What's the matter with the lot of them, I thought, as the traffic slowed and Birmingham began sucking us towards its centre and Dad and Jeff's date with greed.

* * *

D'you know how cool gold is?' said Jeff, as we waited for our van to be checked and to be given an official parking space round the back of the jewel market.

'Listen to this stuff, Lukee,' said my dad, quickly.

'It's what makes things *real*,' said Jeff. 'Gold. It's the heaviest metal, man, so there's like the least atomic movement in it. Back in the day when it was just men and dinosaurs they reckoned the heavier something was, like, the more it existed. So a cloud was like, you know, half way to being not real, and the soul was like…'

'Alright, get on with it, Jeff,' said my dad. 'We're here to talk money, and to educate Luca, not fill his head with the sort of mumbo-jumbo his mum would actually *approve* of.'

Jeff laughed. 'Right. Fair point. Aye, okay.' Then he turned to me. 'Economics it is, see, Luca my boy. When they invented money, it worked coz it was made of precious metals. Then when they invented banking people didn't need the metals coz they could just use notes from the bank.'

'IOUs,' said my dad.

'Aye, that's right. IOUs. That's all a bank note is. A "promise to pay". Read what's written on a tenner. Technically, see, a tenner's not actually *money*. It just means if you ever handed that thing in to the bank and actually formally asked them, then they would change it for some metal. A tenner's worth. If you *insisted*, like. Which no one does.'

Two men in security uniform were standing by the van now, tapping codes into some handheld device. I could hear one calling out our number plate to the other.

'Thing is, though, see,' said Jeff. 'All that money that it says the bank has got, all the numbers on your dad or my bank statements – they have to equal something *real*. That's where gold comes in, see. Britain and America's whole banking system is built on foundations of the stuff. Literally! That's how it works. There's a big reserve of gold hidden in each country's banks, underground in places like Fort Knox in America and in the Bank of England's vault, and that gold is used to "underwrite" the numbers the banks play with. Brilliant, in't it? They play with make-believe numbers, but the gold in the cellar makes it *real*. Gives it *substance*, like, innit.'

'Long as it actually exists,' said my dad, trying to pretend he knew as much as Jeff.

'Exactly, Steve. Long as it's actually there.'

The men were waving us through. We weren't even worth bothering to search. Must have been my dad and

Jeff's outfits, or maybe the fact the open window probably meant all of Birmingham was hearing Jeff's crappy gold stories.

'Rumour has it, see, boys, that some of the gold in Fort Knox, and other places, might not actually exist. The surface of all those bars is gold, but we don't know what's actually in them. Clever, eh? People have become so happy to trust a piece of paper that they are happy to *believe* in something that's not there.'

'Bit dumbass of them?' asked my dad, trying his best to talk like Jeff.

'Well. Long as no one checks then it's fine. That's the beauty of gold, see. It's the metal that makes *ideas* real. It makes things exist.' Jeff tapped a closed fist on the dashboard, to knock his point in.

'Looks good, too, mind, gold,' said my dad.

'Aye! That too. Plus it sells, genuine, on the cheap to people like you and me around here if we play our cards right.' He was reversing the van into an underground parking bay, guided by another man in security uniform.

'Start with the basics, though,' said Jeff, like he had the remotest idea what he was on about. 'Basics first. Turnover, see. All about turnover. Just keep schtum, boys. I'll talk for us. Look like we're interested in nothing at all – and if there's gold market games to be played then my contact will find us a way in.'

'Got that Luca?' said my dad.

'Got what?'

'F…' He went to curse at me, then saw the grin.

'Aha! Good boy. Funny when he wants to be, see, Jeff.'

Jeff laughed and thumped me soft on the shoulder, just like Gaby did.

'You have got it, though? Right?' said my dad.

* * *

The market was in some kind of hotel or officey-type building. We had to go up some escalators, and came out at this big room which was like a lobby. It had a front desk, and we signed in, putting Jeff's contact's name down, then we had to sit down and wait for the guy to come and fetch us.

I spent about twenty minutes watching each of the people who arrived, showed IDs and then got waved through, while my dad and Jeff talked more crap together. Most of the people were wearing suits and ties, posh, shiny shoes and had little metal suitcases, like the ones my dad sold a trillion clay poker chips in once for about a quid of profit. There were loads of foreign-looking people, too, and they were always really neat and clean. Still, it didn't stop Jeff moaning about immigrants taking over the country.

'We're in England, Jeff. That makes *us* immigrants, too,' said my dad.

Jeff's mate arrived – a tall guy with curly grey hair tucked behind his ears and a round, tanned face, who was not dressed in a suit but a tight jumper and faded jeans. He introduced himself as 'Haz', short for 'Harry'. Jeff rubbed his hands against his trousers nervously before shaking hands, and then Haz took us through.

Beyond the double-doors to the main market, we hit a wall of chilled air. There was some noisy machine blowing it across the hall, so the whole place felt like the frozen aisle of a supermarket. On each side of us were little rooms, often dark, with stacks of glistening jewels, necklaces and rings inside them. They had notices pinned besides their doors, like menus.

'You guys got to pay in and show you can shift before you get a bigger deal,' said Haz, as we turned into one of the rooms. He walked behind a glass desk filled with rings, and then added, 'So you reckon those stalls you can run in Wales are busy then? Tell me what your customers are most likely to lap up, and we'll get you a big batch, below wholesale. Make it worth your while, like. Then you'll make a wedge as you shift that, and if it goes okay then I *can* get you a sniff of something a lot better, like I said.'

'Good,' said Jeff. 'Me and these two boys here, we're good for it, see.'

Haz looked at me. 'Young?' he said.

'Not really,' said Jeff. 'He's eighteen.'

'Is he bollocks.'

'He is, mate, I can tell you. He's sharp with figures.' Jeff could spin a slick fib when he wanted, you had to admit. I'm pretty sure he knew about the extra Maths I was getting forced to do in school for being so *dull* with numbers. 'Steve's son, this is,' he added, and it seemed only now that Haz properly noticed my dad.

'So what's Steve for?' he asked, dead serious.

'Sales. He'll sell ice to an Eskimo, this fella. And his kid, Luca, is tight with numbers. Between them they can work discounts in, while raising prices, and you'd be none the wiser.'

Haz laughed. '*I'd* be all the wiser.'

'Plus, Steve will pay in,' said Jeff. 'Long as you show him the end product.'

Haz stared at us again. He pushed air out of his nostrils, and then said, in a lowered voice, 'Well, we're a mile past security now so fine.'

He reached down into the bottom shelf, and pulled out one of the metallic cases people had been walking in with. He lifted it to the glass counter, and it made a *thud* as it landed. He reached for a key in his trouser pocket, and unlocked the case on two sides, then lifted it open. A glow seemed to slip out almost before the lid had lifted. Underneath, on a surface of foam, was a chunk about the size of an iPhone of metal so bright, so reflective that it could have been made of early-evening sun. I wondered if it would scorch you to touch it, and I had to breathe soft, long and slowly to stop myself wanting to reach a hand out.

'Congolese gold,' said Haz. 'Highly pure.'

The three of us just stared, waiting for whatever he wanted to tell us next.

'Twenty-two carat,' he explained, his voice gentle, as if the wonder of it had got to him just as much. 'Soft, and shiny. Same as doubloons or bullion bars.'

'Thought they were twenty-four?' said Jeff. 'Bullion. It's normally twenty-four carat.' *Bullion. Doubloon.* My mind just flashed images of pirate legends and sea-shanties at the mention of those words. Weren't doubloons the coins that poured out of treasure chests in all the cheesy pictures you'd see as a little kid?

'This is blended with silver, though,' said Haz. 'We can fetch copper blend in from the same suppliers, but it's not as bright.' He looked at me, and said, 'How much you reckon you get for that, then? It's meant to be two and a half grand for a hundred grams. That's eight hundred there…'

My dad looked at me like he was about to cry.

'Er… A lot?' I said.

Haz exploded with a throaty giggle immediately. 'Funny kid.' My dad's face shifted to almost proud. Then Haz added, 'Shit at sums though, isn't he!' and then we all laughed.

When his face went serious again, so did ours. 'This stuff's *way* cheaper, anyway,' he said. 'Remember I said it's the same mix-up as old doubloons from back in the day? Well, that's coz it *is* doubloons!'

Jeff nudged my dad and said, 'Yeah, man, Steve. Listen to *this*!'

Which of course my dad was more than willing to do:

'It's not Congolese at all,' said Haz, 'although we'll get the paperwork to say it is. It's actually salvage gold melted down, though. That's where it really comes from. Off wrecks hundreds of years old. And that's why we're willing to go to start-up investors, see. Guys like you can help shift this into the main gold markets as clean metal.'

'Salvage is illegal, see,' said Jeff, now fully finding his flow. 'Can't go into wrecks and draw up treasure anymore.' Haz dropped three battered but equally bright coins out of the bottom of the case.

As if *Jeff* was in a position to raid shipwrecks anyway. I mean, look how much of an army of divers he had to help him. Me... My dad...

'Oh salvage is legal alright,' grinned Haz, putting one of the coins into his palm. 'If you can get permits. That's where this stuff comes in. It's *un-licenced* salvage. Only going to reach full value if you can melt it down and turn it into something legit.'

Great. Un-licenced meant stolen, right? Not to Jeff and my dad by the looks of it.

'So how do we get involved in helping clean these doubloons up, then?' asked Jeff.

'You don't. Not until you sell *watches*.'

The coins and bar went away so quickly it was as if Haz needed to hide them from someone coming around the corner. Still, though, he had the two grown-ups who'd brought me here virtually hypnotised, and by the time he began showing them through a range of chavvy watches, they just looked like they wanted to buy something for the sake of it.

'Coupla hundred units, fellas,' said Haz. 'And that's gonna bring you back with a coupla grand! Plus I'll give one doubloon of copper coated in leaf to your boy, to get him in the mood, like.'

He reached under his desk and flicked a chewed-up coin at me. It shone like the other bits of gold he'd shown us, and had the same worn-away markings on it – some sort of shield or badge with a 'V' and a '+' sign under it.

'Worth a hundred quid that,' laughed Haz. 'Keep it, Luca. Fake of course, but you don't have to tell people, do you? It'll bring you good luck anyway.' He turned to my Dad and Jeff and winked. 'So, we in then, gents?'

'Bring it on,' said Jeff. 'What you reckon, Steve? You keen?'

'Keen as mustard,' said my dad.

I wondered if these watches were 'un-licenced' too, as I watched my dad sending a text to Mum. It was right then, with freezing air-conditioning all around us and this grey-haired conman grinning, that I suddenly felt unbelievably, heart-stoppingly sorry for him. The nerves crackling in his body were causing his face to twitch slightly, as he waited for her to reply. Despite all his stupid plans, he always tried to make it feel as if she was in on it in some way, as if she had the final say. Gold laced with cheap copper, I could see the blend of metals in his heart – hope, fear, excitement shame and, somewhere, mixed badly in amongst the rest, was some sort of love. He wanted to do this stuff *for us*. I knew it. My mum probably knew it, but still, what could she say?

His phone pinged, and he tapped at the screen.

'Well,' said Jeff.

'Hang on... Yeah. She's cool. Got the go-ahead. Let's do it.'

*　　*　　*

Talk about purity? This place had nothing of the kind. The lights of the city made even the darkness seem somehow dirty, as we drove the van out of the security gates, the back loaded with four boxes of crap watches.

I thought about texting Gaby or trying to find a tune, but the shaking van was making me travel sick, and I couldn't forget the way my dad had seen my mum's permission as being so important. Feeling the copper doubloon in my left hand, I watched Dad steer the van through traffic. I was looking for any more of the worry I'd seen back there in that creepy office. It was gone, though. I was struggling to imagine my mum really coming back to him with such a positive reply. It wasn't what normally happened, and I wondered why he found the need to claim she was on-side. Unless she actually was? In which case, something definitely wouldn't be right.

It was about ten o'clock when we turned off the motorway at the Chapel Shores sign, and Dad phoned home to plan dinner about ten minutes before that.

'Got you on speaker phone,' he said to my mum as soon as she answered. 'So don't go slagging Jeff Rafferty off to me now coz he'll hear.'

'Me? Slag Jeff off?' she said.

'Hi Hannah,' said Jeff, laughing and leaning towards the speaker.

'Hi Jeff.'

'You alright?'

'Yes, fine. So how'd things go today then guys?'

'Good,' said my dad. 'Got some really good possibilities for deals on the go. I can tell you more about that when we get in. What have you done for dinner?'

'Nothing. Been waiting for you. Didn't realise you're gonna get in so late.'

'Ah, we're nearly home now. Howabout I stop off for a Domino's – that one in the Marshes?'

'Fine.'

'Cool. See you in a bit.'

And he hung up, turning to Jeff. 'You up for that then mate?'

'Nah. Going down the pub, I am. Meeting that bird I was on about.'

My dad grinned and winked. 'What. The young one? She still like you?'

'Course,' said Jeff.

'Ah well, fair play then,' said my dad.

I wondered why on earth anyone would want Jeff eating pizza in their house just before bedtime – or even why on earth someone would want to meet him in a pub for a date. At least my time with him was nearly at an end, for now. He'd be back, though. You could guarantee that.

Maybe it was the Domino's that sweetened her, but somehow, when we got in my mum was being really soft on my dad too. Could have been the bottle of Mount Gay Barbados Rum that he bought her, mind – despite Jeff telling him he should never buy a drink with the word 'gay' in it.

With ice and rum in their glasses, pizza on their laps and me sitting off to the edge making do with value lemonade, Dad explained to her all about the deal. He pulled out several of the watches, which was the sort of thing that normally made her roll her eyes and scold him for being too keen to buy stuff. This time, though, she seemed to be taking an interest in it all.

'They seem a reasonable buy,' she said. 'They'll probably shift okay on eBay. Nice margin, too, even if you sell them for only 65% of their RRP.'

'Exactly,' he said, filling his face with a slice of Hawaiian.

Her real excitement, though, was spared for the idea of gold. Of course. He'd texted her from the market, hadn't he?'

'*That's* why we're drinking Mount Gay, isn't it?' she said, tipping her glass my dad's way. 'You remember that place we went in Barbados where they were flogging gold. How cool was that?'

'I remember, Hannah! Of course I do. That's what I was thinking. Remember how cool those stories we heard about those guys scoring gold in that wreck?'

'Yeah!'

'We should have dived with them, I knew it,' he said. 'That stuff about not having our scuba licence, it meant nothing, I'm telling you.'

'Well, who cares,' she said. 'That was then. This is now. Did it have that look? You know, that kind of liquid shine? Like those coins we saw that they'd cleaned up?'

'Probably. We only saw one little bar of this stuff and two coins. 99.99% quality though, it was. Looked good, don't you reckon, Luca? And *heavy* too. Jeff was really positive about it.'

'Ah forget Jeff,' she said. 'Didn't you ask to see the rest?'

'All in good time. Need to move these watches out first. Are you keen to help?'

'Not really.' She laughed and took a slice of pizza. 'But I'm sure you can manage to do it.'

'So you're think these watches are a good idea, then?' he said, lifting one out of the box and winding its turning face.

She didn't reply, but took a sip of the rum.

'We should do a family holiday to Barbados once I turn the gold over,' he said.

Mum spluttered slightly through her nose, then half choked on her rum and had to sit forward to stop anything spilling.

'What?'

'Once you *turn it over*?' she said.

'Ah come on – don't be like that now. You're on-side and you know it.'

'What makes you think that?'

My mum turned to me. 'What d'you think, Lukee?'

'I think the pepperoni dipping sauce is okay,' I said, and they both looked at me like I was from outer space for a second before laughing their heads off. I laughed with them, and got stuck into another slice. After dipping it, of course.

'He's good value sometimes isn't he, Steve,' said my mum.

'Who? Lukee? Yeah. He's gonna be a neat little gold merchant one day. I can tell.'

'He can be whatever he wants,' said my mum.

'Yeah, but I can teach him to want the right things.'

'Can you?' my mum laughed. 'Like you taught me? Well, I'm looking forward to watching *that* happen.'

*   *   *

They put reggae on not long after that – 'Good Thing Going' – remembering when they travelled the Caribbean the year after they met. Just before they had me, and then responsibility. It was on loud, too, so that when I left them with their rum and his watches and her fake support, to go upstairs, the beats were rumbling through the floorboards.

'Thanks for the pizza,' I mumbled on the way out.

They had to know what they were doing, surely? There it was: *my* music. I know it was their music once but they'd given it to *me*. The only thing of theirs I didn't mind having.

I opened the window and tried to get noises in from the street outside, but all I got was freezing air the flavour of saltmarsh and rust. It was all I could think: my parents were using my music.

I slammed a pillow to each ear, and tried to think of words that didn't link up. I needed to take my head apart to fix the bugs before they realised they could seize control. Even now, they were everywhere, trying to get in the way of my reboot. I pressed cushions into each temple, and tried to tell myself stories that made no sense.

Long, long journey to settle from here. As big a task as DJ Luca could ever take on.

Chapter 11

D'you know when Wentloog used to creep me out the most? It was when he'd come by really late in the evenings – like after midnight.

I found out just after why he was doing it. Apparently he wanted to understand more about how I got to sleep. He had a theory that I got too alert to nod off properly. Then he reckoned not catching enough z's was getting me down in the day because I had to get up early for school whether I slept or not.

I'll pause there just the let you realise the genius of that conclusion... ... ... There you go. Amazing, isn't it? That'll be a couple of grand probably, judging from the car he drives.

Anyway, I wonder if he ever picked anything up by watching me? It made me realise that the guy was sort of, loosely, in a roundabout way, almost snooping at the right stuff. Good sign? Bad sign? No sign, I hoped.

Also – even if he did spot something 'wrong', who was he to call it wrong? All the best people on earth do their stuff by dark. I realised that ages ago. It's when your brain can forget the rules you spend all day telling it to stick to. There's a music for the day and a music for the night. I reckon the people who hear them both are the ones who should run the world. They'd get *everyone*.

Anyway, I found out the one thing my mum did right in her whole life, too. Did anyone else know Wentloog offered to write them some kind of note saying I didn't have to go to school the next day anytime I didn't sleep well?

They were planning to keep that from me, too. Probably because my mum told him to piss off and that I was going back to school anyway, as soon as I was allowed. Does it sound like her?

It was all there, in the notes I'm allowed to read, anytime I want.

Thing is, I'm not sure yet whether to be happy about that stuff or not. Part of me kind of likes her telling him to stick it. But then free days off school? Would have loved that idea a few weeks ago. Now though… Well, we're not meant to get everything about ourselves, anyway, are we?

*　　*　　*

Somehow, I eventually got away that night and drifted. My earphones found their way to my head even though it seemed impure to play reggae at the same time as them downstairs, and I'd fired my brain back on track just about. Their borrowed music only, but up here in my room it was still playing on my terms, in my space.

'Good music helps you see,' I said aloud to myself. 'In the dark, too!'

It was about three hours later when I pinged awake again, my heart and chest and head and soul all trying to tune into something else not too far off. I could still hear music from downstairs and looked at my bedroom clock. It was gone midnight and Mum and Dad were obviously yet to turn in. I listened out to see if I could recognise the tunes they were using. That might give me an indication what sort of mood they were in by now. I couldn't be sure, though. It was something heavy, and lead guitar driven with a fast pace. I couldn't hear either of their voices, either, above the din.

Now I had options, though. At least they'd left my music alone – for me and only me again. Now I could think. Now I could search out whatever else was calling for me.

A drum-roll and bout of guitar-feedback came through the floor from the living room. Maybe I should bang on the floor, to make them shut up. No. That would tell them I was up, then she'd stress out and get on my case.

I listened a little more. They had to have the stereo cranked close to full volume.

And that was when I realised I could probably sneak out again.

Why had I only just thought of this?

My cammo outfit was slumped over a box at the bottom of my bed, just where I'd left it after going down to the shoreline last Saturday night. It was all there, right where I needed it. The brown hat, the dark jeans – with Haz's doubloon in the back pocket for extra luck – and hoodie. I put three T-shirts on underneath, over the warm one I'd been sleeping in. Snug and ready, I began tip-toeing downstairs.

I got past easily. The door to the living room was shut, with the key right by the front door. It was open, so I locked up from the outside, slipped the key into my hood pocket and fastened it to the sewn-in loop, like before. When they finally went to bed, Mum and Dad would go to lock the door and probably just think they'd already done it.

So, like that, I was out – into the night. And it was *perfect*.

There wasn't a cloud anywhere above me and the stars were scattered overhead. The ground was so hard it felt like you could bounce back off it if you ran too heavily. It wasn't a frost – getting a bit too far into Spring for them now – but the little lumps in the soil didn't squash properly under my feet either. The gravel path at the bottom of our street felt somehow more solid than usual. Maybe it was just the blackness all around, making it so things didn't need to worry about how they looked. The pavements, the mud and stones, and then the dunes – maybe with this lovely darkness to hide them from sight they could all just concentrate on *being*.

The moon was almost down to nothing, now. Where it had been a bright ball of gemstone light the first time I'd seen the men, now it was just a tiny, tiny crescent – a lost shaving of bleached lemon peel. It cast no reflection on the sea, although its illumination meant there was just enough visibility to make out the horizon, the sand, the wet shoreline and the troop of figures already beginning to rise from the ocean surface before me.

This time the tide was a bit lower. It must have been high earlier in the night, and had been dropping back for a couple of hours. That was why the sand was covered in soaking patches. It made their footprints really easy to make out.

The lead figure was just getting his feet to the sand, and the guy behind him was out up to his waist. The third was just a head starting to lift his beret-capped forehead out of the water. The beach slanted less when the tide was this low, so although they were the same distance apart as before, there was room for more of them to still be partly in the ocean at the same time. It meant that once the first had stepped clear of the shore's last trickle the fourth was also starting to rise.

Having sunk back, free of the odd groups of rocks that normally swirled beneath the high-water mark, the outline of the sea was now a neat arc across the bay. As my eyes grew a little more used to the dark, I could make out mini waves as unbroken lines, travelling in horseshoe shapes towards land.

With the beach wider than before, more of the men could stride across the sand at once, and for the first time I was able to look at them as a straight line of marching people. The climb up the pebble bank – where I was sitting now – and the immediate start of the dunes behind meant that the other times I'd seen them their line was always rising and dipping. Now, though, I could see them slowly treading, one after the other along the level beach, the line of their footprints marking out a gradual bend towards where they could arrive at the dunes in the same place as usual.

They were close to me now – as close as they'd ever been – and despite it being so much darker, I could still make out the eyes of the lead figure. He didn't move his head, or let his gaze slip at all, and went methodically past, up and behind the first of the dunes with that same, uniform pace. Behind him, as if programmed or towed by an invisible line, the second also followed.

All nineteen were there. With the further distance from shoreline to dry land, I counted seven being able to all be on the sand at the same time. Not one of them looked my way as they felt out the pebble bed beneath their careful feet. Not one head turned as they took their first sinking steps onto the ancient, dry sands of the dune – and like with their leader not one hint of distraction could be seen in any of their fixed, frozen gazes.

To the nineteenth man, yet again, they kept their routine. Over the wet sand, up the boulder shoreline, over the dunes and then merging with that wall of sand – each sinking smoothly into it, disappearing from sight again, and leaving me alone in the sweet night air, to lie back soothed by the sounds of the shore and looking at the stars.

Again, I thought it – *You can't walk into a dune like that* – but again I had to stay, had to try something, whatever it might be.

*　　*　　*

On a small, flat, grass verge at the foot of the dunes, and right where the band of pebbles marked the start of the beach, I planted my back hard against the floor. My knees lined up with the ledge of earth and roots, leaving my feet dangling down. If I swung them back and forth slightly, my toes would brush gently against the boulders below.

As more and more pins of light seemed to turn on in the sky above, I felt my back sinking further and further into the cold floor of planet earth. I rolled my eyes up and down, feeling the nearly freezing, dry air in the corners of my eyelids and noting how many individual dots there were out there in the jet black sky. Stretching my sight to each horizon, there seemed less stars, as the oranges of the Chapel Shores streetlights diluted their flickering glow. But right overhead, the sky was awash with constellations, dancing as luminous dust.

I closed my eyes and gently hummed the little riff from 'High Tide or Low Tide'. The lyrics rose in my mind, too. How someone was going to be a friend whatever. Couldn't apply that to Gaby, I thought, or anyone else in my life. Perhaps this troop of maybe-ghosts that had just passed me by would be my friends no matter the tide. They were certainly looking for something. I hummed the riff harder, letting the tune take over the words. Closest I could get to relaxation tonight. Sleep was overrated, anyway. This was all I needed. This and to wait out the moment when my nineteen figures would return and mark out the path.

A noise, nearer than anything before, broke my non-concentration.

It was the fox, and without thinking I stood up to greet him.

He was close. Maybe ten metres. I could see that he was wet, at least on the legs, and there was a little bit of blood around his mouth.

'Hey,' I said. 'I'm Luca.'

'So?' he said back. I heard him. It didn't matter if he really spoke.

'I'm waiting,' I said.

'I know,' he said. 'But why not go onto the beach?'

'You're right,' I said, and stepped across the pebbles towards the track of footprints coming out of the shoreline.

'You're welcome,' he said, except that when I turned around he was gone.

I was tracing the marks in the damp sand that the men had left. The prints were always the same distance apart, and it seemed as if the men had all stepped in exactly the same place every time. It meant that I couldn't make out any individual marks at all.That changed when I reached the actual shoreline itself, though, where the receding tide had allowed the last two or three men to step onto fresh sand. Their prints stood alone before joining the rest. They were wet, and gradually filling with water and silt, but the shapes were still as clear as I needed them to be.

I put my own foot over one, and noticed theirs were a lot smaller. The outlines seemed to go into a much sharper point at the toe ends, too. I remembered the way their boots had looked like they might be made only of cloth, or of leather so wet it had lost its shape. I was a size eight, so these guys must have been a five or six at the most. When I stepped away, my own print had left the grooves from the sole of my shoe as a perfect mould. I waited for it to fade, but it didn't. The sand was hard enough to preserve it. That meant the men's prints were probably unchanged too. Theirs had no rivets in them at all from soles, so it meant they weren't wearing anything that had rubber or plastic on the underside.

I started walking back up the sand along the line of footprints, trying to take the exact same steps that they'd all taken. A quick rush came over me, like I was someone else for a moment, and then, just as I was getting used to the rhythm of the paces they had used, I looked ahead and saw the first shadow emerging back over the dunes.

The troop was returning.

And I was right in their path.

There was no option besides stay put, and find out once and for all if they could see me – or if they would react. It was going to be useless to run to the side in either direction. I'd just look like I was doing something wrong. Plus, the way they always walked, looking *way* ahead, meant they must have seen me already. Those empty white eyes had to have better vision than mine in the dark. I'd made them out, so they must have made me out, for sure.

The rhythm was draining out of my mind again. Breath was about to come in gasps. The hot feeling in my head wanted to rise and drag me down.

And then it all went. It all kind of, dispersed. As if my mind suddenly knew what to do, I stepped sideways, two clear strides, and put my hands in my hood pockets. Mum and Dad's house key was there in my fingers, a little token from the real world back behind those dunes, anytime I wanted to return. Then I felt the doubloon in the back pocket of my jeans, rubbing my thumb against it, feeling the temperature and texture.

Like before, it was a different figure leading them down the beach.

They started passing me by, so close I could have touched them, and now I began to hear the sounds they made. Each one was the same: heavy breath firing out of their nostrils with every step of the left foot; lightly breathing in whenever they put forward the right. The careful regulation of breath, to each pace, was what was causing them to pause slightly every time they put a foot freshly on the ground in front. It wasn't enough of a pause to stop them moving, but it gave their progress this stunted look as they stooped onwards towards the ocean behind me.

I started noticing the crunching, squelching noise their feet were making, too. Sand and saltwater, mixing around inside those shoes that looked like slippers made of super-worn, floppy leather. They had sand in their hair, and in their ears, sand spread finely along the velvety material of their jackets, sand everywhere.

It wasn't until the nineteenth man – the one who'd led them up into the dunes in the first place – came back that I decided to try and make eye contact. And it was him I chose because he was the one who'd beckoned to me last time.

Again, he appeared out of the grey dunes about a minute late on this return leg. All of the others were well into the water by the time he reached me. I shuffled slowly sideways the other way, back closer towards the worn path of footprints in the silvery, wet sand. Closer to his way than I had been to any of the others, I waited for a reaction – and as he approached he slowed.

By the time he reached me he had *almost* stopped. But he didn't. He stepped past without catching my eye at all – except he did it all with several seconds of stillness between each two strides.

Step.

Step.

Stop.

Pause.

Step.

Step.

Stop.

Pause.

I had to do something. If the chance would ever exist, this would be it.

So I started humming Bunny. 'Dreamland'. The one I listened to earlier, and the other night. The one I always listened to when I really needed to be in control. The one that could lift me somewhere else more than any other track in the whole world. I just whistled the tune, but in my head the lyrics were rolling along, telling me about the land that was rumoured to be somewhere over the sea, where everything was perfect and nothing bad could get you.

The man had started beckoning, and his pace was picking back up, so I moved after him until the shoreline was in front of us and he stopped again.

As he turned to face me, a little surge in the surf bounced its way up the beach, and I could see the white foam ride up his heels, leaving a tiny trace of silt behind on his soaking socks. I watched the thin film of seawater carry on running along the sand, two metres from my toes, then one. My feet were going to get wet. Fifty centimetres, and the water was slowing down. Forty. Then thirty. Twenty. Still moving softly, now only a trickle.

I braced myself for the cold.

But when it touched me it wasn't cold at all. Not in the slightest. No. The water was warm. And I mean warm like a bath.

The man up ahead was in just below his waist, now.

Water so warm you just wanted to sink into it and float or swim.

Or dive.

I was still whistling and the lyrics in my head were going through the glories and the heaven of Bunny's dream land, while my legs were wading into this patch of gorgeous, cosy water somehow shivering with heat in the middle of the Chapel Shores night.

I realised then how they waded out into it so easily, without flinching. This little current was running deep, too.

In beyond my waist, and still my feet were wriggling in the reassuring warmth of the water running along the bottom. This was like climbing into a hot tub, or a sauna – a really deep bath.

I wanted to see how far down it would go – the warm – and just before I reached the point where the water was up to my shoulders, couldn't hold off anymore. I pushed my hands out above my head, cupped the palms together like some kind of prayer to the ocean and plunged forward. I popped my head up a few strokes further out, and the night air was immediately chilly and harsh. But under this sea, towards where the men had gone, it was only getting warmer.

I dived down again, swimming deep so my belly was brushing gently along the seabed. There were little currents of slightly warmer water mixed with wriggling streams that had a fresher feel. Then one current, even warmer again and more soothing than the rest, pushed me upwards towards where the surface should have been. I wondered how long it was before someone my size and age needed to breathe – but everything felt so comfy and the water was so good for my soul and the music in my ears was so loud that I just kept on swimming right where I was. I kicked my feet gently, first together, then in opposite motions. Then I let the beauty of it all take over. The warm currents would lead the way. I knew it without needing to be told.

The music was strong in my mind again. Yes, I thought, lead the way, alright – all the way – to the land across the sea.

Part 2

Chapter 12

Ah, the weight of water, when it presses down. And the noises too! Behind the ocean's swirling, humming song grinding at the warm sand beneath me, I could hear something else. The darkness felt so safe. Push on, push on, I thought, feeling the softness of the water around. Kicking my feet, I felt the warm water shivering off the tips of my toes.

Now I was deep. And moving so fast. Ten, twenty, a hundred – who knows, maybe a thousand miles an hour. Nothing could hurt, nothing could get in the way. The whole ocean was moving with me, so warm, so heavy and so comforting.

The voice, though, was behind everything else. And the moment I heard it, that voice became the only important thing.

It came out of the deep, deep hum, but straightaway it was all around. Like whale-song, it could have been miles away or just behind me, beneath me, on top of me or even in me and running through me. It came, again and again. A voice, muffled by saltwater and bubbles. And it kept repeating itself – over and over. I could tell it was saying the same thing because the rhythm was the same. Each time, the same six or seven words.

Luca! My name! That was the last word. The only one I could make out.

Its tone, soothing but certain, I wasn't worried at all about whether I could understand. If it just kept repeating the words, sooner or later they'd make their way into my mind.

Rising and dipping, the voice grew louder then softer, vibrations shaking the water. That voice, wherever and whoever, it was after me – and ahead of me. It wanted me, and nothing coming from that warm, soothing depth of salt water could possibly be bad. I knew it, as sure as I could ever be of anything.

'I'm coming,' I tried to say, thorough the weight of water. It was out there, just beyond but I knew I could get to it.

The same murmur, stronger, louder, nearer. The same last word:

'Luca!'

A bright light flashed, almost too quick to notice, but so intense and so sudden that it was impossible to forget. The warm began to lift, the current pulling away from the bottom. The thinning water started cutting away and, as the brightness filled in, slowly this time, the sounds sunk to the background.

'Luca,' I head it say again, and then at the last moment, one other word, easy to make out, in a sure, growling tone. 'Come!'

* * *

I opened my eyes when I'd felt the water getting shallower and saw the outline of the city from just beneath the surface. Its colours had lit up even from beneath the sea as they wavered and trembled before my underwater vision.

Where I broke the surface, it was at the edge of a waterway between the two halves of the city. As I waded ashore, the new buildings were to my right, and the old ones straight ahead. The skyscrapers were a mile off – maybe even more – but even from there they imposed themselves across the hot and hazy air.

It took my clothes about five minutes to dry in that sun. Plus, it was so hot I didn't even mind it when they were wet.

Behind the dirty city wall, a giant, yellow dome rose tall from the other buildings. It had bright trims of white running around it, and a small turret off its top. Orange and red shone out of anything that wasn't yellow or grey. The wall ran neatly in front of the coloured buildings. I was walking towards it from the patch of deserted sand and shoreline out of which I'd swam.

I was heading towards the wall, though. You could see ramparts all along it, and its moist, dark colours made the whole thing look ancient straight away. The old city. You knew it, too, because the buildings were all of them rounded and pillared, painted and unique. There was an entrance through the great wall, with a tower or gate-building just over it. All along the approach I could hear the sound of reggae, in either Spanish or French, holding my familiar beat, calm and relaxed in the heavy, hot air. Then, at the gate, the music faded, and another beat started to creep up on me.

Boom-b-b-boomboom. Boom-b-b-boomboom. It was faster and shook the ground around it. It was asking me to accept it.

I walked through, into a clean square of bright churches and there were those strange iron statues of animals that didn't seem quite to exist – a giraffe with the head of a shark, birds with arms instead of wings and a jaguar whose smile had in its corner a giant, wooden cigar.

There was some sort of parade going on inside this, the fort part of the city, too. Girls with glitter masks in bright purple dresses were dancing to this new drum beat. I tried to guess their age. Bit older than me... maybe... It was massive too, the parade – and everyone and everything was in Spanish. Drums were hitting this music again, which *sounded* like it should be reggae, but it had this kind of aggro energy to it.

Behind the girls came a marching band, younger – like twelve years old, apart from their leader who was also about my age – and then a little cart playing some sort of electronic drum-n-bass-type noise, driven by a middle-aged man. It was the two of these tunes together – the marchers with their brass and the portable DJ – that made this new sound, the sound that was pulling me onwards. The rest of the column of people behind, families, teens, older people, was walking, same pace as the band, further in, away from the outer wall.

I was fully dry now, and my hoodie was starting to be a nuisance. It had to be something like thirty five degrees here – way hotter than you'd ever get in Chapel Shores – and everyone else was just wearing T-shirts. Some weren't even wearing that, and they had super dark skin that had been in the sun and the outdoors forever. I pulled the hoodie off, and could smell the drying seawater from my journey as it came up over my head. Then I flung it, along with the two extra T-shirts I'd put on, to the side of the road, and pushed into the crowd.

The tower and turrets of the churches and other buildings got taller and brighter in colour as we headed further in. Any buildings that were flat or square would have these wooden shutters and white balconies with hanging baskets of flowers and flags striped with the colours of no country I knew.

At the centre, right up ahead was yet another big, familiar plaza, but just as it looked like we were going to go right through it, the procession changed direction and headed left – away again and out towards the parts of town where I reckoned you'd find the fort wall. That was when the sudden urge to check where I was hit me and I found myself breaking away from the crowd. Wandering down a shady alley, I was immediately alone but with my head still running smoothly to the fading beat of the mystery music.

Another, smaller square, darker and empty, lay at the end of the alley.

Well… empty except for two statues.

The first was a shining, metallic impression of an enormous lady lying naked and on her side. I knew this piece! It was in Rogoff's file. I tried to remember the name of the woman in the sculpture, but it was just beyond me. She was smiling a cartoon smile, as folds of fat sagged towards the edge of the white-brick block she had been placed on. I wanted to try and decipher the inscription, but my eyes were too quickly taken off her and drawn to the other statue in the square.

This one, I didn't know.

It was charcoal black and, unlike the lady, exactly life-sized. It had been erected on a crude, wooden block about three feet high. The statue was of a boy – maybe my age, maybe younger, it was hard to tell. He had a metal ball and chain attached to his left foot, and another broken chain around his neck, made of iron or some other metal. The statue was so dark you couldn't quite tell what the main bit was made of.

The boy's expression was the most intriguing bit, though. He looked like a real child who'd been turned to stone just a moment before he started crying, and yet behind the drooping mouth and closed eye-lids there seemed to be some gesture of hope. I couldn't say where it came from, but looking at him made you feel it.

And then there was the sign below. Someone had written in fresh marker pen, on the wooden block under the statue's feet. A crudely drawn arrow pointed to a small hole in the box, and next to that was scrawled in English:

xxx~~~PLEASE GIVE A PESO FOR THOSE WHO LOST EVERYTHING TO THE SPANISH~~~xxx~~~EVEN MORE TO THE AMERICANS~~~xxx~~~AND WHAT WAS LEFT TO OUR OWN PEOPLE~~~xxx

It was written twice. On the floor, just to the side, the same message was on a creased piece of card, which had fallen flat but face-up so that it could still be read. I looked around in all directions. Who would put this kind of thing in the middle of a square that no one used? Also, how could you lose *everything*, then *even more* and then after that still be able to lose *what was left*?

I looked back up at the statue, raised like he was, several feet above me. Ah well, new land, I thought and went to walk away. But then he winked.

I mean it. He winked. Winked, as in his eye, which I could now see was wet and had the pink edges of an eyelid all around it, fully scrunched into a wink and then opened again.

Looking down at his sign again, I had another go at working it out. Okay, Spanish, then Americans… what was left… made *sort of* sense, if you tried. Plus the three x's on the end, in the middle, at the beginning. A kiss?

'I have to write them in English, my signs,' said the statue. 'Because… this is the only language the people who come here understand. Sometimes French, but I can't write in French. Can you?'

'Uh, I … I'm doing it for GCSE,' I said, finally. 'But your sign is kind of…'

'I'ss a *translation*, Luca,' he said, his accent stopping him from being able to say either of the 'n's. 'My father, he help me.'

'Did you just say my name?'

'Yes. You're Luca, no? I knew you would come here sometime today.'

'Really?'

'Of course,' he said. 'Look, I stay here more half an hour and then I can explain to you many important things. You like to wait? I'ss hot, my friend. Maybe move to dark first.' He pointed to the shade a few steps away.

'What about you?' I said.

'I'm used to the sun,' said the statue. 'I'ss no problem for me. Also my name is Alejo. You can call me Alex.'

Then he winked at me again, and straightened to look ahead. His eyes were once again the only hint of being human.

I walked slowly over to the steps he'd pointed out, and sat down. The stone floor was warm under me, even though this was completely in the shade. The air around felt thick and soft – a hot day, but comfortable once you were out of the sun. Resting my elbows on the steps behind, I leaned back and looked at the sky above. That kind of blue never happened where I lived. It was full, rich and deep. I remembered Gaby telling me once that the sky got its colour from all the water that hovered in it. That was why sunsets went all red and orange. The sun was shining through the water at a different angle. She reckoned the blue of a sky was something you could never paint properly, even if you mixed the shades up perfectly. 'Never got the *life* when it's only paints,' she said.

The noises of the parade had faded right into the distance and all I could hear was the cooing of pigeons. There was a flock of them on the edge of the building's shadow, walking in and out of the direct sunlight. The half hour drifted by and Alex stepped down from the wooden box. He walked straight over, dragging it behind him. When I jumped up to give him a hand he gestured for me not to. Once the box was into the shade too, he let go of it and, after gently shooing the pigeons away with his foot, walked over and sat down.

'So... *Bienvenido,*' he said. 'You know where we are, Luca?'

'Colombia?' I said.

'Yes! *Cartagena de Indias,*' he smiled – hitting the 'g' sound with a 'h' instead. 'What tells you this?'

'The pesos,' I said. It seemed embarrassing to mention Mrs Rogoff's Art lessons right now. Not fair on the real life Cartagena that was all around me, along with its real life people.

'Lucky guess, my friend,' Alex laughed. 'Seven other countries use pesos too.'

'I suppose I just had a hunch.'

'Well. You are happy to be here anyway,' he said. 'Cartagena is most beautiful city in all of Colombia, and maybe in all of north of South America.'

'Why am I here?' I said.

'You've come from the sea,' he said. 'Tell me about this first. About how you're finding the way through the sea. You tell me *how*. Maybe I tell you then *why*.'

'I swam,' I said. 'I think I chose it.'

So I told Alex everything I could think of, trying to speak slowly and staying away from English words he might not know. As I gave him the story of the figures on the sand, the maybe-false dune, the warm water, the music of Bunny, Alex kept nodding as if it was all a story he knew well.

'Have you seen these guys yourself?' I asked eventually.

'Not seen,' said Alex. 'But I hear them. I hear them all the time, and you are not the first boy or girl to come here with this story. Always either they see these men, or they are hearing the voice.'

'What does the voice sound like, Alex?'

'A man. I think. But it is very low. It sounds like the deep water thinking very hard. It's like a vibration, no? You hear it too?'

'I think I do,' I said.

'I have not been to swim in the sea, though,' he said. 'I am not sure if I can. Maybe one day. How long were you swimming?'

'Oh, not long,' I said. 'It couldn't have been. I mean, I'm alive, aren't I? So how long can someone hold their breath?'

'I think breathing is okay when you journey with this style of swim,' he said. 'Can be normal to swim for hours.'

'It wasn't hours,' I told him. 'It just sort of... went light straightaway, then I knew to swim up, and then when I felt for the bottom it was shallow and next thing I'm walking up the beach here. Why have I come, Alex? Why were you expecting me?'

'My father paints me like this,' Alex said. 'I'ss hard work! But this what I do. My father, he is same. We are *artisanos*. My father is poet, and he is playing guitar, and he is singer, and he can sometimes dance in the ballets.'

Alex frowned at me, and patted me on the knee, his hand sticky with tar-like paint. It left a little smear on my jeans, next to the salt powder from where the ocean water had dried out of them in patches.

'It is a hard way to live.'

'So why do you do it?' I asked.

'We need the money.' Alex smiled. He was getting surer. 'I think this is why you have come from the sea. You have come to help.'

135

＊　　＊　　＊

We cut through the narrow streets and up to the edges of the fort. This part was right on the edge of the sea. From here I could see the coastline bending away to the right, and more of the city over to our left.

'*Mar Caribe*,' said Alex. 'Caribbean Sea.'

The ocean looked dirty and frustrated. It was muddy brown and windblown into hundreds of crumbling white-caps. The breeze felt salty and the air was thick with it – a warm breeze. In Chapel Shores, the wind coming off the sea normally meant it got colder but here you could feel the heat crank up every step closer to the shoreline.

'Look, Luca,' said Alex. 'This is where you can swim back to the sea.' He pointed at a little swirl of even muddier water, with patches of churned sand and foam around it. 'Water here, it move. Swim and pass. Other side, who knows.'

'How d'you…'

'Everyone here say this is place where you can swim to another country. But nobody tries it.'

'Why?'

'Because we must help Cartagena to be a great city. We must try to build our *artisans* here. You understand? Yes, you understand. Now, I am to show you…'

He led me back from the ramparts again and down a slope of concrete to a smaller square. There was a church on one side of it and what looked like an old hotel on the other side with balconies and people sitting drinking from tall glasses as the sun got lower in the sky. The reds, yellows and oranges of the buildings were thickening in their colour as the blue overhead dropped into a deeper dark. The rumbling drums from the procession were in the distance again, but so quiet it would take them ages to get anywhere near.

'This corner,' Alex said. 'This is where we work many of the days.'

There were four pairs of shoes laid out neatly along a cracked kerb. Next to them was a box similar to the one he had stood on in the other square. He fiddled with the side of it and suddenly the box popped open like a chest.

'I can explain,' he said, and began pulling objects out of it. First came a set of facemasks, held together with a ribbon that had been bound over them in quarter-knots, like you'd wrap an important gift. Under this were cloths and hats, waistcoats and then a pair of shoes that had yellow and white strips of leather, polished perfectly like some kind of 1920s gangster outfit.

'These are how we perform!' Alex said, lifting objects out quicker, and shorter of breath.

'These also, nobody else can use but my father!'

And then he pulled out four batons – like wide drumsticks made of metal – and without realising it, suddenly I was interrupting him, just as excited myself. I knew what they were right away.

'I've *seen these*!' I yelled at him. 'Amazing! I've seen these.'

'Where?' he asked.

'Well, I've seen one of them. It was old and rusty – but it was definitely one of these. Can I hold it? What are they? I think one of these was…'

'These,' interrupted Alex, bursting with pride. 'These are for eating fire.'

'They're yours?'

'No. They are property of my father.'

Feeling the weight, and the shape of the handle, I was sure this had to be the same thing me and Gaby had seen on

Bunkers Beach. Would they get to Chapel Shores though, these fire sticks, as Alex was calling them, without someone carrying them there?

Alex showed me how the top end, the bit that had covered itself in rust on the one we had, was rough because it could be dipped in fuel. It had some kind of thick, wet cord wrapped around it at that end, while the rest of the baton was smooth metal, coming down to a small rubber covering at the bottom so that the hands didn't get burned by the metal heating up. The handle fitted tightly around the square-shaped end and made it easy to grip safely. It must have fallen off the one Gaby had found.

Alex was pushing one end of it towards his mouth and tilting his head back. He showed me how there was an angle at which you could lower something almost straight down into the stomach. Next he showed me their juggling cords, packs of cheater cards for magic tricks and knives that had false handles. He showed me magnetic blocks that looked like model books and which could stack end-to-end in a way that looked like they'd beaten gravity. He had a saw that oozed fake blood. Under those objects were various mini carpets and cloths for marking out on-the-spot stage areas, and then, at the very bottom, the polishes and paints for when they made human statues.'Yes!' he said, tossing a pot of black tar in the air and catching it behind his head with the other hand. 'My favourite. The statue is best. Always. When we do this, people pay well. Hey, where's *your* dollar?' He tried to pull a serious face at me, but dropped it straightaway, along with the pot which he flicked back into the tub. 'I'ss okay! I joke. You're not taking a dollar in the sea. I know this.'

I rubbed the rear of my jeans, feeling the outline of the doubloon through the crusty denim. Could I give him this? Would he want it? Could he even do anything with it?

'Yes, the tourists, they *love* the statue,' Alex went on. 'Me and my father don't love it because wearing statue clothes and paints is very, very hot. The dollars make it good work, so we learn to love.' He laughed. 'It's six hours sometimes. I can stand six hours without to have a piss.'

'In that sun?' I could feel the cruelty of these rays even now, late afternoon. Earlier it had wanted to scorch everything underneath its gaze, and even now the land and sea both seemed to sigh with warmth from its energy.

'And so you are here,' he said, turning to me, and beginning to put the objects back in the chest.

'I am,' I said.

'To help,' he said.

'Right,' I said. 'To help.'

'Yes,' he said, again, nodding.

'You are to help me find my father. I know places he might be. One of them is with the police.'

'That doesn't sound good.'

I thought about my father with his dodgy deals and his false hopes.

'No. See, Luca, the problem here is they are making what they call "licence". We – me and my father – we have to have "licence" now or we cannot make our life here. We are now getting ten dollars a day. Without licence we will be getting one or two dollars a day because then we can only perform in Cartagena city *outside* of the walls, where there's no tourists. Local people will not pay us well. But to be in tourist streets we need licence. '

I thought about my father with his dodgy deals and his false hopes. Maybe I'd be in Alex's position one day. But he was looking even more worried.

'There is a possibility even more bad. My father, if he is not with the police for his licence, he is trying to be a farmer, and this is terrible.'

We were back now in that square near the city gates, where these crazy sculptures were watching their own shadows grow long in the dropping sun. The colours from the bright painted buildings, at this time of day, were so thick they might burst or melt, while the sky overhead had filled out into a blue even darker than the murky sea out front.

'Why is that terrible?' I asked.

'Because if he is farmer again, he will be killed,' said Alex.

*　*　*

If you thought *my* dad could get himself into some scrapes then Alex had it on another level altogether. He had come down from the inland mountains when he was a little kid, along with his family – three sisters who were all younger than him – to perform in the streets of Cartagena with his father. Before that, his dad had been a farm hand, a worker on some local coffee field, eventually taking charge of a whole crop.

That was when they got into trouble with the army. Only, this wasn't the army we'd all think of as fighting to keep us safe. No, this was a *militia*. I'd heard the word in school from Mr Lloyd, but now Alex was telling me more about what it meant. Hired soldiers were throwing farmers off the land if they refused to grow drugs instead of coffee. The militias were making all sorts of violent threats, and Alex looked like he wanted to cry when I asked him to tell me more. He was sure that if street-performing didn't work out, his father would try to farm again and get into trouble with these soldiers.

'Why would he do that?' I asked.

'Because he cannot live as a father who is not able to find money. If he cannot find it on the street he will return to mountains for farming because he wants to help his family. But if he is farming with the people from before, we will lose him,' said Alex. 'He will be killed quickly because they will not trust each other. This is happening to my friend's father too. He is now dead.'

'Where do I come in?' I asked him. 'I don't think I'm gonna be much use to you if we have to hike into the mountains looking for armed militias who sell drugs.'

'Not necessary. You can do something simple, by talking to the police,' said Alex. 'They are not going to listen to me, but you are a tourist so you can walk in and they will make you coffee!'

'Really?'

'Yes. Colombian policemen will be very kind to a *Gales*. Speak English with them. They will like it.'

'You just want me to go and ask the police to look for your father?'

'Yes.'

'I'm fifteen.'

'I'ss no problem. They listen because you are tourist and they are to listen to tourist people.'

'So, go into a police station and get them to listen to your story?'

'Yes please, Luca. This is kind.'

'Okay,' I said. 'No problem. And that's all?'

'I think. Maybe also… maybe you can say you think fire eaters and human statues in Cartagena should have licence for performances without paying much money to the government!'

'D'you realise how cool you'd be, eating fire or dressed in that stuff in Wales?' I asked him. 'You could go to London or Cardiff or Birmingham. You'd be "cool" as in "look at that guy, he's amazing".'

Alex looked thoughtful. Eventually he spoke again.

'I have tried to swim like you have done. This is not working for me. I can hear the voice but I cannot go under the sea.'

'Can you hear what the voice says?'

'It told me to wait. I am believing the voice is a good man, because it is helping me. The voice tells me today you will come and see my statue. Then you come!'

'How's that make it good?'

'I asked who is speaking,' said Alex, stopping walking and standing square to face me.

'And they say "Wait" and then no more.'

'Wait for what?'

'I don't know,' said Alex, shaking his head. 'No answer. But another day the voice comes back and says I cannot leave Colombia before the *Ingles* and the *Gales* help me.'

'There have been others?'

'Yes. I meet lots of *Ingles* and *Americano* young people, but you are the first one who comes from the sea! This makes you special. You come from the voice!'

'I heard it,' I said. 'But I couldn't understand what it said. D'you think it's one of the men I saw on the beach, the voice?'

Alex shrugged his shoulders.

'I will maybe use the sea someday too.'

He nodded back towards the coast, where, over the rampart, that swirl of turbulent water supposedly marked my way out of this town.

'I'ss dark soon,' he said. 'In Colombia dark will come quickly. Cartagena outside of walls is not nice when is dark. Better you at home country.'

'So can we go to the police now then?' I asked.

'Of course.'

*　　*　　*

Alex was right. The Colombian police were over the moon to get a visit from a 'Gringo'. As for my new human-statue mate himself, well, he got more and more terrified as we approached on the station. 'Yes, Luca. I am scared. They are not nice to Colombia people, these police. Thank you thank you thank you *thank you*.'

'No worries, Alex,' I said.

I felt none of the inferiority I would have done strolling up to a policeman, or any grown-up in authority back in Chapel Shores. Here with these once-in-a-lifetime people, I was free to speak and laugh with confidence. This wasn't Mr Kleener or any of the many who had it in for me back home. The tunes of Bunny wandered into my head…'Cool Runnings'…

'Welcome Gringo!' shouted the chubby and smartly dressed chief of police, smiling at me, before snarling something at Alex. Alex winced as if he was about to get hit but I said, 'No! He's with me,' and they calmed right down and fetched a load of old newspaper to put across the office chairs so that Alex could sit on them without his black polish going over everything.

The police station was echoey and empty, but the chief of police's office was carpeted and furnished and had air conditioning that you hit into like a wall as soon as we went in and which made Alex gasp.

His happiness didn't last, though. His dad wasn't in their custody, and they didn't know anything else. It took about twenty seconds to find out, from the grinning, white teeth of the chief.

I watched the dark paint on Alex's skin dry in the cool air and start to crack, kept moist only by a trace of a tear from his eye as he scratched some details about his father into a missing-persons report. Then came the process of sticking an old Polaroid picture Alex was carrying of his dad to the top of the page. He looked somehow familiar, like someone I'd always known. He had the same dangling curls of hair as Gigi Carranero in Gaby's sketch, or that man, Haz, from the jewel market. Lately everyone I'd never met would stare at me as if they were one of those nineteen ghostly figures on the nightime shore at home. It doesn't mean anything, I told myself. Nothing at all.

'You like tea-coffee-CocaCola-Fanta?' asked the chief of police.

Alex scratched the tarry tears from his eyes, and pointed at himself.

'Lo?' he asked.

'Yes. Very cold and sweet,' said the chief, sticking to English and winking at me.

Light began to come back to the space behind Alex's eyes.

'Okay. I would like,' he said, and was handed a Fanta out of their fridge. It was in a big glass bottle with a straw coming out of it. Alex slurped the whole thing as if was going to be taken away from him any second, before standing up and heading towards the door.

'Come back anytime,' said the chief.

And then we were back out into the heat and the darkening skies of Cartagena. It would be night any moment now.

'Where do you sleep?' I asked Alex, as a food cart near the city gates started playing 'Ninety-six Degrees in the Shade'. Three girls of about our age were waiting for the seller to cook them something, and shook their hips against the slow beat as they watched.

'Outside the fort,' Alex said. 'We have a cabin near the beach. My mother and my sisters will be there. I need to go back and collect my box from the plaza. There may be a few pesos in it. We can eat fish if the old man who lives in our cabins has caught one.'

'And if not?'

'He has always to catch a fish this season. I'ss no problem. He will have fish and we will have rice too.'

'So, aren't you worried?' I asked. 'About your dad?'

'Of course. I am worried very much. Nothing we can do after telling the police, so I must do the same things. Tomorrow I will make this statue again, then maybe try to do some showing-off tricks on my own. I have never done these without my father, but I cannot only be a statue.'

I wished there was more I could do to help.

'Luca, you should swim home before i'ss nightime,' said Alex. 'If you don't is *muy peligroso* – very dangerous – because you can maybe lose the spot in the sea.'

'But I…'

'You see me again soon. If I find my father, you will see me. If I do not, it's same. You will see me. Now you must go to the shore. I can take you. Is very important to find the right place in the sea.'

'I'll know where to look,' I told him. 'It'll be warmer than the rest.'

'I am coming. It's important I am saying thank you to you for being kind.'

'It's only kind if it works,' I said. 'If it helps make the police get off their arses and find him.'

'This not true. Kind is kind. Any person is kind and it helps.'

Alex walked me to within sight of the shoreline, and hugged me before pointing towards the swirling patch of sandy water just beyond the beach. He turned and walked away, trudging a few steps then skipping a few, as if great forces of happiness and sadness were fighting inside him, taking it in turns to have the upper hand.

When the water hit my toes it was bathtub warm. I waded slowly out, waving at the disappearing Alex. Then the comforting luxury of the heated current began persuading me to sink in. When I could resist no more, I made a final wave at the section of road where Alex had been a minute ago, and then let the ocean draw me under.

The swimming felt so good. I stretched my shoulders and arms out ahead, felt the tiny trickles of colder water flick past me, then turned and kicked with my feet, downward, to the warmest parts of all.

'Well done, Luca,' whispered a voice in my ear. Maybe Alex's voice, maybe someone else. 'Well done. Now *go!*'

There was an off-beat starting to dance in my head. Like the music of Cartagena but older. Somewhere out there, my tune would play any moment.

The water was getting warmer, and I could feel it moving, fast along the ocean floor.

'That's it,' whispered the other voice, even quieter than before. 'This way. You know it already.'

Chapter 13

The current may have been warm, but the air was *freezing* once I waded up the shore back home. It was still night-time and my clothes were dripping wet. Being without my hoodie was better at first, because the wet clothes seemed to be making things even colder. As a sub-zero breeze whipped across the dunes, my soaking T-shirt and jeans seemed to fill with the frozen air particles, clinging against my skin.

All of this was shoved right to the back of my mind by the time I'd ran home, though. What would my mum think if she saw me drenched, with squelching feet and muddy hair? That would pretty much be the end of the world if it happened.

The streetlamps were still off, so I figured dawn had to still be a little bit away. Knowing my parents, that didn't automatically mean they'd be in bed. Sure enough, there were lights on in my house, and that was when I realised that the front-door key was still inside my hoodie.

Inside my hoodie, on the floor, by a kerbside, in the walled city of Cartagena de Indias.

Now, I did have a problem.

It was time to weigh up which was going to be the biggest disaster of my life. Knock the door to get let in…? That would wake one of them, if not both. Dad would be the better option, but even he would throw a mental if he saw his son strolling out of the night looking like this. Other option was stay outside until one of them got up and opened the door. That might involve actually dying from the cold – and *still* getting caught anyway. Of the two, staying out still made kind of the most sense though. No streetlights, no horizons glowing at all. It was going to be a long one.

First thing was to get out of the wet clothes. I went round the back of our house where there were a few layers of tarps and old blankets that my dad would use to line his van when he shifted dirty or splintery objects around. One of them was a big cloth drape, almost as thick as a rug, and it felt dry compared to my sticky skin. I threw my T-shirt and jeans off, taking a moment to take out and grip the doubloon, which was still there, then wrapped the huge curtain round myself at the neck. It was no good. I was seconds from teeth starting to chatter, and once that happened I was going to be done for.

Done for, in this case, meant knocking my parents' door. Suddenly death by hypothermia had fallen into a close second.

The cloth was around me like a robe when I wandered back to the front door and tried it again. Of course it was still locked. The rear door too. Why wouldn't they be?

Another gust of wind shook through the trees between our house and next door.

Then I got the idea of running to keep warm.

I turned out of our drive, and hoisting the whole sheet of heavy cloth around myself, jogged to the end of the street, where the dunes began. I turned to go back, and did three laps of the street before thinking this would look too weird to anyone looking, so I headed back into the dunes.

It took about twenty minutes but eventually I was starting to sweat – this weird kind of sweat that felt hot on my face, but with my core still cold. It was the best I could do, though, so I headed back to the house and rolled myself under a tarp in the back garden. Pressed close to the wall, I asked whoever was listening for daybreak. The cold is your friend, I tried to convince myself. It feels good. It is good. People last days like this. Come *on*!

There was no sleeping before dawn came, but time still seemed to skip with a kinder pace than before. Maybe Alex, or my ghostly friends, were turning the dial a little. Or maybe I was getting good at discomfort.

First out was my mum. She stepped out of the back porch to smoke. Nice one, Mum. A roll-up first thing in the morning. Must be taking it outside so Dad didn't realise the smell. He wasn't into her smoking unless they were on the rum together. Didn't look like she had rum in her coffee, although knowing this pair it probably happened from time to time.

I crept round the side of the house, to see if she'd opened the front, but she hadn't.

What time was it? Surely still too early for…

'Luca!' I head her shout, long and friendly, somewhere near the stairs.

She had gone back in, and was waking me up for school.

Crap! I yelled under my breath.

'Luca! Did you set an alarm? I can't hear anything? Come on. Attendance, attendance, attendance!' I wondered why she hadn't said that dreaded word three times in a row yesterday when Jeff and my dad were lining up my 'apprenticeship'.

I was going to get one chance to get this right, anyway, and then that would be it.

Throwing the tarp to the wall and the blanket into a corner, I opened the back door behind her, trying super hard not to make any kind of latch noise.

I was in, and, leaving the door open slightly to avoid the noise of it shutting, I made straight for the shower room

149

under the stairs. I got there just as she headed up to my room.

'Luca? You up? Come on!'

I threw my wet boxers in the bin, and turned on the water current.

It was so warm I wanted to cry. I could get my clothes from the garden later without them spotting, no problem. They didn't notice what I wore when it was on me, let alone scrunched up and covered in sea water in our weedy flower beds.

'Luca? Lukee?' She was coming back down.

'In here, Mum,' I yelled. 'In the shower!'

'Really?' she asked. Then I heard her mumble something else, but the spraying water, cleaning and heating my soul, was too loud and too lush.

'Have you been outside?' she asked, as I came out into the hall again, my waist wrapped in the toilet's hand-drying towel that they never washed.

'No,' I said. 'Have you?'

'What kind of question is that?' she said.

'Back door was slightly open when I came down,' I said. 'Maybe we've been burgled?'

'That's a horrible thing to say,' she frowned.

'Well, someone opened it, Mum. And anyway, what's there to burgle here? The watches?'

She looked like she wanted to cry, but that was probably the sore head. They'd been up late, hadn't they, intoxicated with tales of gold bullion and their traveller memories. Oh, and rum. Now one of them would probably try to offer me a lift to school to show they could still be responsible...

'Your dad will be up in a bit. If you want some cereal I'm sure that will give him enough time to get ready to drive you.'

'Nah, I'm alright,' I said. 'Don't feel like breakfast.'

*　*　*

First prize out of a huge field of entries; that school day took the award for the longest in the history of the universe. I missed being late by seconds, which made me feel just as crap as if I'd been caught. It meant I had to go to assembly, where I swayed, on my feet in a line watching some visitor talk about joining the army.

Friday brought us Art, too, but Gaby wasn't there. At least that was one less thing to think about – and I wasn't allowed to stay in the lesson anyway. Kleener had marked me out to spend the morning in a revision group for kids who might not get enough exam results to make the school look good. Instead of doing what we sort of enjoyed or being left to just be us, I had to read over a Maths exam.

Then came lunch, so I went over to Mrs Rogoff to say sorry I'd missed her lesson for the extra Maths, and then asked if I could look at the Cartagena pictures she kept for our 'inspiration'. She looked amused and then said, 'Oh, want to *finally* do some work now then, do we, Luca?'

I flicked through the photo booklet she'd made, fighting a yawn big enough to probably break my jaw. There didn't seem to be much that could help me in there apart from some web links on the back page, but I stuffed a student copy in my bag anyway and left to go and wait outside the Maths room for the afternoon, and Catch-up Class Number Two.

'Not going to actually sketch anything, then?' said Rogoff, as I left.

'Sorry, Miss.' I said.

'No you're not.'

I pretty much slept through the Maths then, which left only just enough energy to push my tired legs home across a grey afternoon of cold fog. I was out like a light until Friday had been and gone, my parents had partied again, and my messy house was shaking first thing in the morning to a sound I hadn't heard for years. A sound which was telling me right away that stuff was happening in Luca Land which I should listen hard to.

Luca Land – the one place I might never get away from, no matter how badly it doesn't seem to fit my size and shape.

Chapter 14

'Lucifer son of the morning!' yelled a husky old voice from downstairs.

Saturday and what a way to start.

It was coming from my parents in the living room. They hadn't played this in years! Sure, it might have been shuffle, but, really? This song? Now? This morning?

'Lucifer son of the morning!' – then came the drum roll and scratching of a wood-stick shaker. The reggae sound, but they must have known what they were doing... 'Lucifer son of the morning!'

The song pushed on, and I stared at the ceiling. I couldn't make out the words once the instruments kicked in, but I didn't need to. It was only the first line that mattered to me. This was it, the song that had started me. 'Lucifer son of the morning!'

Looking to my phone to check the time, I saw a message had dropped in from Gaby:

'Alive? Me neither. What u doing today LLcJ?'

I slid the screen open and went to reply, but the song was still too strong with its hold over me. Plus, I had nothing decent to say.

It must have been there, in my sleep, every time anyway. The song my parents were playing right now, the song that once made me think *I* was the devil. My mum reckoned it was the funniest thing I ever did, but I just remember being shit scared.

My thumb was thinking of something to text back, but my mind was stuck on the rumbling beats through the floorboard.

'???' was all I could manage as a reply to Gaby, but immediately she messaged back.

'Come on. Let's get outdoors. Bunkers? Or what about marsh markets. Bet that's where u are already lol.'

Through the throbbing of the muffled music, I thought about the places I'd been since I last saw her in the tiny world of that misty beach. The jewel stalls in Birmingham seemed far enough at the time, but the other place? Yeah, as if I could really tell her – or anyone else, ever – about that.

Thumbs twitched for the best reply, but there wasn't going to be one. Not for the next one and a half minutes.

'Lucifer son of the morning...' The song was on the bit where it went over and over that line. 'Lucifer son of the morning...' And like it always did, my mind was fighting not to hear the words as they had appeared to me for the first years of my life... *Luca son of the morning!*

I rammed my thumbs against my ears and tried to roll towards the wall.

It was no good. *Luca son of the morning!* He was coming for me. Whoever he was. The devil in me was calling.

I put my face in the pillow, yelled 'COME ON THEN' into the total silence of the feathers and fabric, and then turned back to the world. Best take it on, I thought. Head to head. Sliding Gaby's message off the screen, up and out of my way, I searched out the same song, and stuck my earphones in. Let's deal with this, before anything else gets in the way. Or before *it* gets in the way of anything else.

Yeah. Back at the controls, steering through the storm. Me choosing when to press play, how many repeats.

Five turns, five repetitions and I was getting somewhere.

My parents hadn't been to bed yet – they *must* be in a good mood about this gold-buying business. Through the music I could pick up their footsteps, plodding up the stairs.

'Luca?' my mum called out.

'Yeah,' I pulled the headphones off.

'Yeah, he's up,' I heard her say to my Dad.

'What is it?' I called from behind my closed door.

'We're just gonna catch up on a few hours sleep,' said my Dad. 'We're in, though. Had a bit of a late one. That's all. Think Jeff Rafferty's coming round for lunch. Will you let him in? And wake us when he calls. If we're not up before then.'

I didn't reply.

'You got that, Luca?'

'Yeah.'

'Cool.'

The song had lapsed. The spell was lifting. Maybe.

I left the earphones on the bed and sat up, then grabbed Mrs Rogoff's Cartagena pack. The 'further information' websites were at the back. Flipping my phone sideways, I went after the first suggested link. Couple of pics of the walled city. Nothing to help me though.

The second site was no more use either, so I went on Google Earth, then clicked on the little orange man to go into street mode. You could do it for Cartagena! Suddenly I was gulping the air. Did I really want to play with this stuff right now? As the screen blurred and began to resolve into the plazas and that old, stone wall, I had a sudden shudder. OFF! OFF! OFF! I couldn't let myself see it all like this, in such an unreal way. Not after being there like I had.

I didn't want to see Alex again, either. Not like that. It didn't seem fair.

Somehow at that moment, the internet and everything it could bring into your own home seemed, like, wrong, I suppose. It felt like Alex had the right not to exist online. I didn't want to put him to that test. Also, did I really want, or need, to compare the place as a Google truck had shot it to the place where I had been? If they were totally the same, then that would be kind of freaky. But then it would be just as freaky if they weren't, too. The pictures I'd seen in the Art pack were close enough already to be sure it was the same city.

Back on Mrs Rogoff's list now, I worked through the rest of the links, until one had another link inside it about the performing arts of Cartagena de Indias.

I rolled through a gallery of street performer pictures, which you could tell from the clothes of the tourists in it was, like, twenty years old. Typical school resource then. Welcome to the digital age, teachers. With your pictures of 1975 or whenever.

A text from Gaby slid into view. It was a copy of mine from earlier:

'???'

I flicked it out the way without opening. What I needed was only a few clicks away, I was sure of it. One pic flashed up, then another. A gallery of performing artists from Cartagena de Indias. This was going to be the right link. This method of connecting my journey to the real world would be okay.

Sure of where I was heading, I tapped back to Gaby's message, and knocked up a reply:

'Fine. Gonna be ready to come out in half hour. Where u gonna be?'

'Town. Buying paints. Come to the Quarters.'

She meant the square of shops just before Chapel Shores ran into Chapel Marshes. Fine.

'Ok. 1hr?' I typed back.

The thumbs-up emoji arrived as a reply. I pulled on my

spare hoodie – the one perk of having a dad who bought and sold wholesale crap; having two hoodies that had both fallen off the back of the same truck. Leave one in Cartagena and my folks wouldn't notice, because he'd given me two at the time anyway. I slipped my shoes on too, ready to go out.

Tough luck, Jeff, I thought. If he's that keen to come for dinner then he'll have to knock hard and wake them himself. Why on earth would I want to hear more of his crap anyway?

Ready to head out, I returned my focus to the gallery. Could I find a picture of one of Alex's fire sticks? I had no idea how Gaby would react if I could show her evidence of what it was, but it seemed important to be able to do that. Maybe the sticks were the thing that could link our daytime world and the stuff that was happening in my nights. Yes. That's why this was important. No music needed. My 'Art' research. Yeah, right. It had to be possible to find something. Just a few more clicks. More important than Maths. More important than me. More important than Lucifer.

* * *

It was getting easier, somehow, to see through Gaby. This seemed, in some sort of messed up reality, to make her keener to hang out together.

'Why didn't you come to the office on Thursday then?' she asked first.

'Call it "school",' I said. 'If I end up in an office one day, I'm not gonna have it linked to *that* place. Anyway, why didn't you come Friday?'

'Come where?' she said.

'School. Come on. You know what I mean.'

157

'I didn't want to. That's what I do. Trust me. I need the days I miss. Maybe one day I'll tell you...' She looked upwards, as if weighing something up, but then her gaze dropped sharply back to me, and she pushed on. 'But *you*, Lukee – you're always in school. You never have a day off.'

'How can you be so sure?'

'I know you don't. Like I said, you're always there.'

'No I'm not.'

'Come off it, LL Cool J. You're super consistent.'

I thought about the one month that my mum had made me take off school, after the Skunk incident and the bleeding knuckles. Mind you, at least I'd been consistent then, too. Consistent in not going outdoors, not speaking to anyone. Consistent in refusing to tell her why I didn't want to eat. Consistent in sticking to my shrinking world of bedroom and garden. But that was the only time. And maybe it didn't really count. Gaby was right. I was consistent.

'You were somewhere interesting on Thursday, though, weren't you?' she said, still pressing to know more.

'No.'

'Bet you were.'

'Fine. Went to work with my dad,' I said, out of the blue, boldly as I could. 'He needed a hand.'

The tiniest trace of a laugh came over her face, before she chickened out. *Yes*, I thought. *Yes!* Go on, Gaby Carranero. Laugh at him, the guy you keep telling me is cool. Laugh at me. Go on. See where that puts you.

She straightened her face and looked down. 'Doesn't matter, anyway,' she said. 'We need a plan for what to do after the exams. I'd rather die than work with *my* Dad.'

'Yeah. Don't think it's gonna come to that for you though, is it? You'll be able to do your A-levels. You can take Art.'

'Dunno. I'm not feeling it right now,' she said. 'Been trying to mess around with that rusty stick thing we found, and then I thought to myself, like, what *is* the point? All I'm doing it making weird stuff and it doesn't really mean much.'

'I know that feeling,' I said.

'Not like *I* know it,' she said.

'Try me.'

'Careful, LLJ. You'll get more than you wish for.'

'What's that supposed to mean?' I asked.

'Me to know. You to find out.'

'Whatever.'

We were arriving in the little strip of old shops that Gaby liked to think was her 'mall'. She mocked the way kids our age used to go and hang out at the shopping centre over on the motorway side of Chapel Marshes. She reckoned they'd just got the idea from American television and were copying what kids in the bigger, cooler country did. Or what they did on TV, according to Gaby.

'You and me,' she used to say, in a fake American accent. 'We got more imagination than that. You listen to REGGAE (she'd say this with a big, booming Caribbean voice that made me cringe) and I go to the art shops!'

'Neither of us is being particularly creative by doing either of those things,' I said.

'Yeah we are. We're doing it for ourselves, see. Not so we can show others.'

'Is that all it takes to be creative?'

'Pretty much. "Live in the moment" equals "to create".'

'Sounds too simple.'

'It is. Creative stuff is always simple.'

The 'art shops' as she called them, were in a little loop off the side of the main road, where workers from a row of warehouses would come for a lunchtime baguette. There was a big, trucker-type bakery at the start of the street, then a Costa Coffee and a Greggs, some garden shops, a boat showroom and then at the back end, right out the way, a paints shop, an antiques shop and a little café that joined onto both of them. It was always quiet, usually dark and had mellow jazzy music playing in it. Gaby would bring money for a 'flat white' there, and a cookie. That meant I watched her drink and eat. All my pocket money had been cancelled forever to pay the bills on the iPhone that got weird messages from the friends of its old owner. The phone did let me look music up and stream, though, so I'd just remind myself of all that as Gaby drunk coffee and pretended she might buy little dresser tables from the antique shop, or rolls of canvas from the other one.

'I wanna check out the acrylics,' she said, finishing coffee number one. Going to browse the paints shop, just after telling me how much she felt 'over artwork' was typical Gaby.

'Okay,' I said. 'Ready when you are.'

'No rush,' she said. 'Just letting you know. That's why I wanted to come here.'

'Okay,' I said.

She slid the plate with her seeded cookie on it over to me.

'Wanna bite?'

'Nah.'

'Okay. Suit yourself. It's lush mind.'

'Had a big brekkie,' I lied.

She sat and looked out the window, at the daylight which this place seemed so good at squeezing down to a minimum.

'I've been finding out more about grand pappy Carranero,' she said.

*　*　*

Gaby's morning coffee ran to early lunch, which ran to another coffee after lunch, which ran to a five-minute flick through some tubes of paint, which ran to more coffee time.

She wasn't here to mess about with her art supplies at all.

But I knew that, right?

I wish. Hours after that first mention, she finally came back to the topic.

'So anyway, old great poppa Carranero,' she said 'Well, there's a bit more to him than we knew about.'

'Really?'

'Yeah. Loads of cool stuff. Did I tell you he was into kidnapping too?'

'You know you didn't.'

'Well, he was, Luca. Made a fortune, too. Half the money my dad bought his hotels with, they reckon!'

'Whaaa?'

'I'm serious. My mum's sister said it when she was pissed off with my dad the other day.'

'She said what?'

'Honest. She comes over and she's all, like, shouting at my mum, saying "leave him leave him leave him", which is fine.'

'Hang on,' I said. 'Rewind. *Leave*?'

'Yeah. My auntie always tells my mum to leave my dad. In front of me too. She doesn't care.'

'But I thought your folks were…'

'Nah. They hate each other. Serious, Lukee. My mum can't stand my dad, and he ain't nice to anyone, so that's kinda okay.'

'Yeah, but that doesn't mean they're gonna…'

'Split up? Course they won't. Don't be silly. My mum would never be brave enough to do that. Imagine the crap she'd get trying to have enough cash.'

I laughed. I imagined how my mum and Rachel and Amy would love to hear this, and how I'd never, ever, ever tell them for that exact reason.

'My mum's a proper diva,' said Gaby. 'I hate her.'

'Bit harsh?' I said.

'It's not. I really do, honest. I do… hate her. But anyway, who cares about that. Thing is, I found out something cool *as*, just the other day, by listening to her whine. My auntie's come over, and she's giving it all her usual "Think of Gabrielle, you can't let him make you into a doormat" rubbish, and then my mum says her usual "Back off, he's a hard-working man, he gets stressed, so would you if you had as much on your plate as him" reply…'

Gaby shuddered, rubbed her hands on the sides of her arms like she'd suddenly become cold.

'…Then… Well… That's when my auntie goes, "Come off it. The whole Carranero fortune's bad money anyway. Get your slice and get out!"'

Gaby paused again, like she was weighing up whether to say more. I kept still. Waited.

'So,' she carried on, 'my mum says to my auntie "*You'll* be getting out in a minute!", which makes my auntie press on and my auntie tells it then… Well… hang on… more like reminds her. Seemed as if my mum knew it already… Anyway, my auntie says something about great-pappi Gigi, and how everyone knows his money came from some big kidnap, and that his whole side of the family basically has money only because he was such a nasty piratey-kidnappy-robbery type and like a full-on bad guy from history books and then my auntie's shouting at my mum, "Who would want to be married to that money, so why not get some

162

lawyer to grab you a wedge of it and get out while you still can before it makes you into a devil like the rest of them!" How cool is *that*, LLJ?'

Gaby's breath was coming faster. 'Seriously! How about it, then Lukee! And that's not all.'

Seriously, this girl had no clue. She still thought hearing bad, behind-the-scenes shit about your family was something to be excited about. Mind you, she was new to it. She always went on about how she thought my dad's dodginess was cool, and now here she was hearing about dodginess from her own dad and almost pleased. It wouldn't last. I could promise her that, if she wanted the free advice.

'Anyway,' she said, 'I pulled out my iPad straight away and went researching. Because the other bit I overheard was my auntie calling him something else – like a secret name! Gigi Carranero was known as "Gerald" Carranero too, and if you hit that into a search engine you won't believe what comes up. It's awesome!'

'Really? Another name? Like an English version of it?'

'I dunno. Yeah. Maybe? Anyway. Check it out,' and she pulled out her iPad, cased in its Nintendo Game Boy cover, and swiped it. Have a look at this!'

I flipped it so the page went horizontal, and had a look:

CHAPEL SHORES MARITIME LEGENDS: 'GERALD' CARRANERO

Gerald Carranero was a small-time runner of contraband goods between the old Welsh port of **Chapel Shores**, Ireland, Asia and the **Americas** before finding infamy for the successful kidnapping of the wealthy widow, **Lady Melville's** only son, **John**. Carranero was believed to have amassed a large fortune from that and other unknown kidnappings, before successfully laundering the money into the **Carranero Family's catering and hospitality empire**. He was believed to have been stowed away in officer uniform on the **HMS Pictor** when it wrecked in high seas in **1909**, although his body was never found and sightings of Carranero continued up until **World War One** when a much less likely theory was formed that he had gone to battle in **The Somme** and was killed in action. Given Carranero's vast fortunes at the time and the fact that front-line action was rare for wealthy men, this theory has been widely discredited, leaving death at sea in 1909 by far the most plausible explanation for his demise.

Carranero was born in 1871, the son of **Cardiff dock workers**, before getting a reputation as a seaman. He arrived in the then bustling port stop of Chapel Shores in 1896, which is when the earliest accounts appear of his ruthlessness and capacity for criminal activi... *continue reading...*

'Have you read on?' I asked. She lifted herself up and swung, hips first, onto the sofa-type chair I was sitting on. Then she shuffled along, just to the edge of my personal space and touched the iPad, scrolling down for herself.

'What do you think? Look. Hit this link here, Luca. This has to be what my auntie was on about:'

KIDNAPPINGS OF 1902 AND OTHERS

In 1902 it is widely believed that Carranero was the orchestrator and chief beneficiary of the famous kidnapping of John Melville the Second, the only son of a wealthy widow living on the Ceredigion coast in the now derelict **Melville House**. **Lady Melville** was reported to be worth enough money to purchase the entire Chapel Shores shipping and military manufacturing industries, and Carranero had developed the idea of using ransom money to buy into these growing trades. This money would later be used to acquire restaurants and hotels across Wales and Southern England, allowing Carranero's grandson, **Riccardo**, to become Chapel Shores's first multi-millionaire by the age of thirty. Allegations that his starter funds were derived from ancient kidnap money would dog the early years of Riccardo Carranero's business empire, before stock market flotation raised further funds and effectively ended any serious chances of the **Melville** family's instigating any investigations into the hotelier or his descendants.

Key to Carranero Senior's kidnapping plan was the ability to keep the victim safe and comfortable, whilst ensuring the immediate family still believed severe and imminent harm was likely. Along with ensuring that Carranero could never be proven to be involved, these methods are alleged to have afforded Gerald the opportunity to become extremely clinical and successful as a kidnappe… *continue reading…*

Gaby snatched the iPad away.

'Anyway. That's all you're gonna care about,' she said. 'You get the gist of it, eh? A full-on nasty, crooked pirate and hard-core kidnapper! And we're drinking coffee with his money!'

Well, you are, I wanted to say. She hadn't bought me one.

'So how cool is that!'

'It's pretty heavy,' I said. 'If it's true.'

'It has to be! Luca, there's loads you can read into it once you know the right names to google. It's insane! It says the Melville family had made slave money anyway, so that's why Gigi wanted to target them. He used to go to the South of the USA, see, so he had strong feelings about equal rights for the slaves.'

'How d'you know that?'

'I worked it out,' she said. 'From stuff written about him. He had to be into it.'

'Okay,' I said.

'And anyway, the Melvilles grew their money back. They sold loads of land and sailed to America themselves.

'So you feel okay about it all?'

'About what?'

'Like, about the way it's making your, like, great ancestor out to be, you know…'

'Yeah, it's totally fine. I'm finding it exciting. Haven't told my mum or dad about it, though. None of this is in the family history stuff they keep.'

'So how did you say you found out about it? How to look up the other name? And anyway, maybe it's not the same person?'

'Shut up; of course it is! I heard my auntie say 'Gerald' to my mum, then looked it up from there when they weren't around. And it's the same boat he's meant to have died on. Same dates of his life. Almost. Same… you know. It *is* true. I'm telling you. It is. When you read on it's even got my actual grandpa's name in there, who's still alive even. Plus I never heard about it because they wouldn't want me to. My dad sues people who write bad stuff about our family, so it must be true or that site would be out of business by now. So it's all true, true, true. It has to be.'

'And you feel okay about it then?'

'Why wouldn't I? What you trying to say, Lukee?'

'Nothing. Just…'

'Just what? Okay, maybe I shouldn't be telling you this stuff then. Just what? Are you okay about it?'

'Me? Why would I be…'

'So that's fine then. Anyway, I don't need you to make me feel okay about that stuff. That's not your job in my life.'

'Not my *job*?'

'No.'

'So what is it, then? My job?'

'Haven't decided yet.' She winked, and shuffled across the sofa seat until she was pressed unusually close to me. It was like the temperature in my body had suddenly gone up a few degrees and my heart thumped three times, loud and excited, too.

'What else is news?' she said, leaning her furthest arm across my lap to the iPad and pressing the home button.

'Er. Okay… Well, I got something to show you too, anyway,' I said.

'Ooh yeah?'

'Yeah.'

'Sounds fun!'

'Er, maybe.'

'Well come on then. Don't leave me hanging.'

Even though I didn't want to, I wriggled a little bit to push just the tiniest gap of personal space back between us. I wanted to tell her what I'd found out about the metal stick because of what it meant, not for any other reason. She just leaned over again, though, and I gave in. Fine, Gaby, I thought. Stay close. My heart hit three more off-beats.

'I worked out what the rusted thing we found at Bunkers is,' I said.

'So did I,' she smiled, lifting the iPad back off my lap and onto hers. Now she did edge away again slightly. And now I didn't really want her to.

'It's a wand,' she said. 'Belongs to a sea god. That's what it's gonna be in my sculpture anyway. I'm gonna make a big spirit of the sea thingy out of metal and wood and fishnet and plastic. That bar's gonna be his wand or sceptre or something like that.'

'It's a fire-eater's baton,' I said.

'It's a what?'

'It's from a fire eater. They light one end and hold the other. The rust is growing on the end they light. There would have been a rubber handle on the other bit. Look.' And I slid open my phone, pulled up my browsing history and zoomed in on the photos I'd screenshot just an hour before.

She peered over. Leaned over, too. Like that, her head was on my shoulder.

The photos were impossible to argue with. There it was, right in the guy's hand. Not Alex's father, but a different fire eater, in a different time. The baton, though, was there, zoomed in on for Gaby to see. I'd found a page of instructions for how to use them too, with close-ups of how to slide the rubber handle over the square end.

'Nooooo waaaaaaaay!' she whispered. 'That's so cool! How the *hell* did you find that?'

'Mrs Rogoff's Art pack,' I said.

'What? *She* had *this*?'

'Well. Kind of. It was in a gallery off some web link on the back page of her study pack.'

'The Colombia one? But Luca, *nobody* in our class looked in those packs. What came over you?'

'Dunno,' I lied, before layering it with a shred of truth. 'Got a panic-on coz of the Maths classes they're making me go to instead, I think. Realised I was, like, six months behind in Art so I'd better do something.'

'That's sooooo cooooooool,' said Gaby again. 'Send me that screenshot! Please?'

'Yeah, no worries.'

'Cool.' She pulled out her phone, and unlocked the screen, while I pressed 'share' and ticked each of the photos to pass on. They were with her in just a minute or two, with that whooshing 'send' sound.

'Nice one, Luca.'

168

I tipped my phone her way and winked.

'LL Cool J,' she said, and barged me with her shoulder.

'Whatever.'

'Anyway. Wanna know what else I've got for you then?'

'Maybe.'

'I think you do.'

'Okay then.'

'It's the coolest thing ever.'

'Go on. Try me.'

'Luca,' she said. 'I've drawn him again, too. A copy for you. Of Old Gigi. Wanna look?'

What could I say to that? Sure Gaby, let's have a look. Why me?

She jumped back to the other chair and started rummaging in her backpack.

'You'll be able to make him out better, this time,' she said. 'I liked the way your face went last time you saw my drawings of him, so here's a proper good one. Hang on... Here you go... Ah, here it is. Ready? Luca, meet Gigi!'

Now my face *did* go. Despite me trying to keep it together. And why? Because there he was, and this time there was no doubt about it.

'Like it?' she said, as I made out the row of figures trudging behind him. Or was it a row of figures? She'd done that cryptic thing again, where she rubbed and smudged it all so much you kind of wondered if you were just imagining what you wanted from the picture.

'Well? What d'you reckon, Lukee?'

I had no reply.

'Like it?'

I tried to nod, catching dryness in my throat as I moved my neck.

'Wicked,' she grinned. 'I thought you might.'

Chapter 15

How funny is it that Wentloog asked me to try and sketch the Gigi pic? Of course, that's never gonna happen – because if I did then it would probably cause all kinds of crazy stuff to come to life. But I will have to give the Doc something one day. He wrote it into that behaviour contract he wanted me to sign up to.

Contract? I know. I did have to do one, though. Brilliant isn't it? More value for money from Wentloog the Wonder.

I wanted to tell Gaby that I had beaten her to an official contract to draw something – but then I realised that she'd probably try and sue me because it was her concept. Intellectual theft, she used to call it. Also, the more I learn about her... well... who knows? She's been super tense about how much detail I've given them about this guy. Come on, Miss Carranero. As if I'd go and tell them everything about him. She doesn't need to worry at all. I've told her this. They won't join those dots. I've promised her.

'This man – this "Gigi" – he can go in your blue booklet, anywhere you like,' said Wentloog, when I finally realised he wasn't giving up on the idea. 'He's such an important character in our tale. We all recognise that. I think it's important you feel what it's like to sketch him. It's such a liberating thing to do. Lots of young people in your position have found that the case. I've seen it work in my own practice plenty of times. You can even do it in pencil and rub him out afterwards. Some like to do that, while others are still a bit afraid to take such a step. I just think the process of creating this person with your own hands is the crucial bit, though. Realising that *you* control this character. It's something I really do want you to do.'

'It's only properly creating if you do it for yourself and not anyone else,' I told him.

'You are going to do it for yourself, Luca,' he replied, legs crossed and his hands on his knee. He was doing the look-right-through-you thing that always meant he wasn't being straight.

'Except you'll see it,' I said.

'Only if you want me to.'

'I won't want you to.'

Dr Wentloog smiled and said 'But you will'. Only he said it without moving his face. He just meant it – which for him was as good as saying something.

'Nothing in that blue book of yours is shared with anyone until you're ready,' he added.

'Good. Because there's nothing in it yet,' I joked. His flat smile trembled for a second and he laughed, light and forced. 'I told you I keep the pages of my notebooks blank, didn't I?'

'Okay,' he said. 'If you're not ready, then try to sketch him further in your mind's eye first. That's just as effective. That way you can make him more complex, and that comment you made about being creative will be true. It'll be just for your own observation if it's in your mind. True creativity, as you yourself just called it.'

'Did you say "complex" though?' I asked.

'Yes.'

'Ah. See, it's only creative if it's simple, too, see. So that won't work either.'

'Fine. Well then, Luca, you tell me what will?'

'Okay. Tell you what, Dr W,' I said. 'If you promise to believe me, then I'll do your drawing. Do we have a deal?'

It wasn't in the contract, of course. But why not ask, eh?

He left the room shortly after that, and I scratched the first few lines of 'Gigi Carranero by Gaby' into the next page. For me, of course. I ripped it out and got rid of it nearly straightaway. But then again, we don't need some pencil lines to bring him out, do we? Gaby did that for us anyway with the charcoal.

Wonder if she was proper 'creating' when she did that? I mean, she did plan to show it to me, didn't she? Maybe that's how it happened.

Ah, maybe we can just ask him sometime, anyway? No, not Wentloog. HIM. The man in the pencil lines. Except we can ask the real him, rather than the charcoal version, of course.

Probably easiest, right?

*　*　*

Jeff was still there when I got back. He and my dad were hatching a plan to take the watches to market the next day – Sunday.

My mum was sitting in the kitchen listening to dance music and baking.

'Macaroons,' she shouted, over the din.

I went back into the living room. It was dark in there. The day had been pretty bright, but the curtains were closed and the air felt stale.

'What's happenin' Lukee Boy?' said Jeff.

'Nothing.'

'Good one. Gonna come with us tomorrow then? Five a.m. start. Swansea. Bit of a drive but should be a good un. We'll sell most of these, and then you know what happens next.'

I didn't. And the thing is, neither did they, really. I knew what the *reply* was, but that didn't make it true.

'*Amser Aur*!' Jeff grinned. Dunno why he needed to say it in Welsh.

'Gold Time,' translated my dad, just in case I hadn't managed to pick up two of the most basic GCSE-level words out there.

'Great,' I said, rolling my eyes.

'Lookin keen there, Lukee Boy!' laughed Jeff.

'He is. Don't you worry about that,' said my dad. 'Just needs to catch up on a bit of kip, doesn't he. Teenagers. Grumpy about anything.'

He could talk. How many hours sleep had my folks had last night?

Seemed Jeff was claiming even less:

'Ah, no sleep's good for ya sometimes,' he said. 'Only had an hour myself. Was, er, busy, like, if you know what I mean.'

'Met up with *her* again did you?' said my dad.

'Ooh yeah,' said Jeff.

'Yeah, well that's all you're gonna tell us, Jeff, mate. Not with Lukee here. He still thinks babies come from a stork.'

'What d'you mean,' said Jeff, winking at me. 'They do, don't they?'

Then both of them laughed.

'Anyway,' said Jeff. 'Let's get on with these labels. Lukee, you gonna help us?'

'If I have to.'

'G'boy,' said Jeff. 'Right. You've seen how it works. Here's a sheet with the trade price on them. We need trade plus thirty per-cent plus VAT minus a fiver. That's our bottom line. Add twenty to that if it's under forty. Add thirty if it's over. Then we know how far down we can haggle. Got that?'

'Yeah.'

'So go on then. A watch is labelled up at eighty-nine,' said my dad. 'What can we drop to and still make our share?'

'Fifty-nine.'

'Good, Luca. And they write us these letters home saying they're worried about your Maths!'

'He's doing great if you ask me,' said Jeff. 'So then, Lukee Boy. Howsabout this one... Watch price is eighty-nine, but you can see it's already been reduced a tenner from ninety-nine... What happens then?'

'Er...'

'Go on, Lukee Boy. Be bold!'

I knew what was coming here.

'Go on. Say it.'

I sighed: 'Sixty-nine.'

'Wahey!'

Both of them laughed again.

'Childish twat,' said my dad, and Jeff winked again.

* * *

Back in the kitchen, my mum was arranging some CDs, as she waited for her macaroons to crispen.

'How's Lukee then?' she said.

'Alright,' I told her.

'They finished their price indexing?'

'Yeah.'

'Good.'

'Mum,' I said.

'What?'

'What made you put this on the other day?' I held up the *Thickest Thumps of Two-Tone* CD, and ran my thumb along the track list. There it was. Number nine. Max Romeo.

'Chase the Devil'. That was it. The one that used my line in its intro and outro.

'Oh, did you hear it? I thought you were still asleep! I dunno. You know the way it is. It was its turn to go on.'

'Really?'

'Yeah. That's how I run our CDs. Just change them over every now and then. It must have come from upstairs. Why? Does it still make you feel creepy, then? God it must be ten years, now, Lukee.'

'I don't know if it does or not,' I said. 'But I heard it and then it was, like, kind of stuck in my head afterwards.'

'That's coz it's such a catchy tune, Luca,' she said, smiling and flicking the kettle on.

'Wanna put it on?'

'Nah.'

'Okay. Cup of tea?'

'Yeah.'

'Don't blame Max Romeo, anyway,' said my mum. 'It's not his fault you spent like two years thinking he was singing your name instead of Lucifer.' She chuckled again at the memory.

I could have sworn they had it on a tape deck back then.

'How old was I?' I asked her.

'Gosh, like four? Maybe five? You have to admit. It was cute. You thought it said "Luca, son of the morning" in the first line and you used to come running when it went on. Then you used to dance in circles to the beat. You can see why we didn't want to tell you what the lyric really said.'

Yeah, nice one, Mum and Dad. Lovely touch. Let your kid think there's some catchy song on the stereo with his name in it.

And then one day tell him it's actually about Satan.

Yeah, good one.

'It is about the devil though, isn't it?' I said to my mum, remembering how I screamed through the night as my dad tried to explain the complex details of a reggae legend's lyric choices. They might recall me as a dancing baby instead, but I could still feel the fear of first finding out.

'Kind of,' said my mum. 'That first line isn't by a songwriter anyway. It's from the Bible. Ask your dad. He'd know. It's Isaiah, verse something or other. It means the morning star, like, as in Venus or Mercury. You know they called the "star of the morning" by that name – "Lucifer" – too, see. So it was a star's name, anyway, as well as the devil. A star, Lukee! Someone who brought light to people's worlds. The one that was shining brighter than the others. The star that ended the night. The bringer of dawn. The morning.'

'A five- or six-year-old kid isn't really going to get that, though, are they?'

'Doesn't matter,' she said. 'You were our star of the morning anyway.'

'Not much chance of that now, eh?' I said.

'Of what?'

'Me… being star of the morning.'

She laughed and grabbed me into a hug.

'You're a funny little bugger when you want to be,' she said, reaching across the table and grabbing the cup of tea she'd made me. 'Sugar?'

'Two.'

'Two! Cutting down then, Lukee?'

'Saving the higher doses for the mornings,' I said.

She laughed again. 'Good idea. So you going to go with them tomorrow?'

'Probly.'

'Use it as your song,' she said. 'Your wake-up track. It'll be perfect. Star of the morning! Come on!'

'What's the next line?' I asked.

'You *know* that. Come on, Luca.'

'No. I mean from the Bible verse. Not the song.'

'Oh, I dunno. Ask your dad once Jeff's gone.'

'Nah, it's okay. I can look it up myself sometime.'

* * *

It was ages before Jeff left, and by then my mum had turned back to being full-on buddies with my dad again. I couldn't figure out at all why she wasn't giving him the usual grief about buying crap goods and fetching wrong prices. These watches didn't seem any better than any of the other junk which he sold for so little profit that there was never any pocket money for me and I had to watch Gaby drink coffee down at the Quarters Cafe.

Anyway, for some reason that I couldn't get anywhere near, my mum had gone soft over him on this latest deal. That kind of messed with the balance of our household. My mum always put the daggers in if Dad set himself up for another bum deal, and I was sort of missing the reassurance of seeing that happen this time. I know people don't like their parents arguing, but my parents arguing meant all was well.

Hearing them in the living room that night, though, the reason for her being so easy on him was getting nearer, now lingering somewhere behind that cloud of smoke as they puffed on a few roll-ups and drank a bit more rum.

So I listened in.

'Really gonna sell enough for us to put a stake in some gold then, is it, Steve?'

'Ooh, dunno. Gold costs a fortune, Hann.'

'I bet it does. Costs the earth.'

'Aye. Literally!'

My mum was laughing.

'Unless,' grinned my dad, leaning right back into the darkest edges of our tatty sofa, '...unless you know a source who can get you some for a mega cut-down price. Some that can easily melt and get sold again on the markets clean. Some *salvage* surplus!'

My mum giggled, again, and then drank another sip, judging from the way her laugh was cut short. 'Now that would be cool,' she said.

I went upstairs.

I didn't try listening to or googling 'Lucifer son of the morning' that night. Like running Street View on a map of Cartagena, it was as if there was some sort of living lump inside me, waiting to rub cotton wool on my brain or poke out my eyes from within, any time I entertained the idea of clicking on the right button to do it.

Instead, I ended up listening to Bob Marley's 'Concrete Jungle' while reading some online stuff about Satan in music. There was stuff about Voodoo and the formation of jazz – music my mum listened to often. Then there was something about a Rolling Stones song, which I clicked on to listen to. It sounded familiar but then my heart started thumping and my breath sped up and I felt hot in the face and needed to go back to Bob to hold the right rhythm in place.

Then, a few links later, it came round to the same guy. *My* song! Max Romeo. There he was and then there the verse was: the lines from the Bible that I was scared to search. The singer himself was saying some pretty cool stuff about how he wrote the song because he thought people had it wrong believing the devil was a person or something living. 'The Devil is in all of us!' he was saying, and somehow I could cope with hearing it, because Max had that soothing voice that reggae singers do, and all the while Bob was winding down his lovely riff with that jiggy shake of guitars in the background, and the harmonies of The Wailers were locked in his trance.

I was learning something here.

Wonder if Dr Wentloog is actually going to ever read this stuff? Hopefully not. He wouldn't get it, anyway. So how's this for a theory?

The devil... Lucifer... don't matter what we call him. Well, he's just the evil in each of us. We create him with our own bad thoughts, the ones we keep to ourselves, the ones which we can't do anything about because they're just our own mind's rhythm. Then God, and you can call him – or her – whatever, too. That's just the good in each of us. How simple is that? Surely it's simple enough to count as creative, if we're still going by that rule?

Anyway, it was what the guy who wrote my song was on about. That was what he meant. *That* was its message.

I still wasn't going to click the Bible verse link, though. No way.

My sixth run of 'Concrete Jungle' was coming to an end, and through my now silent earphones I could hear some kind of indie pop from downstairs.

I wondered how much good there was in my parents. How much evil, too?

Were they where I got mine from? And how much of it all was in me?

How much of my mum's good? How much of my dad's? And how much of the evil in them? Was there evil in them? And was there evil in me, then?

Was I really Lucifer, Son of the Morning, some of the time?

Maybe not for me to say, you know. Maybe I should let the Doc decide. Would be interesting to hear what he thought, anyway.

*   *   *

Next day was all about keeping my good and bad under control. Funny how it worked out like that, don't you think?

I woke up just after lunch and there was my dad, chewing on a pie from the chippy that he always went to round the corner. My mum was digging into a sandwich she'd made, and you could see on their faces the moment I came down that something had happened which they were going to rate as good.

The watches had sold. Sold quickly, too. They only had four left, and my dad was eyeing up a wedge of cash on the kitchen surface.

'Add this to our savings and we're over the line anytime soon,' he kept saying. 'Ell of an appetite for wholesale on those babies at the market! Dropped in price a bit, but I can shift more of them next week. If I did this for a month we could buy twice as much of Haz's gold!'

Jeff Rafferty was on his way over, too.

I looked at my mum for some kind of sense, but you could see there wasn't going to be any. No use. This was happening.

I thought about what this might mean for me now – more trips to Birmingham, more sketchy geezers trying to flog stuff through my dad. More afternoons like this, with Jeff and the pair of them playing loud music and singing like kids in the year below me.

That seemed to be Sunday in the Lincoln-James house these days. Parents counting money from market watches and planning to spend it all, and more, on dodgy gold – as they sipped rum and swayed like they were on an ancient galleon in high seas.

Perhaps they'd all kidnap someone soon, too, and hold out for a huge ransom from some posh family with too much money of their own. Then my parents would finally be as bad as Gaby's. Or as bad as Gaby thought hers were since less than twenty-four hours ago.

No. Hang on... Kidnapping? Ransoms? That would make my folks just a little bit clever. They'd never do anything like that, then. My folks and clever didn't go together.

There. That's the main part of them that was in me: not being clever. Good or evil were too ambitious for this family. There you go – the real reason I was bad at Maths. I wasn't evil enough!

Maybe that was my destiny, I realised. Was I meant to be one of these people who couldn't create because you were neither good, nor bad, but just grey and boring and empty? Maybe that was it, I thought, dragging myself upstairs to wait for the day to be over and Monday to come and get me with all the savage glory that it seemed to have no problem creating out of nothing.

Chapter 16

I didn't feel like Bunny in the mornings the next week. There was too much out of sync in my head to even dare approaching the gates of Chapel Shores Comp with my usual routine. Mr Kleener would need to be warded off with something else.

I flicked on 'shuffle' for most of the Monday walk to school, only settling on 'Many Rivers to Cross' by UB40 right at the last minute. It seemed to have just the right message for where I was heading right now. Long shadows cut their way across the yellowy dawn ground, as the herd of kids pushed through the gates. It was one of those cold, crisp mornings you get in the spring, with no wind and the air really sharp.

We had a new supply teacher for Reg, and this time it was a much older woman who wasn't going to put up with any crap. She was thin and tall, dressed in blue trousers with a white shirt and a long, dark green coat over – one of those coats you could kind of wear indoors and not look silly. Her hair was straight and neat, dyed dark brown with grey roots just showing. Straight away, I missed the grumpy young teacher we'd been having for Reg. She never bothered us to do any of the stuff we were meant to. This lady, though, was working through the register checking up stuff like who'd missed lessons in the week before and asking them questions about where they were.

It was my turn to get it easy for once, or so it seemed. I was on time this morning, and my only day off – to go to the market with my dad and Jeff – was authorized by the last supply already. Still, it wasn't much fun listening to her laying into us all first thing in the morning, when everyone knows kids my age are crap.

'I taught for thirty years,' she was saying. 'Retired and happy to go. But your Mr Kleener is a dear friend, so I've agreed to come back until the summer and you lot are through your exams. Don't worry. I won't go away. It's going to be stability from now on.'

Stability sounded okay, before I realised it was just a decoy for something much worse.

'Oh, and…' reading off a screen, she squinted and announced: 'Luca Lincoln-James, Bethan David, Harrison Storer and Robert Singh? Are you all here?'

Three of us were. Harrison Storer we had never actually met. We wondered who he was, ever since he 'joined' in year nine but hadn't ever actually showed up. But the rest of us were in, and she knew it.

The rest of our form piled out for the day and me and the other two sat, tired, behind our desks in this dim room for someone we'd never met to come out with exactly what we were expecting.

'Now, you three – we don't know where Harrison is, do we? – no. Never mind. You three are here now, because the school has asked me to keep an eye out. You're very important to Mr Kleener and to the school, and I've promised him I'll check in on you every couple of days. You see, you three have been flagged up as kids the school's a little worried about, as in you *might* be at a little risk of maybe not quite meeting your potential in one or two subjects…'

And I drifted off. It was the only way to cope with that

speech. We'd had it off a million adults by now. Ride it out until they reach the bit about…

'…Now your attendance is very important at this stage, and well done for being here…'

…and then you knew they were near the end.

*　*　*

Break rolled round and as soon as I saw Gaby my head was filling up with questions, but there she was, quiet and oblivious to my existence once more. She wouldn't even catch my eye.

I wanted so badly to talk to her about the picture she'd shown me, but Saturday to Monday can be *such* a long time in Chapel Shores for a kid like me, and it was as if the person who had shuffled up to me in that coffee shop, sharing secrets of her family's criminal history was long gone.

Now, there was just this smart-looking girl, whose uniform was ironed and whose hair had been straightened to cling close to her cheeks. This girl who seemed like five years older than the rest of us, riding a taunt of 'Gabo, give us a kiss' from some muscle-bound rugby kid with a gentle sneer in his direction, while two of the other girls who were too grown up for anyone to approach called her 'Gabe' as they showed her some pictures on a phone that seemed to be of immense interest.

I had a *theory* to hit her with, though, and it wasn't fair that I couldn't just ask to speak to her. Those other girls with her – they looked kind of sound, didn't they? Maybe they'd be like Ella Bowen, who had turned out to be fully approachable and nowhere near as scary or hard as people claimed. Maybe, through some sort of weird mixture of pity and general humanity, they might also decide it was fine to hear me out, and that their great mate 'Gabe' should be cool to me too.

No. Never going to happen.

'Fair' was an idea that got left at the gates of Chapel Shores Comp. I knew that by now, and no amount of Bunny Wailing or UB40-ing or anything else would ward off the natural order of things. A natural order that said *No*. She *is Gabrielle Carranero and* you *are Luca Lincoln-James and you two cannot mingle when the social order is at play*.

But what about my theory! Come on, Gaby. It'll interest you! It will.

If only I could get to tell it to her.

I reckoned she knew it already, anyway. She had to. Otherwise she wouldn't have been able to knock out that picture the way she had done – with it seeming so real. With the silhouettes of the other guys following him. With each figure in the queue casting a shadow down onto a surface that, even in the shaky charcoal of Gaby's 'impressionist' style, looked so much like sand at night that it couldn't be anything else.

We had Art two lessons later, as well, which they let me go to this time instead of extra Maths, and where it should have meant I got a break from simultaneous equations. Instead it came as even more of a stress as I had to watch her being perfect, getting told so by Rogoff at every opportunity. Gabrielle Carranero the impressionist. Gaby Carranero the sculptor. Gabe the fashionista, the avant-garde, the prodigy. Gabe the genius. Gabo the girl the rugby boys took a pop at from time to time because sooner or later one of them thought they were going to get somewhere.

'All Art chicks are mental,' I remembered Joe Poundes saying once in a corridor, behind her but so that she could hear. 'It's *so* sexy, innit!' I'm sure he'd been rewarded with a chuckle from his mates for that one. I hadn't seen her reaction, though, and knew by now not to meddle if she was getting grief in school – not that I could have done anything at all about it. In Rogoff's room, though, she had her refuge, every single time.

It was the highlight of my day, that Art lesson, as they always were whenever Kleener let me go to them instead of Maths. How sad that this kind of thing is my highlight, though? Getting to sit there watching Mrs Rogoff rave about Gaby's work, and a few others' work too just to make it look balanced, while feeling like a moron myself for having such a crap idea. I sat there, adding pointless licks of paint to my pop-art collage, while Mrs Rogoff occasionally 'popped' by and pretended she was trying not to look disappointed or unimpressed.

Yeah, Gaby was right to steer clear of me in school.

And then my parents ignored me once I got home too.

*　　*　　*

The next morning I was back in the extra Maths classes – which was just as crap, because it meant missing Art, where being an underwhelming failure was kind of cool, to go to a place where being at any risk whatsoever of not succeeding meant you got harassed and hassled to the point of near death.

'Any of these mathematicians getting near that C-grade yet?' bellowed Mr Kleener, when he visited half way through the lesson. 'It's the golden ticket, Year 11!'

Golden ticket? Did that make it real, then? Did that help it exist?

'What was that, Luca Lincoln-James?'

'Er, nothing, Sir. Just talking under my breath. Sorry.'

Then it was BTEC Science again, and that meant my

second chance of the week to imagine a world where kids in my year were kind and sensitive, where people liked you for who you were and had no secrets or motives to hide. In other words, it was my second weekly hour sat next to Ella Bowen.

'It's LL Cool J and his sweetie music,' she laughed, as I arrived and unpacked.

'How you doin, little man?'

'Alright,' I said. 'You?'

'I'm good. Thanks for asking, *brawd*.' She smiled big and flicked a curved thumbs-up at me, her finger nail, pearly-white today, rising out of her tanned hand like an antennae.

'Anyway,' she said, 'been hearing a lot about you.'

'Really?'

'Of course?'

'What, from Gabrielle?' Not knowing which of the shortened versions of her name to use in this situation, I just went for the full one.

'Obviously. Yeah, man! Gabe won't stop going on about you.'

'Doesn't seem like it when I'm in this place,' I said. Somehow, it seemed okay to say those kinds of things to Ella.

'Ah, don't worry about that,' said Ella. 'She's a funny bitch with all of us here. She'll tell you herself. It's always been like that, though. She's got funny ideas, see, hasn't she.'

I didn't say anything more, but flicked to the next page of my BTEC booklet. Ella did the same, then added:

'Yeah. Thing is with Gabe, see, she's all into this thing about how she only comes here to pass her exams and get a job and all that, like. Suppose she's kind of right, isn't she?'

'Yeah, maybe.'

'She just wants to get amazing results then escape Chapel Shores and become like some kind of famous designer or something.'

'Does she say that?' I said. 'Coz she's always told me about how she likes it here and, like, the way it's, like, you know... The way it's kind of quiet and dead-endey here.'

'Nah. She don't really believe that, though. She's changed her mind now anyway. Did she tell you about her parents arguing?'

'Er, sort of.'

'Bad, innit.'

'Uh...'

'I mean, like, her dad sounds like a full-on murderer waiting to happen, don't you reckon?'

'Er... I've not really met him.'

'Yeah, but getting all in their faces like that? You know? Like he did the other night. That's harsh, eh?'

'Er, yeah. It's pretty bad.'

I pretended to know what she was on about.

'Did you hear about the crazy shit she discovered about her dad?' Ella went on.

'Uh, about...'

'Yeah, that he's like some gangster guy whose great grandpa was some sort of, like, money... What's the word. You know, "money laundromats" isn't it?'

'Money *launderer*,' said our teacher, Mr Powell, arriving just late enough not to hear the rest.

'Yeah, that's it! Thanks sir!' Ella grinned and fluttered her eyelids at him.

'Not quite sure where money laundering comes into the BTEC Science syllabus,' said Mr Powell, frowning and smiling at once. Ella could get that from people. Teachers loved her, especially male ones. She just had that way that meant they couldn't stay annoyed with her.

'It is, sir. Trust me.'

'I'm not as sure as you, somehow, Ella. Come, on. Get on with your workbook.'

As he strolled away, Ella winked at me. 'Cool, though, int it! Gabe wants to run away and earn her own money now. She don't want her dad's, see. That's why she's so on it in school, like. Why she's so intense at the moment.'

I wanted to say that she'd been that intense in school for, well, since *ever*, really, for me, but I didn't want to incur Mr Powell's wrath for distracting Ella during the one sentence of the hour that she'd decided to write into her workbook. He wouldn't be so cool with *me* for not getting work done. So I just turned to my own workbook, and waited for her to choose when to lose her concentration next.

It was about thirty seconds.

'Hey. She's gonna have a break at Jackdaw's party next weekend, anyway. You're coming, aren't you?'

'Party?'

'Yeah, man! You know Jackdaw, don't you? From the year above us. He didn't stay on, though. Works with his dad now. They're builders. D'you know him?'

Of course I knew of this guy. He'd been a proper badass when he was in Year 11 last year. They kicked him out before his exams, so working with his dad was probably his only option – if he didn't become some kind of drug dealer or other crim.

'His full name's Jack Dooley?' said Ella, as if I didn't know of this local celeb. 'His dad's van has Dooley's Driveways written on the side of it? Me and him used to go out a bit but then we worked better as friends. He liked Gabe, too, but she was only with him for like a week and nothing happened. He wasn't her type. Anyway, his mum's going away and it's only him and his dad in the

190

house, so his dad said he could have a party. Last one he did was *mega*. They had hot tubs and live music in the garden.'

'It's not very warm right now,' I said.

'Yeah, but that don't matter. Have you been in a hot tub on a cold night? It's lush.'

'Yeah,' I lied, again.

'Anyway. Gabe wants you to come. She told me to tell you.'

'Really?'

'Course she does, LLJ! Bring some booze too.'

'BRING SOME WHAT?' yelled Mr Powell, timing his pass perfectly.

'Sorry, sir. I said bring some, er, clues, sir. Like, clues for how to find the melting point of, er, aluminium. Me and LL Cool J're gonna catch up after school.'

The class buckled with laughter, and Mr Powell couldn't stay mad at her after that:

'Catch up? You pair have hardly started! You're getting on too well, I reckon.'

The class laughed again, with a few hoots and whistles.

'I don't mean...' said Mr Powell.

'So what, sir? Maybe he *is* my boyfriend.'

Then she grabbed me with both arms and hugged me hard in front of the class. It seemed to shut them up, and Mr Powell too.

Ella had that power. The natural order had given her the right to make herself the butt of a joke, and to end or grow the joke whenever she wanted. For me, it was a freebie. I could get laughed at here, and because it was Ella, there was the kind of unspoken rule it couldn't get picked up outside of class by anyone.

Apart from Joe Poundes, who nudged me hard by the gates at the end of the day – just enough to make sure I knew it wasn't meant to be friendly – and went, 'Bowen would eat you for breakfast, mate. Honest. You wouldn't know what hit you.'

He wasn't in my BTEC class, which meant someone must have told him. He had no audience at the gates with him either, and must have known Ella had been joking. So what he said, well, it was meant for me and only me. Or maybe just him. Was *he* being creative, then?

It worked, anyway. I had to walk home pulling hard to get the cold air into my hot lungs, as 'Many Rivers to Cross' played over and over to keep my heart from knocking its way up and out of my throat.

The mists were drawing back in over Chapel Shores as my breath and pulse made it back into their right rhythm, and I could hear the grey rapping of the sea on the beach at the end of my street.

It might be time again, soon, I thought.

* * *

I had the text drafted like ten times. Never sent it, though. Imagine the risk? Imagine the parallel universes filled with her possible reactions, only one or two of which were anything that would make my world any easier. Or hers.

It was dark, but I had my curtains open anyway. The orange streetlamps were lighting soft rings of mist and drizzle for several metres around them, like really dim versions of the sun floating, in miniature along my street. The lamp by my bed pushed the dark out almost as far as the window, which was only there to keep the room warm. I was letting the night in. It felt like the right thing to do. Under the floor, the rumble of some nineties indie music reminded me my parents were still in a weirdly good mood about life, the universe and everything.

My thumbs twitched over the screen.

It would be such a leap to send this. More than I'd ever have in me.

Still, though, I typed it, again and again, in loads of different versions, and hovered a fingertip by the 'send' option:

'Got to ask u Gaby. who were the people behind him in the pic you drew.'

Or…

'Hey can you tell me coz its bugging me was it his crew from the boat that sunk. The people following your pappi up the beach in that pic you did?'

Or…

'Hiya any more nice sketches today? Rogoff properly loves u eh. Was it people he'd kidnapped in a line of shadows behind ur grandgrandpapa in that pic, been workin on a theory about him and cld tell u if you wanna meet up?'

And maybe:

'Hey Gaby-Gabe plz can we meet up I GENUINELY think I met ur grandpa the pirate type and I really mean it. U believe in ghosts right so maybe I can take u to him? LLJ'

You can see why they always got deleted in the end, right?

I'd just have to wait. The natural order couldn't be messed with. It might throw everything into the mix. One day I'd get a message instead probably saying something simple like 'Bunkers?', and then I'd go and then I'd pike out of managing to bring it up, yet again.

Or maybe I could head to that party and manage to actually walk in and be someone else and tell her it all, and more, and then I'd be free of me forever and she'd be free of her.

And we'd go to Bunny's land across the sea.

Dream on, dreamer. I laughed at myself for the idea. So hard my mum called up the stairs to see if I was okay.

I called back, 'Fine!', because that's all the natural order would allow for an answer to such a stupid question.

*   *   *

As the weekend drew nearer, the things Ella had told me drifted around my mind.

We had BTEC again one more time, and then all she did was go on about how nice and misunderstood this older kid, Jackdaw, was, and how I really should just come along to this party because he'd love me, and Gaby definitely thought I was going to be there, too.

Still, though, there was not a word from the mighty Gabrielle Carranero herself, great granddaughter of pirates and mega-crooks. Even Ella reckoned the girl had gone into her own little world and wasn't speaking to anyone apart from teachers.

In the meantime, I couldn't stop thinking about my two theories either, and I wanted to know why Gaby had drawn Gigi's latest imagined portrait the way she had. Or was it more than something imagined?

In the end I did send her a message, but it was nothing like I wanted to write. I just said: 'Howsit going? Been busy? Might wander down Bunkers tomorrow after "work". U keen?'

She never replied, though, and 'tomorrow-after-work' came and went, and still Gaby set about the tiny moments we were near each other in school as if I was someone she had never met.

Friday came, one week out exactly from the party that more people than just Ella were starting to rave about now, and there I was trudging home, bored and forgotten, but maybe safe once again.

So I thought instead about Alex, the boy in Cartagena. How long had it been for him now? I wondered about his father and his life, working those hot streets, painted black in the bright sun. And because of those thoughts on the way home, I dared myself to do something risky. Stopping the tune I had on, I hit 'Third World' instead, and found the other track I shouldn't dare touch because it was almost half the way towards street-viewing that place anyway. The tune I heard when I was there: 'Ninety-six Degrees in the Shade' spread through my ears, and immediately Alex and his town and his dad and the warm sea and the cold clothes and the police and the drug dealers and the army and the fire eating were right around me – real life visions, there on the street corners of Chapel Shores.

Now I *knew* it was time.

There was takeaway pizza on order at home, so I had a few slices before heading up early. Once it had got dark and I was again sealed up in my room for the night, I went online and started looking at ways to help 'street performers'. It was a better option than pretending to sleep.

Cartagena was in one of the links I found, and then there were more, newer images of several fire eaters. Stuff someone had uploaded since I collected that image to show Gaby at Quarters. They were on a corner together and looked like they could be in some sort of troop or team. I squinted and stared at their faces until there was one who I was convinced was Alex's dad, because he had a face somehow different from the rest – with the same dark hair and sad eyes as the kid I'd met.

Then I tried my bravery, and went onto Google maps again, but each time I was about to drop the little orange guy onto the streets of the walled city from above I couldn't quite make my frozen hand move. Instead I drifted onto a promoted link, which must have been suggested to me because I had been on these 'humanitarian' sites about helping the people of other countries. Only this one was about Japan, and had some petition you could sign about saving the seas near Tokyo from fishing. They were catching too many fish there, and it had a YouTube clip of the millions of tons of living, slimy sea life that was being dragged out of the ocean every day, including all the little things that couldn't be eaten and so had to be thrown in the bin, and the dead dolphins that had got mixed up with tasty tuna. It made me feel a sadness that was almost beautiful. It was so clean, so pure and so right, I realised, to hurt in some way when you saw what people could do to each other, to the world and to its amazing wildlife, just because they felt like it. There were so many other things to worry about on this planet, and somehow to me, right then, it seemed a comforting thought. Does that make me weird? Because it didn't feel weird at all. It felt like the least weird thing to run through my head in months.

I drifted off in minutes, then, and woke late on Saturday, still with the gorgeous sadness, but also kind of buzzing that there were already only a few hours to go till dark again. I spent them lying on the couch watching my dad count more shoes and more watches, before he roped me into helping him price up a few. Then he bought me chips to say thanks, and went out to the pub to meet Jeff, while my mum switched on the telly and reached for the rum.

Still no word from Gaby either. But by now I'd forgotten to care.

My next shoreline night was moments away.

Chapter 17

This time it was only music. Nothing to look at, nothing to watch, or read – instead I let the dark come from outside and with no lights or lamps indoors laid out my clothes and waited for the right time to come.

Bunny was calling the mood, and his 'Dreamland' was my theme tune.

The few more hours crept in under the door and, one by one, eased themselves out the window and into the night air, until it was time for me to follow. I stuck my mum's spare key under a flat stone round the side of the house this time, so that if this outfit of hood, hat and jeans had any trouble coming back with me then at least I'd get into the house okay. Then I shoved the doubloon Haz had given me into my back pocket again – since I knew for a fact luck didn't exist.

The wetness had gone from the day before. The mists had drifted back out to sea, over the horizon and it was once again clear, starry and moonlit. The ground was dry and the dunes soft. I felt sand slipping away from under my steps as I half walked, half slid down to the pebble bank that met the shoreline. The tide was in, and the big, round moon stood right at the top of the sky, throwing white and silver patches across the surface of the inky sea.

The shore was swishing against the looser pebbles, with perfect time passing between each little whoosh and crackling drag-back.

Everything else was still.

In case I'd shaken the balance by walking up so clumsy, I worked at making myself still too. I stretched my back, knelt down and then eased myself into a sitting position with a smooth boulder under me as a seat. Then I drew deep breaths with my nose, pushing them out each time a wave sloshed up the shore and the sand, rocks and pebbles ground together noisily.

A few minutes passed. Things settled again, and I drifted into the trance offered by the hypnotic, dancing light of the moon on the surface of the water. This was the patch of light I knew they'd emerge through.

And then, sure enough, up came the first lump of dark, rising steadily from the water. Here they were. Here *he* was.

Head and shoulders up and out, his body continued emerging, until you could see the gentle rhythm of his steps. Again, those even paces lifted him up and forward, each pushing him further towards the moment when he'd break free of the murky ocean and begin to wade up the dry land in front.

Behind him followed his number two, then his number three.

The leader of this silent army was right by me now, and I looked up into his eyes as he began to pass.

Are you Mr Carranero? I wanted to say – but his eyes were the emptiest I'd seen them. Should I try to show him my doubloon? It looked as though there was no person, no soul, nothing living guiding this figure as he kept his focus ahead and led his followers up and over the dunes, towards the streets.

I couldn't follow, though. I was fixed to the spot. My legs were folded, chin at my knees and my arms were looped around them. No part of me wanted to move, and like all the other times I let the whole troop pass, before the sound of the sea returned and my body relaxed, telling me it was okay to move.

Had they been going quicker this time? I couldn't be sure. I looked up at the starlight, so unimaginably far overhead, then at the horizon beyond the shoreline. Stepping down to the water's edge, I swept my hand through the foamy water to check its temperature. Cold. That settled it. I turned and made for the dune as quick as I could.

As I ran, I looked around to see if I was alone – maybe the fox would be about – but like every other time, it seemed *I* had complete control over the whole universe for as long as the presence of these men was near.

Over the brow of the dune, one of the men had stopped to wait for me. It was him, and he gently raised his left hand to me in a silent, firm beckoning motion.

'Mr Carranero?' I said, the sound of my voice exploding into the night air around.

No answer. Just the beckoning, every bit as steady and empty-eyed as his walk.

When he strode into the rising ground and disappeared, I went straight after him. The sand seemed to move away from me. Beneath it, as I sank further, was softer sand, then a swirling torrent of dust and air – and then water which was warm in a way I already knew from somewhere else. My neck and head relaxed in its undertow, and all I had ever wanted was to be in it and under it as fast as I could.

The sand was now gone, and warm ocean had taken over everything. Breathing out long and content, from my nose, I sank, and with a stroke of my arms pushed under, and forwards. I found and felt the bottom with the palms of my hands. The trickles or warmer and cooler water were pouring out of the sea-bed, and I swam along with them, sliding my belly along the ocean floor as I went.

Then the warmth moved through me, right to my core, and I was on my way again – through the deepest parts of the night-time, and the whispering voice which sounded like it knew every answer that had ever existed.

* * *

'Hello. I'm Cee and you're *late*,' said a girl's voice, as I crawled across the sand, squinting at the weak sunlight above.

'Sea?'

'Yeah. Like "sea" – the ocean – or "see", with eyes – but spell with letter "C",' said the voice. 'I am "C-E-E". Is short for "CHIE-EH", spell "C-H-I-E", but you won't be able to say that, so you call me "Cee".'

'Okay. I'm Luca.'

'Yes. I know. You're Luca. You're late. Market starts in *three* minutes. Come on. No time to dry!'

Through my blurred vision, I looked at the girl, and blinking several times cleared my eyes to make her out. She was shorter than me, but about my age, and had neat black hair in a ponytail. She looked Japanese or Chinese, and was wearing loose, grey overalls – the kind a worker would normally have on. She had wide, dark eyes and she'd lifted her eyelashes out high and straight. Apart from that, she was pale skinned, pale lipped, thin-faced and wore no make-up. Her smile though, which came and went almost too quickly to notice, looked warm and beautiful.

An electric speaker barked some announcement in another language, and so crackly I couldn't make out a single sound. It drew my eyes up to what was around. A narrow bay of dark sand, walled on both sides by huge rows of light-coloured, concrete boulders. Behind me was a busy waterway. Boats were passing and seagulls chasing them in packs. In front, the small bay rose quickly to a strip of concrete steps, and then a massive building made from strips of metal that had the look of plastic or Lego. A bright yellow and pink sign was on the building, in writing that was, again, in Eastern characters. As I saw the sign a seagull bleated loudly overhead and a bell rang on one of the small boats that had been dragged half up the shoreline. That was around the same time the smell hit me.

This time, I'd come ashore somewhere dirty, and I mean properly dirty – like, scared to stay in the water once I noticed. There was a thin surface of rubbish floating on the sea, which was sticky warm as if it didn't actually contain much real water. The smell was a disgusting mix of things going off – maybe fish, maybe cheese, maybe bin bags or rotten meat – and burnt plastic or fuel. In fact, you could see a rainbow film of oil binding all the floating dirt together.

It stuck to me as I walked the last few steps out. The muck on my dark jeans was shining like the vinyl on an old record, and there were millions of bits of broken plastic or rope, almost the size of sand grains, clinging to the dirt from my knees down. I shook each leg, and only some of it fell off.

'You can take a bucket of water from the harbourside,' said Cee. 'Throw it on your legs. Good like new.' Then she laughed. 'You'll stay wet but we can say it was raining.' Her voice was soft, and as she said 'raining' she drew the word out. 'Raaiiiiineeeeng…' Either she was about to burst into song or she was trying not to laugh more. Then she reached for my hand: 'Come on. You make us *late*!'

'Is this…?'

'Tokyo Japan! Yes, you know the answer. Why ask?'

She led me, running, up the stone steps where I held us up for a moment to take a look back. There were five boats in this little bay, which was a tidal harbour of some kind. From the pink and orange brush-strokes in the sky off to what must be the east, it looked like dawn had been pretty recent. The whiter light of the sun was hidden for the moment, though, behind a dull cloud that sat low on the horizon.

Three of the boats, the bigger ones, were moored just far enough out to float. The two smallest – which only had outboard motors and little wind-shields rather than cabins – had been pulled onto the sand and roped to iron rings on the wall of boulders. A passage of deeper water flowed past on the other side of one of the walls, and another even bigger, red-hulled boat was cruising slowly through it, along the back of the wall to the sea beyond.

We were at the front of the grey building, and by a small door were a row of tall, white buckets, each filled with clear water. The one at the rear had a hose plunged into it, which you could tell was still discharging water from the way a tiny ripple of twisting current was making its way around the surface.

Cee gestured to me to pick up the front bucket.

'Throw. Like this!'

She mimicked chucking the pale of water over my jeans. I did what she said, pouring the heavy water down my legs. It was cold, but it felt so relieving to see all that grime and debris come off me and wash towards the gutter at the rim of the building and back to the sea.

A small, electric buggy – like a golf cart, but smelly and dirty – came around the corner, driven by an older boy wearing the same one-piece overalls.

'This is my brother! He speaks no English, but you can say *konichaaawa* to him!'

'*Konnichiwa*,' I said, carefully.

'Hello,' said Cee's brother.

'Come on. We must go quick!' Cee pushed me towards the rear seats of the buggy, and we both hopped in. The electric motor engaged, and we skittled along the wharf, turning around the side of the big grey building. On this side of it there was a series of metal shutters, each half way open, so that I could see the well-used tractors and boats stored inside.

'Where are we going?' I asked Cee.

'To MARKET!' she yelled excitedly, over the noises of the port at work.

'Which market?'

'I have important job to do, and not much time! I must show fish market to Luca. My father and brother and I all work in fish market many times in one month. Today my father is at sea, fishing, so today me and brother can take you and father won't catch us.' She grinned. 'Father catch fish? Yes. Father catch us taking *gaijin* with us to fish market? No!' And she winked at me, her eyelashes flicking up and down as quickly as the smile that went with it.

Her brother looked ahead and kept driving.

We ran up a concrete ramp and onto a busy, city street. It was crammed with buses and cars, all held together in a jam, but on our buggy we could ride through the gaps and close to the pavement. At a set of traffic lights we had to wait for the pedestrians to cross, before sneaking around to the left. This new road was clear, and ran parallel to a huge river, which suddenly turned and flowed under us, as we drove out onto a wide bridge. On the other side, we were immediately swallowed by tall buildings, with big shops and restaurants in the ground floors, and everyone was hurrying about in suits. Then we turned again, and were in a narrow lane.

'Sorry. We must go fast,' said Cee, as her brother began weaving in and out of people.

The lane was dark – buildings were holding out the sunlight – so the rows and rows of red, puffed-up lanterns that illuminated the way seemed to float in the air above us. Signs in Japanese writing fluttered down on homemade banners outside the stalls that lined the sides. The lanterns stopped, before starting up again, this time with their own black, unreadable writing running vertically down them.

When the lane forked, we followed to the left, and then came to a sign written in several languages, including English. It was the size of a big shop window, and had a cartoon figure of a man in a hard hat and overalls like the ones Cee and her brother were wearing. He was standing in front of a very basic colourful drawing of a fork-lift truck, and was holding three fish, heads down, in one hand and raising a thumbs-up with the other. A speech bubble was coming out of him for each language, forming a circle of little word-clouds around him. The English one said:

'WELCOME TO TSUKIJI FISH MARKET.'

'Don't worry, Luca. I know way back to water. You can go home same day.'

We were turning into a small, open zone where lots of buggies like ours were being parked in rows. On the other side of the clearing were stacks and stacks of wooden pallets.

'I work here every day in month except three. Market very busy now. Come. Must show you all before time finish. Market open already.'

She tapped a cheap Casio watch on her wrist and held it up for me to see the time. It was 8:01am.

I quickly tried to do the maths in my head. Did that match up to the time I'd left Chapel Shores? I used to be good at knowing these... What was Tokyo? Like, eight or nine hours ahead of where I lived? Anyway, it didn't really matter. I couldn't hold Cee up any longer, whatever I did.

'Tuna fish coming now. You must look!'

Half the stalls were already being hosed clean by the time we'd made it to the back of the room – a distance of about two hundred metres, I reckoned.

'They sell everything in one hour,' said Cee, proudly. 'Markets very busy now in Tokyo.'

'Yeah. Looks like it.'

At the back wall of this massive warehouse, we started tracking along, pausing to peer at the various creatures that sat staring up at us from the tables of crushed ice and stainless steel that hadn't sold out yet.

'Too busy, Luca.' Cee was shaking her head. 'Far too much busy. It makes me and my brother very sad.'

She stopped – up until now we'd been moving so fast it was almost a jog – and turned to face me.

'Luca, I have read a lot about fish in the sea. *Beautiful* fish. In Japan we eat fish all mealtimes. We are not looking after them. This very hard for me to think about.'

She pointed at a stall in one corner. 'Come see.' We walked over to a small square of metal tables, set up around a hole in the tiled wall. Behind the hole was some kind of washing room for the plastic trays the fish were coming in and out on. This stall was full, and Cee began identifying the fish for me. Each one was staring blankly up at us with eyes like those of the men marching on my Chapel Shores beach at night. They looked so lifeless, so dead, and yet the way they fixed on you, every time, made you think there was still a soul in there somewhere, suffering on this bed of ice.

'This is sardine, this *buri*. Here is *saba* – mackerel. Now *this* fish very beautiful; barracuuuuuuuuuuda! Also here is sea bass – which we call *suzuki* – and this is eel, and, over here, *tai* fish, which you call red snapper.'

205

A small, perfectly formed shark lay at the end of the row. It was the length of my arm at the most, but so streamlined and so detailed. Everything about it said 'predator', but here it was, stone dead and frozen solid.

'Ah, you see the salmon shark?' said Cee. 'This one very small. Maybe baby salmon shark. Many people like eating salmon shark in Japan and in world too. Now come. Tuna fish ready.'

She took my hand and walked me back up to the first table, where the barracuda lay. Next to it was an empty metal surface about ten feet across. As we arrived there a man in the same grey overalls as Cee came out of the hatch in the tiled wall, and dragged an enormous fish out of a big, plastic water vat– a fish about half the size of the man himself.

The man rolled the tuna into place, and I saw its eyes, so still they could have been painted onto its head. In fact, that was the first thing I thought – this was never something that lived. This was a torpedo – it was too round, to bullet-like, too perfect. The fish was dark and, like the eyes, the rest of its features seemed to be fading into its smooth surface. The fins were stuck to its body, and the overalled man lifted them outwards, rubbing gently behind each flipper with a knife about the length of his forearm.

Then he started to cut.

He ran the blade deep around the back of the head, then fiddled hard with the handle until there was a hollow, popping sound at the top of its spine and the head lifted neatly off. It looked like he was removing a helmet from a suit of armour, the whole thing seemed so lifeless. I was waiting for the fish to suddenly flop, or shake, to resist somehow. Next the man shoved his knife deep into the fish's back, and then rammed it along the side of the creature's body. A few more runs back and fore with the blade, and he was pulling off the biggest strip of meat I'd ever seen – no cow, no pig, nothing you'd find in a butchers back in Britain, could have this much flesh on it. The man kept his focus, and slid four more of those enormous chunks away, until all that remained was a strip of spine, covered with purple and red goo, attached to a tail that still had nothing wrong with it – a tail which still seemed to be reflecting all the colours of a rainbow across the grey table covered in blood.

The skill of this man made me feel a weird kind of joy. He'd spent his life learning to do this. But the sight of the fanned tail, at the end of a little pole of gore and bone, was crushing that feeling with pure, heavy and hot sadness. This was all that remained of the giant tuna now. Seconds later, it had been thrown in a nearby bin.

'Luca. You know my father catches this tuna fish?'

I looked over, and could see her eyes slightly wet in the corners.

'Beautiful fish,' she said. 'Very sad.'

'But it's been sold now, right? Someone will eat it.'

'Father brings fish to market in many ways. Father sometimes brings fish with boat from Tokyo Bay. Sometimes using boat in Shikoku – *long* way away from Tokyo – and put fish in train or on other boat for going quick to market. Sometimes father is in the market, sometimes father sends us. We learn to choose good price for fish when very young. Important. Choose right price, can take much money. Father has three boats. Sometimes we need to choose right price for many, many fish at same time. Big prices. Cee *little* and get scared choosing big price for thousand fish to going for sale together.'

Her voice had slowed down, as if she needed to find or check the right words each time she spoke.

'But you *like* it, don't you?' I asked.

'Cee like to help family. But this is not what I want to do.'

'Beats choosing prices for trainers or watches,' I said. She either missed it, though, or didn't understand – or didn't want to bring my own market-pricing skills into it.

'Father catch fish. Father's father catch fish. Whole family *love* sea! But we're killing the oceans. Look.'

The chunks of meat were being neatly carved and stacked into floppy strips of steak, deep reds, purples and shades of orange streaking their way through the skin; uniform lines across the surface of the meat that looked like the layers of a chopped onion, or the grain of a smooth piece of freshly cut wood.

'So how am I going to help you, then?' I asked.

'Help?'

'Yeah. Isn't that the plan? Why I'm here? Isn't this the bit where I help or there's something only I can do.'

It was the first time Cee had to really properly think before saying anything. Her eyes and mouth flashed with that smile, before she twisted her forehead into a quick frown and blinked several times.

'Luca is not here in Tokyo to help Chie!' Her energy was straight back, and she used her proper name in her excitement at how wrong I was. 'No-no-no. Luca is very kind, but not *necessary*.' After the momentum her voice had gained from going back to the right version of her name, she almost choked over the last word... '*Ness-a-saaaaa-reee*...'

I didn't reply, and that smile flicked across her face again.

'Luca! Cee is helping *you* this time. I don't need help because another boy has already come here. Alec has been here.'

'Do you mean *Alex*?' I said, suddenly wanting to talk with the speed and excitement of Cee. Alex! It had to be him. Surely.

'Yes,' she said. 'His name Alec.'

'Ale*X*,' I said, stressing the 'x' again. Al-*ecssss*.'

'Maybe. Boy from Colombia.' She lifted one eyebrow, expecting me to agree.

'Yes! That's it. *Alejo*!'

'Good, yes, same boy. *Alexo*.' She repeated the name close enough. Neither of us could say it like he had anyway.

'He was *here*?' I asked.

'The day before yesterday. He has gone home now. Yes! Alec helped Cee already. And he asked me to help *you*.'

'How did he help you?'

'It's hard to explain. He came and helped me to understand the words in the sea.'

'You mean the voice?'

'Yes! The voice!'

'I've heard it,' I told her. 'How did you find the voice?'

'One day Cee was sitting on the beach and thinking about how sad our catch of fish is. So many beautiful fish all dying for us to eat. Some of them have been alive for years but it takes five minutes to eat them, and we eat four times in a day. I am not sure if eating fish is right for me, and not when we catch so many at once either. Maybe if we eat only the fish we catch with the traditional methods and not the big boats that look like evil spaceships... But for me, I would love to eat more fruit – but fruit, my father says, is so expensive in Japan. Fruit is also beautiful but not alive in the same way a fish is alive, although my brother says fish have only a little more life than fruits. It is not easy for me to understand or decide what is right. But I am thinking on the sand about all of this, and then, as Cee is feeling sad, the sea begins to speak! I am not joking. It speaks and says...'

She paused and frowned.

'Says what?' I asked.

'Problem to understand the voice. Funny, Sea spelt S-E-A speaking to Cee spelt C-E-E and C-E-E cannot understand because S-E-A is speaking in English and very strange voice, very hard to hear.'

'That's exactly what happened to me!' I said. 'I *still* can't understand what the voice is saying, and I've swum in there.'

'Yes, so this is where Alec helped. Alec came out of the sea, and tells C-E-E what S-E-A is saying!'

'And?' I asked 'What is the sea saying?'

'That you are coming here. Boy with father who sells something bad and that I must make him listen.'

'Got that right,' I said. 'Jeez, Alex has been moving some, eh?'

'Alec doing very well now. He will speak to you himself soon. He swims to you in UK or you swim to him. He helped me to think about what I can do with my life. That I could go to a big city school and learn English and many languages. I don't want to work killing fish. Now maybe one day...'

'Hey, it's tough, man,' I said, 'when your parents do stuff you're not into.'

She looked confused, like maybe I'd said it wrongly. Then she smiled and said:

'So. You want know how *I* help *you*?'

'Yeah, sure.'

'Luca,' she said, her voice going soft and leaning forward, out of earshot of her brother.

'Alec asked me to help you understand a beautiful girl.'

'*She's* not speaking to me,' I said. 'Water or not.'

Cee laughed. 'The girl is very busy! She is working *hard*. She thinks the same thing I am thinking. Work hard for *self* and then no working for father when older! You must talk to girl!'

'I do talk to her,' I said, 'but she doesn't answer anymore.'

'This is no problem, Luca. You understand. Go home and understand. Understand girl very busy. One day she will rest. Same like me. Only three rest in one month. Maybe girl rest. Luca talk. Make girl-friend be girl*friend*!' She winked, and the smile lasted. 'Very easy in UK. Wish was easy like this in Japan. Only boy Cee can talk with now is brother! But this change. Going to school in big, exciting, Europe or America city one day. Life make like new for me. Very soon. Very good. Live like Alec or Luca; going away from home and find adventure! This is my goal.'

'It's a good goal to have,' I said. 'Better than my goal. I don't even know what mine is. Maybe I'll never even have one.'

Her brother was watching as another tuna rolled its way onto a table, fat and shining and sleek, only to get dragged off as a piece of smelly, bleeding litter, its meat gone to the freezers and fridges of a hungry human world.

'Talk to the girl! Ask the girl about important things! Girl is also *very* important for people like us, but she is not hearing the voice. Luca talk to her instead. Must do this! Cee tell Luca. Luca listen. Okay?'

'Okay,' I said. 'I'll listen.'

'Good and then you can be okay for swimming again. Come. Brother can drive back for catching tide and warm water. Luca remember where is swimming in right place?'

'Yeah, I'll remember.'

* * *

The water still looked dirty, but as soon as I felt the warmth rising up around me I wanted to go further in.

I wondered when the voice was going to start, as I stretched out through the deepest parts of that cosy sea and swam on, into the currents. Would I get another chance to try and make it out? Was there time to look back, and see the silhouette of Cee, rippling through the surface, waving and bowing, bowing and waving? There was that point again, as I turned and kicked downwards, when there was no need to see anymore, where only the hearing really mattered.

It had been quieter on the way here – maybe because I'd entered through the dune. But now, as I drew myself along the sea bed, with the current all around me, that deep echo started to fill the water again. 'Luca,' I heard it saying, and then more words, but coming just too thickly through the water for me to make them out. It was saying something different, though. The rhythm wasn't the same as last time, and there was more urgency.

I was scared to say his name. Each time it sat on my tongue – *Gigi* – it would get stuck and stay there, as if the sounds themselves were holding onto my mouth, trying not to get flung out into the open. *Gigi? Is it you?* Through the weight of water, I tried to call it out. I wanted to ask other things, too. *Can I trust that girl? Can I trust Alejo?* That, and much more. Could the source of the voice hear the questions in my head?

Cee had talked about Gaby. What did she have to do with all this? *If you are Gigi*, I thought, and tried to say, *then why can't you just reach Gaby yourself?* Perhaps he already had. Maybe that was it. Maybe she had seen those figures and heard this noise – sorry, *felt* this noise – because that's what the noise was; a feeling as much as it was waves of sound. From the dark depths beyond, the vibrations kept coming at me. The same incomprehensible words, on repeat again.

You're her grandfather, aren't you?

I tried again to ask it, as clear as the swirling water would let me. *Or great, great-grandfather, or whatever it is she called you. What do you want me to say to her?* Then the words started coming out of my mouth, and I could feel the bubbles of water carrying them away. I wanted to know so much. Why was he walking onto the beaches every night? Who was it walking with him? Was something trapping them, forcing them to keep going, or was it a choice? *Are you a ghost?* I blabbed the words into the ocean, but the deep hum of his voice came back, my name the only word I could hear. Now the words were pouring out of me, so I added my first questions again. *Can I trust that girl? Can I trust Alejo?* Why were these kids from other countries involved? And why were we all trying to help each other? It seemed that was what the voice wanted from us. *Can I trust you, whoever you are, Gigi?*

Surely, if the voice was something to do with Gigi Carranero, then it would be stupid to trust him. A criminal, a thief. I knew that. But the way that voice of his throbbed through the water, so soothing, so disarming... It was almost as if it was the source of the warmth around.

Trying to force words through my throat and into the thick water, I noticed it was getting warmer. I hoped the ocean was hearing my thoughts. I tried to call again, but something had changed and I'd lost the ability to do anything but breathe gently out of my nose and drift forward with the movements of the ocean, as the cold trickles started to wind in and out of my path. Then I heard the vibrations, growing slowly, until I could make out the voice, clearer than before.

At last, my ears were tuning in. A whisper, rising gradually to something more, seemed only to say, 'Swim straight, LLJ. Swim through, Luca.' Was that all? Maybe I should have listened harder. Or maybe I shouldn't have listened at all.

The water grew even warmer, and the cold patches rushed through me and over me. Then the sand started to mix in again.

'Swim straight, LLJ. Swim through. Almost there. Almost...'

Chapter 18

The water was like treacle in the end, which is when I knew it was almost time to emerge. There was a whoosh upwards and then I was in this thick, mud-type stuff before I could feel the grains of sand and was on hard ground, walking forwards through what felt like a waterfall of the stuff. A *sandfall*! Cool, eh? And it was so dry, too. There was this warm, warm wind, tearing through the dust at me and then, just like that, I was stepping clean out of the big dune at Chapel Shores.

The night was cold and the men were nowhere in sight. Running would keep me safe from the chill.

When I got in, my mind was full-on tunnel-vision. I had two things to do. Number one: get into the house without causing any trouble; and number two: psych up and go the party next week.

Number one went pretty smooth. I kept feeling my jeans and hoodie as I jogged home. They were still a bit damp, and my socks and boxers were still wet, but this time I was nowhere near as sorry a sight. The key was still there, under the flat rock, and there was no one up. I looked at my watch as I pulled the cold socks off my feet, and slipped into bed. It was ten to four. My feet were sticky and chilly, and I could feel salt and sand clinging to my skin, but I was too tired to do anything about it. If I showered now my mum *would* think something was up.

Just before drifting off, I went to google 'time in Tokyo

now', but, like trying to hit Cartagena on street view, something stopped me before I could press 'Go'.

Then I was out. No music in my head, nothing. Out until Gaby's text woke me, mid-afternoon the next day.

*　　*　　*

'HAPPY SUNDAY,' it said. Nothing else – apart from four smiling emoji in a row after the words.

I reckoned I'd wait an hour before replying, but sent one in ten. That was pretty much the time it took me to wake up enough to type, anyway.

'You too. What's up?'

'Nothin much, been busy, u?'

'Nothin much, not busy tho,' I replied.

'You shld be LLJ, work is important nowadays innit.'

I mimicked throwing the phone at the floor – in front of an audience of nobody, so it must have been a creative act. Work! Why was I still full-on lying down to this no-speak-in-school rubbish?

'Good for u,' I replied.

'Aw come on, u understand sure, come on, dont wanna hav to kidnap like poppi gigi when im older do i!'

I wanted to say 'You don't need to', or something about school not being 'work' at all. Instead I just stared at the screen.

'Anyway, gonna be at Jackdaws party on fri and ella says u comin!'

'Dunno,' I replied.

'U should LL Cool J be COOOOL to catch up innit.'

'Maybe.'

I shoved my phone along the carpet, under my bed, and got up.

Downstairs, Dad was counting money again, and lots of it.

'Lukee boy!' he grinned, getting up from his seat behind the table. 'Check it out. Markets here sold up, and Jeff flogged a load in Swansea, too! Drove up there last night and slept in his van to get a good stall. We're quids in. Going up to Birmingham this week, now, to pay in for some doubloon melting.' Then he laughed. 'Wanna throw a ton in yourself? Hundred quid?'

'Haven't got a hundred quid,' I said.

'Ah, no worries about that,' he said. 'Howbout I lend you a stake, and then you can pay me the ton back when we cash in? You'd make four or five times as much, I reckon. Me and Jeff are gonna pay a big load in. You saw the quality on that gold up there.'

He took a swig of his bottle of Bud. 'Anyway, I reckon you should come with us again. Be a really good education for you. You can say you've done your first metals deal, then, for real, you know. Like, paid in, been a shareholder in it, you know? Plus, I reckon that Haz guy liked us better when you were there.'

'Will you let me have a beer if I buy in?' I asked him, turning for the door.

He laughed. 'Come *on*, mate! Imagine your mum if she comes in and I've got you on the beers with me. Ha! D'you realise how much grief I had convincing her to even let you come to that market last time?'

I walked to the back door and looked outside, at the patch of patio where I knew my mum smoked sly roll-ups without him knowing. Nobody had picked the tarpaulin up yet from that night when I shivered under it, and I remembered the mix of excitement and hypothermia.

'JEFF,' yelled my dad. I turned around. It was the phone, though. He had a habit of answering it so loud you'd think someone was about to step in front of a bus.

That would be wishful thinking I thought. Jeff, in front of a bus.

He was only down the pub, though, tuning hard for my dad to join him.

'Can't for a few hours yet, mate,' he boomed, down the phone. 'Hannah's coming back soon and then we got a load of finances to sort so that I can deffo swing her to give us the thumbs up. Gimme, like, two hours?'

Jeff must have mumbled some reply.

'Ah come on!' said my dad. 'Hang back. I wanna meet her anyway! Heard so much about her!'

I stepped out into the garden. The days were getting warmer, but I'd have stayed out here even in the cold right then. More laughter came from inside the house, so I walked round the front, and headed for the beach again.

By day it looked so... blank, maybe? The dune was about half the size under grey skies and faint sun. The sea looked greyish brown, too, and tired. And small.

In the dark, this was where I could make plans, so I tried plotting now, too. If I was going to take a shot at anything resembling being a normal kid in this town, I would need to turn up at Jack Dooley's house this Friday. I needed to do two things this week. Find out where it was, and line someone up to either meet me there, invite me or even to go there with – top of my list was Ella Bowen. Well, top middle and bottom, actually. Except BTEC was going to be the day Dad tried to drag me to Birmingham. I had it on Tuesday, too, but it would be better to use the Thursday lesson to bring it up – closer to the party, and I'd have to let Ella lead into the conversation.

'Give me a plan!' I whispered to the sea. Then I repeated it, to the dune, and into the grass, maybe in case the fox could hear and was nearby, or maybe for someone else.

No reply. Not even in my head.

None of this stuff worked by day though, so I wandered back to my street, kicking chippings along the path with my toes. Dad was out. Pub with Jeff? Had to be. Least it meant he'd come in a bit pissed up instead of having this meeting with my mum sober. Hey, he might even lose out trying to tune her for a Luca market-pass this Thursday.

Maybe someone *was* hearing me, I thought, and headed upstairs to gaze at the ceiling and listen to Bob. Maybe someone was.

* * *

I was back to earth with a thump by midweek, though.

School trudged by for the first couple of days. Gaby was off again, which was odd considering she was meant to be trying hard in classes, and on Tuesday Ella only talked about her really briefly. Apparently Gaby had said she was studying from home, because the boys in her class were such idiots and the teachers so crap that she could do just as well in most subjects by reading out of text-books or booking a tutor. Ella did start to mention the party, but that was right before one of Mr Powell's passes and so she had to switch to flirt-mode immediately to save us from a bollocking.

'He's not giving us any space today, is he?' she complained.

I looked for chances to get us back to talking about what would happen on Friday night, but Ella seemed keener to grumble about teachers. When it did come up again, by her choice, all she said was, 'People will probably start making a plan later in the week.'

This meant the main thing to get through in my world – and standing in the way of Friday like a giant fence hurdle with a muddy pool behind it – was going to be this nonsense with my dad and his impending gold deal. After my parents and Jeff stumbled back from the pub Sunday, they ended up on the rum again, and Jeff had been over every night since. Then, on Wednesday, as the three of them went through their financial stuff and another pair of giant pizzas at the same time, my dad announced that they were going back to Birmingham the next day and that I was coming.

My mum looked at him and frowned.

Go on, I thought, and clenched my fist in anticipation.

'I'm not sure, Steve,' she said, as a voice in my head went, *Yes! Yes! Yes!*

'Why not, Hann?' asked my Dad in the whiniest voice he could come up with.

'Well, I'm happy with you two going, but I'm still not sure it's the right place for Luca to be instead of school.'

'You wannim to miss out?' mumbled Jeff, who seemed, whenever he came for dinner, to only ever wait until he was chewing food before speaking.

'Course not,' said my mum. 'But Lukee's attendance is *so* important since we got those letters from Mr Kleener, and we want him to be able to get a job that…'

'That what?' said Jeff, swallowing his mouthful.

My mum frowned at them, and then said, 'Luca, d'you really want to hear these conversations?'

Of course I did. This was the most important chat they had ever had about my future. Could I tell them that, though?

Even though I wanted to stay and listen – be involved in their discussion even, although I knew that wouldn't happen – I still trudged up the stairs and away, as if my legs had decided to leave for me. I'd been up there about half an hour when I heard the bad news – from my mum of all people, who must have thought it was a chance to tell me something nice.

'Lukee?' she said, gently popping her head round the door, as I flicked through iTunes looking for some Bunny to soothe the moment.

'What?'

'Can I come in a minute?'

'Can't stop you.'

She laughed, timidly. Then came in.

'I've told them you can go tomorrow, if you want,' she said.

I lost a beat, and my feet throbbed hot for a second. Gutted. Had I ever stood a chance of telling her what was really on my mind? I mean, would *you*? Come on, of course not. Imagine her reaction? *Ah, mum, I need to be in school tomorrow so I can sit by a girl in BTEC to get her to help me show up the right way at a party, coz Gaby's gonna be there and actually*...

Yeah. Course you wouldn't. So what chance did I have?

Yeah. I'll say it again: *gutted*. First time ever in eleven years that I actually wanted to be in school and what was waiting for me? That grimy jewel market, and another day itching in the company of Steve Lincoln-James and Jeff Rafferty.

You might have thought mothers were meant to be tapped into that crap about intuition? Not mine, as you can see. No. She took me at my word. Well, not my word as much as a weak nod of a tired head.

I'm surprised she couldn't hear my soul groan, though.

* * *

The great obstacle had shown up, then. I was going to that hell-hole market with them, right when I least needed it – and instead of being sensitive to this situation that neither of them knew existed, Dad and Jeff seemed determined to be even more hard work than normal. All morning Jeff nagged me about stuff I simply didn't want to talk over with him and Dad: 'Got a girl on the go then, Lukee Boy?' 'Been pissed yet?' 'What about getting a *girl* pissed? *That's* the thing to be trying to do at your age, buddy, I can tell you! Two birds, one stone. Wey!'

They had these cheesy, photocopied appointment badges when we got there this time, too, with their full names on them. I wouldn't wear the one they'd made me, obviously. Jeff also brought one of those metallic briefcases – even though the four lumps of gold they planned to buy would almost fit in your pocket.

'Love it here, don't you, Steve?' said Jeff, putting his hands on his hips and taking a deep breath. 'Makes me realise how small the world of Chapel Shores is, eh? Look at all these people doing something with themselves.'

'They were useless immigrants last week,' laughed my dad.

'Yeah, well that was then,' said Jeff. 'Now's now!'

'Deep.' My dad looked at me and winked, but quivering just behind his dark eyes, I saw his nerves again.

For all the rest of the people at the market it was business as usual; the same cold air-con as you went through, same frosted glass doors and darkened rooms, same light green carpet that smelt too new to be good. Then there was Haz, striding across the aisle between the showrooms to meet us all with a firm handshake. This time he seemed to have wet his mop of long, curly hair and had put on one of those super-tight, fitted suits, complete with a white shirt and the kind of pencil tie that losing contestants on *X-Factor* might wear.

'Jeff Rafferty and Steve Lincoln!' he declared, with a beaming smile. 'Welcome back. Let's get straight to business.'

He meant it, too. Except now there was one extra bit that someone from Chapel Shores is hardly ever going to be ready for.

'Oh, er, gents. Before we head in, now, just a little reminder. Uh, don't be alarmed but it's normal for these guys, some of the time to be, er, uh, armed.'

'Armed?' choked my dad.

'Yeah. Nothing serious. Just for security. But yeah, be ready to see a gun.'

My dad's face went red, then white – almost quick enough to look like a poorly nourished traffic light. He gulped at the air and said, 'What the...', and then Jeff interrupted him.

'Steve! Come on, man. I told you that. Didn't I? Ah. Maybe I didn't. Er, yeah. No biggie though, is it?'

'You want me to take my boy into a room with *guns*?'

'He can wait outside,' said Jeff.

'No I can't,' I said, before even realising it.

'Come on, lads,' said Haz. 'You're making more of this than you need to. All of you come in. It's fine.'

My dad looked like he wanted to speak again, but the words didn't come to him and, pale-faced, he walked on with us. I think seeing him crapping himself meant I'd forgotten to be that rattled myself. I wondered how long that would last, though.

This time we went to a different showroom, still only the size of a small lounge, where the lights were dim and three men sat on a sofa chair.

Immediately, everything went heavy. The air-con vanished and a weight of silence held everything in the room completely still.

These guys were *nothing* like what I was expecting. When Jeff had said Congolese men, I'd just assumed they'd be black – as you would – and that they'd have

African-sounding names and African-sounding voices. These men were palest white, with shaved heads, charity-shop ties and no jackets. They spoke with the strangest accents you'd ever hear. If I had to guess – and there weren't many chances to bone up on your foreign accents in Chapel Shores – I'd have said they were, maybe, like Swedish or Dutch? Or something else like that rather than African, except there was no tone and no humour in anything they said or did.

And then there was the gun. I saw it only after we were settled. It was held by the fourth man, and he was stood at the back of the room, watching. It was only once you were in and your eyes had adjusted that he could be noticed. Just like the others, he was light-skinned and dressed in a shirt and trousers, but he had slung over his shoulder a strap – and the strap was supporting what looked to me like a machine-gun. Both hands were on it, and he could have probably swung and pointed it about as quickly as one of us might blink.

All four of them looked me, my dad and Jeff up and down, looked at each other, then turned to Haz.

'No,' said the middle one, to Haz, immediately.

'What?'

'No. Can't do it today. Something's not quite right about this.'

Already, the tight chest was fighting for control of my soul.

'Hang on,' said Haz. 'These are the *guys*, man! They've got the money, you've got the gold, and so we can fix it up.'

'No,' repeated the man. 'I'm changing my mind. These... *men*...' – he hadn't looked at me yet – 'They can make a deposit on another melt, but no ingots are coming their way. And anyway, I didn't fetch the bars from the bonded warehouse.'

'What d'you mean bonded,' pleaded Haz. 'There's no importing to do.'

'There is. We melt in the Congo now,' said the man. 'So there's importing to do.'

There was an awkward silence, in which I reckon I could hear at least Haz and my dad's hearts going wobbly, too – as well as the breath of the man holding the gun – and then another of the Congolese guys interrupted:

'Hold on, hold on.' His voice was much smoother, but he still had that bonkers accent. 'We can so something today, but first we need to do one more trust sale with these three gentlemen...'

My dad looked up. Jeff straightened, too.

'Come on,' said Haz. 'That's not what we...'

'Tall order to sell bullion to first-timers today,' said the second man. 'You and I both know that, Haz. But... *but*... How about a trial sale of a small bar? Then we can do a load more when we next melt. We'll make the margin good. We'll make it *great*.'

'What are we talking?' said Jeff, just about pushing Haz out of the way.

'Small stake, big margin,' said the man. 'But you go through us, not this guy.' He pointed at Haz, who looked about to object, before the man added, 'He can just have a finder's fee once we sell the lot.'

Haz seemed slightly happier with this.

'How much?' said Jeff.

I looked again at the guy with the automatic weapon, as the main speaker in the group thought about Jeff's question.

'You put in one and a half grand,' said the man sat in the middle. 'We'll show you the coins you're buying. We'll melt. That's a grand for the coins, five hundred for the minting, and the bar you can take will be worth well over six K. Sell it for anything near that – to show us you can

225

run a metals business, and we'll melt as much as you want with your initials on it.'

'Done,' said Jeff.

'Yeah,' added my dad. 'Good, coz we can raise twenty-five to forty, depending on credit.'

'Well, hold your horses, yeah,' said the second man. 'We can't have the stuff not selling, see. Too much risk of comeback on us. If you guys have lumps of this lying around, together.'

'It'll sell,' said Jeff.

'We need to be sure. Our paperwork will be fine for it,' said the man, 'but the whole trick relies on the metals moving quickly. Now, I'll show you the coins, and the bars we turn them into.'

This time there was something much more eerie about the display. 'Seventeen-hundred and a package like this is yours,' said the second man, as he slipped a small, velvet lump of cloth out of his trouser pocket, as the gun behind hovered in the dim, stuffy air. He unfolded the rag carefully, and the glow filled the room. Even from three small coins and a bar the size of a credit card, you could see right away that this was a substance people could worship. The perfectly pressed surfaces shot a glint in all directions, as if light multiplied when it hit the gold. It looked alive – and like it was made with something better than us.

'Done,' said Jeff.

'Cash,' the man added.

'Of course.' And, trying not to look at that fourth, armed man in the back of the room, my dad flicked the notes out of his money clip, five at a time.

I watched the bills go back into the first Congolese man's pocket, along with the coins and the velvet wrap, trying to think of all the other things which that money could have got instead. For my dad and Jeff though, it was only a tiny bit of what they hoped to hand over soon.

The move from that room back to the carpark seemed to sort of pass through us, almost like my journeys through the sea at night. With no words at all, the three of us drifted, zombie-like through the current of traders and suited con-men towards the van we'd come up in. Only once we were inside, with the doors safely slammed and locked, did anyone speak – and when they did, it was a far off the way I was feeling as anyone had ever been, yet.

'I've got bloody good senses on this one, Jeff,' said my dad as he turned the ignition. 'Something's telling me it's a real go. I'm thinking how I can raise more. I'd stake the house on this, way I feel now.'

Part 3

Chapter 19

'Hey, Dr Wentloog, what's the DSM 5?'

My mum was quizzing him in the corner of the room, out of my sight as I tried to watch a telly that was fixed on E4. I'd been out of bed for a couple of days by that point, and the energy to leave was building. This was before his notebook idea, before the contract thingy, before any of his ideas. My mum had been reading around, you know, like, the *mind* and all that. She'd found out all about him by now and his gigs talking around the world about stuff only he could spot.

'It's a basic manual,' he was telling her.

'I know that. But do you use it?'

'It's not something we would *use* as such, Ms James. That's not its purpose. I think self-diagnosing or reading too much at this stage isn't a great idea.'

'I'll read what I bloody want,' she said.

'Of course. It's a hazard of the internet, though, the fact that information which is better explained by professionals is so readily available to anyone. Ms James, the DSM 5 is a simple categorisation system. I think cases should only be correlated to it *after* treatment.'

That was the first time I ever heard him say that word – treatment – and it shut my mum right up for all of ten seconds, so it must have seemed heavy to her too.

'For the time being,' Dr Wentloog went on, 'every case remains unique. That's a pillar of our practice.'

My mum rustled some papers, and then asked him another question:

'So does violent behaviour always mean someone's got something on that list, then?' she asked.

'Violent behaviour needs addressing in this case.'

'But does it mean Luca needs, you know, help? Treatment, like?'

'It means he needs to stay here until he can explain it.'

'I can hear you both,' I yelled. 'If you're gonna call me a psycho maybe say it to my face? And anyway, I haven't actually done anything, have I?'

My mum walked around the sofa to stand between me and the telly, and Dr Wentloog pulled her aside gently. He had a thing about not obstructing things I wanted to look at. That was why he always sat in the side of your vision.

'No,' said my mum, 'but...'

'Luca, are you angry?' said Wentloog.

'No.'

'Have you ever been?'

'Obviously.'

'If I was to ask you to think of one time you were angry, what would be the first occasion to pop into your mind?'

'That question's not fair,' I said. 'You know we're all thinking about the same thing, now. You *know* it.'

* * *

As me, Dad and Jeff drove home from Birmingham that afternoon, with a pathetic ingot and its oversized case in the back, I think I was already looking for ways to pick a fight with him. I watched my dad's hands on the wheel, thinking about how right now would be the exact moment I was meant to be in BTEC sitting by Ella Bowen.

Maybe it was the fact they were ragging on me all the way back about 'where was I when them Congolese men got jumpy' and 'why wasn't there one of your wisecracks that make those guys giggle, Luca'. Maybe it was my dad's own stress at seeing a weapon that had probably killed people in Africa at some point in its history. Anyone thought of that one? And also, he was going back down the motorway having just spent over a grand on a strip of shiny metal off the people carrying that thing. I was also pretty sure he'd just about committed, in front of those men who could have been anyone, to also spending enough money to move house, or buy me and my mum a nicer life, or start a real business or… Ah, I can't think about it, even now.

Well, I went at him, he says, with a hammer. But – if it happened at all – then I think it was because I reckoned he would do for me first. Did he tell Wentloog that? Because it would be pointless *me* telling them. Wentloog and my parents, and others too, are all saying I don't remember things like this correctly, that I can't be trusted, see.

This is how *I* remember it, anyway:

So, he'd been on about how it felt to weigh the gold, and he just kept repeating something about it. Jeff was niggling us to stop at the pub on the way through, and blurting out more of the smelly stuff he says about whichever women he's trying to get it on with. Meanwhile, I was minding my own business trying to forget I'd seen a gun that day by remembering how annoying it was that I had missed catching up with Ella, and stressing about how it was pretty much exactly twenty-four hours now until Friday night. I had so much to try and do before then if I was going to get that invite sorted as real – and I had even more to do before I'd be able to actually act on that invite and find the frame of mind to go to Jackdaw's house and not seem like some kind of little creep sat in the corner.

Jeff – I swear he was listening to my mind – then chose that exact moment to turn on me out of nowhere and go, 'So how come Lukee doesn't have so many friends and when is he going to get into going out and chasing the birds?'

And that was the first key moment, right there.

I'll admit maybe there are little bits I don't remember so well. Jeff's words there... They just filled me with that boiling feeling, and then came the chest, then the fizzing of the veins in the sides of my head. My eyes felt heavy and hot. Then there was a flash, like the ones under the sea, and next thing I knew is that I've fully lost my rag with him and my dad has had to stop the van and pull me out the side of the door into the cold night, because I'm clawing at Jeff and trying to hit him again and again and again. There's more bits that go blank then – but I *know* Jeff was laughing at me and that my dad told him off.

'Jeff! Come on, man. You can't laugh at shit like this. Come *on*! Hannah will lose it as bad as him if we're not careful.'

Then Dad turned to me.

'Get in the van, Luca,' he said, and I waited to see if he would repeat it, firmer. But then he said 'Please?', and all the rage sunk out of me, through my heels into the ground, and I climbed into the cockpit and gazed straight ahead as he put my seatbelt on for me.

Jeff was dropping f-bombs under his breath as he climbed back in, door side of me, and neither of them spoke right up until my dad dropped him off outside the pub back in Chapel Shores.

Once we got home, though, it kicked off again, and this time I remember all of it. My mum was out, and my dad seemed pissed off about that. I think he'd been excited about seeing her and was convinced she would want to hear more about the gold. Anyway, without her around he had no chance of getting his tone right with telling me off – he *never* does that sort of thing – and just got aggro with me instead, straightaway:

'Luca. What the *hell* was that shit all about!' he yelled. 'D'you realise how embarrassing that was? Jeff Rafferty is my *mate*! You just can't get like that. He's only messing about when he gives you a bit of stick and then you go a flip on him like that? Don't ever put me in that position again, or…'

And he ran out of energy – at least as far as words go. He was still trembling with anger, his shoulders square, fists clenched and weight on his slightly bent front leg.

I was stood by the drawers in the kitchen, and I wanted to pull one of them out and make a mess. That's the first thought I had. I looked at the crap he had strewn around our living room, and then the stupid, pointless order that my parents kept in their kitchen, where the CDs were lined up next to their over-sized stereo, and where no plates or dishes or food hardly ever got to lay about because they were always eating takeaways or microwave food, which I knew from PSE meant they were lazy and unhealthy. I thought about how clean and proper they made themselves look, and just wanted to drop something to the floor.

But when I pulled the draw next to me open, there was a hammer inside, and some other tools – an unopened spanner in cardboard case and an electric drill. I acted before I could change my mind, and watched half-interested as my hand lifted the hammer, and flung it, spinning through the air towards him.

He ducked, and it floated in slow motion towards the wall, where it hurt nothing and broke nothing, just leaving a tiny dent in the dirty plaster.

My brain was back boiling, immediately, and the next thing I know was that he was running at me, yelling at me to 'Stop!' and to 'Be still!' His eyes were wide with fear, and I knew he thought he should hit me but would stop before he got there.

Inches from my face, he stood there and screamed 'STOP IT NOW. STAY WHERE YOU ARE!' And then he was yelling for my mum, 'Hannah! Hannah! Please!'

Then he walked out the house, slammed the door and marched up the street.

My mum didn't really need to calm me down by the time she was back. I drifted through a space of no thoughts and no worries for however long it took. When she said, 'Go to bed, Lukee,' I almost managed to reply that I didn't need to sleep anymore – whatever I could think of to make her worry most – but then I started to feel that heat in my lungs again, and the breath came panting out of me, so much quicker than I could suck it back in.

She grabbed me tight, as if trying to trap the air inside me, and whispered to me that, 'It's all okay, Lukee', which meant it probably wasn't.

Three steps up and I was feeling dizzy.

I've been asked about it since, but I can't really come up with anything to make sense of it. When I get like that, the thoughts become kind of a mystery. They always will be. Wentloog can try and guess them but he'll never manage. The way my nerves were buzzing though... Now that is a memory alright. Funny how nerves can remember things, isn't it? It's got nothing to do with my head, trying to recall the rest of it from there. It's all in the senses, and it gives me those little chicken-skin chills even here and now to try and close my eyes, see it, feel it, remember the moments when my mum left me again to go downstairs, trying her hardest not to cry – and the soaking cold that shook me from head to foot once the light-switch was hit and I was shivering in the growing dark.

✳ ✳ ✳

'Have you tried to write about the angry moments with your father, yet?' Dr Wentloog asked me, way back when he first gave me the little blue book. 'And what about that drawing?'

'No,' I told him.

'But you will, right?'

'No.'

'Don't you want to, yet?'

'There's nothing to write,' I remember telling him, for about the fifth time that day.

'You mean you're not ready?'

'No. I mean it never happened.'

He looked at me for a full minute when I said that to him.

'There's no drawing either,' I added, and tried to look back at him, too. Longest I think I've ever stared at anyone without freaking out. Maybe that was the plan, I thought.

'Those things never happened?' he repeated.

'No,' I said, knowing full well the mountain of issues it would probably make him think I had.

'Okay then,' he said. 'If that ever changes, let me know.'

✳ ✳ ✳

'Lucifer son of the morning!'

How many kids d'you know who fix their iPhone to sing them a Bible verse first thing in the morning? Mind you, half the world's best reggae lines are probably Bible verses,

237

or some sort of other famous spell and we just don't know it. I used it that Friday morning anyway, the day after the market and whatever other stuff came after, to charge up for the day – and night – ahead. It was proper creepy, rolling around in this hanging, deep sleep only to hear that shrill cry slamming through my skull after I'd left the earphones in overnight. That's what I'd done, though, somewhere in that crazy fit of love, fear and hate – I'd stuck on the song, jabbed my phone into the mains and listened to it on repeat for at least half the night, as well as setting it as my alarm for the morning.

Now, first thing, it felt like playing the song to myself again might have almost worked.

It needed to have worked, too. It was going to be the most important day of my life. I'd decided it.

I would have to get my plans sorted by seeing Ella in school, but outside of class. A full-on test of whether or not she was genuinely genuine. Today, if any, was the day to take on such tests. Whatever had come for me last night, it had lost – or so I thought – and now the world was there to try and tame.

I went with UB40 again and 'Many Rivers to Cross' as my gate tune, and then, rather than spend hours psyching up to it and probably working down my chances of finding the balls to do it, just went straight up to Ella as we filed from assembly – me to Art and her to Media Studies.

'Um, Ella?'

She spun around, lifted her silky straight hair away from a carefully shadowed eye, and smiled.

'Hey! LLJ! How's it goin' *lad*?'

I sniffed a quick laugh, polite but firm enough to show her I was aware of the sarcasm.

'Okay. How're you?'

238

'I'm alright, like. Hey, fella you weren't in BTEC yesterday. Nightmare! I had to swear at Mr P.'

'Really? Wow. Sorry.' I wasn't sure whether to be gutted or glad that I'd missed that one.

'Yeh. Called him a fuckin perv and he looked like he was gonna cry!'

'Wow. That's heavy, Ella!'

'Nah. He got over it. He was tryin to rip my phone out my hands, so I stuck it on my chest, like.' She clasped her palms together and held them theatrically against her heart, fluttering her long, black eyelashes as she did so.

'He was laughing by the end of the lesson, though, so no harm done,' she added. 'And anyway. Was tryin to find a way of reaching *you*! Dude, you're hard to get to, online, ain't you. And Gaby wasn't replying when I asked for your number.'

'Uh, okay. Sorry. Had to go to work with my, er, dad,' I said, trying to sound way prouder than I was.

Ella didn't seem to notice anything odd or wrong about that, and just said, 'Cool. Well, anyway, I was tryin to get the deal to you about Jackdaw's tonight, see. Coz you weren't in Science I was worried you'd miss it.'

'That's why I wanted to talk to you this morning,' I said.

'Cool. Well, let's make a plan then, fella!'

Inside, as in right down, behind my chest where my rhythm gets set, it had felt all night as if the fact I'd need to go and find Ella Friday morning had knocked me off line. Now though, the way it was coming together so easy had given me a new thing to get anxious about. I'd shaken the morning in with *the song*, and all the risks that came with it, for nothing – put all that energy into building myself up, but for something that had turned out easier than easy. Surely there would be payback for this, some time, I told myself, because it seemed somehow against the rules for something like this to go smoothly.

Ella laid out the plan – come to Bunkers, nine tonight, then I could walk off the beach with her and her mates to Jackdaw's house where this party full of sketchy older kids was going to be in full swing. Gaby wouldn't be at Bunkers with them, but she knew we were coming to Jackdaw's and was going to meet us there.

All of this gave me the rest of the day to worry and excite, with 'La-la-la son of the morning' rolling around my head, helping me take turns at being either Luca or the Devil himself.

I thought about the whole good and evil thing, again. How much of it was in us all? I watched the boys in my Art class – which Gaby didn't show up to even though I knew she'd been in her Reg group – jumping around and pissing off the supply teacher who was taking us because Mrs Rogoff had some meeting. I watched Mr Kleener when he came to collect Joe Poundes from DT for 'stopping others learning'. I watched the History teacher, Mr Lloyd walk towards his car at lunchtime and drive off. I studied Skunk George at lunchtime, leaning back on another teacher's car and fiddling with his phone. I wondered about the balance between devil and good that lay behind his shark eyes. I tried to imagine Rogoff or Kleener, Mr Lloyd or Joe Poundes, their devils and their gods and for a while it all helped stop me imagining mine.

Ella had my number now, and she sent me a message that evening, as I was eating my parents' leftover Indian and thinking about what music to listen to upstairs before going out.

'You PUMPED yet LL Cool J? It's on, gnna be a BLASSST ayeh!'

My mum and dad were at the pub together, already, and that text from Ella came in somewhere around the time I started getting these quick, sharp rushes of something totally different from before. It was coming from the same, like, root, in my core, but this feeling, when it hit my fingertips and made my throat want to fill with cool air, was new. And this feeling was good. It was right.

Breathing out short and hard, then in long and slow, I went upstairs and tried to control it. It was running down my spine and buzzing right back up to the top of my head. I stuck Toots onto my iPod and turned it loud. The tingling in the back of my head met the music in the front and I nearly yelled out. Yes! This is *it*! I was going to go, to be me, to find the best of my soul. I don't know if it was my Lucifer, my devil, my goodness, or some other current – maybe even one I'd picked up under the dunes and sea, but it was going to take me through. Showered, dressed, no need to tell anyone where I was going – mum and dad would probably have had a skinful when they got back anyway – I looped my key over the inside elastic of my hoodie pocket, stuck the bronze and gold-leaf doubloon in my jeans and shut the house up behind me.

It would take twenty minutes to walk over to Bunkers at the right speed, and all I needed to do was keep the rhythm in place. Everything else was perfect. I had the tunes, the air, and the dark of night.

Ella was right. It was *on*.

* * *

Their voices reached me before the light of their cigarettes and torches. The laughter was running in little ripples across the sand. I could feel the wetness in the air – one of Bunkers Beach's fog layers drifting in by night. It helped mask them from view.

The voices of the boys were deep, and the girls could be heard shouting and chuckling. I saw a lighter flick on, then the flame turn into the single, orange point of a cigarette. The rushes of adrenaline, which had been coming and going to the rhythm of my tunes, were free to hit me and last – even after I'd taken the earphones out to be able to hear the group of people ahead.

I was about ten steps away by the time I could make out their faces, and the dark edges of the bunker they were leaning against. There was seven of them. I recognised four boys, all friends of Jack Dooley, all from the year above me at least. Ella was one of the three girls, but I didn't know the others.

'LL-Jaaaaaay!' called Ella, before I had to say anything. 'Yes!'

The others hardly seemed to notice me – until she made them. She introduced them all – her older sister Maya, her sister's friend, Lizzie, and then the boys. 'This is Henry, DK, Lewis and Taylor. Boys, Lukee's in my BTEC class. He's a legend. He's comin' with us.'

'Yeah, man. Whatever you need,' said the one she'd called DK.

I was passed a small bottle of beer – like the ones Jeff used to bring my parents from Europe – and we all started walking off the beach almost straight away. The cold, wet air was punctured by the smoke and the tiny points of heat from their cigarettes. Ella and her sister chatted to me as we trailed the boys and Lizzie.

'So, *you're* the one who gets my sis into trouble with Pervy Powell then?'

Before I could answer, Ella was laughing.

'Yah man, he's wicked when he wants to be, this one,' she said, rubbing my hair so hard it pushed by head forward. 'I need him in BTEC though, to keep me on the ground, like. Lukee pulls some of Mr P's attention off me.'

I loved that version of it. From where I sat, Ella was the one saving *me* from Mr Powell's crappy moods, using her charms to the fullest in the process. Still, she could tell her sis what she wanted. Did it really matter? Ella went on:

'Can you believe Poundes and those rugby mongs from my year give LLJ a hard time? How wrong it *that*! Anyway. I told them to wrap up or we'd get their legs broken.'

Her sister laughed. 'Legs broken! You can't say shit like that to younger boys?'

Ella gave her a gentle shove and said, 'They ain't younger if you're me, are they, Maya. Come on. Sixteen minus sixteen. Can't you count? Anyway, that's such a good threat to make on rugby boys. They love their legs so much, and every other bit of their bodies too. And since they all think DK is a sketchy *mo-fo* anyway, and know I go round with him, then it works anytime I try it. I always threaten to get him onto people who are being dicks.'

'DK? Ha! Yeah, that is funny, actually. He couldn't hurt a fly.'

'Still. No harm done. Can't have the roiders messing with LLJ, can we.'

'Roiders,' her sister laughed. 'The rugby boys in your year are cry-babies. They've probably never even heard of roids. Probably can't even drink ginger beer without bricking it. That goes for all of you, mind. You lot are still kids.'

'Nah, they do go out to parties,' said Ella. 'Who knows, those morons might even come tonight. The creepy little one is Jake George's little bro in't he.'

'Him?' said Maya. 'Sylvester? *He's* one of your "roiders"?' She made the inverted commas with her hands, wedging her cigarette in her mouth to do so. 'He's a weasel! I always wind Jakey up about his little brother. Sylvester. Ha. Skunk they call him, innit? Yeah, that's him.

Jake reckons that kid can't really be his bro, like. Reckons it's impossible the two of them can have the same MDMA.'

'DNA,' corrected Ella. 'Know your genes from your deadly disco drugs why don't you.'

'Ok. DNA. Whatever.'

Ella and her sister may have been on about Skunk as if he was nothing, but listening to this I still dragged a deep breath in through my nose to ward off the fear. Ella noticed immediately.

'Don't worry about him, Lukee. You're with us. He'll realise you're out of bounds.'

Her sister grinned, and dropped her smouldering cigarette butt into an empty bottle, winking at me as it made a hiss-sound. 'It's kid's stuff, the lot of it,' she said. 'Just have a good time tonight, *maan*! And get smashed, too. That's the important bit.'

She reached into her handbag and pulled out another mini beer bottle.

'Alright for beach parties, these, but not really getting me enough of a head-on for a Jackdaw house gig,' she added. 'Better knock one back quick each, or this shit is gonna be *boring*.'

* * *

I wondered what a party that Maya Bowen didn't find boring would look like. As the ocean's mists faded we arrived to an open door and a house which backed onto the dunes, not very far from where I lived. This house, though, was crammed from the front porch to the back garden with kids from the years above me. The girls led us in, and the boys followed. I was sandwiched between them as we pushed through the door in single-file, and the buzz of strolling into a place like this, one step behind

Ella Bowen and her older sister, was racing through my veins.

There was music on loud, and I liked it. Something dancey, with a soft beat and a woman's voice. I couldn't place it – not techno, not house, not pop – something unusual, something older and sort of... *real*, and that felt right. Whoever had put it on, it was their own sound, like saying 'welcome to my space, come and share my rhythm'.

Ella noticed my head moving with it and said, 'Massive Attack. Eighties. You like?'

I nodded.

'Nineties,' corrected her sister, shouting over the noise. 'Hey, Luca. Ella says you got craaaizeeee taste in music?'

'Uh...'

'That's good, man!' she yelled. 'Be bold! We got to be, eh?'

Bold... The word echoed round my head. It was working. I had the buzz under control, and looked around. Boys and girls were mixing and laughing, as if egos and groups didn't matter at all. The three main rooms of Jackdaw's house were bustling with kids from the years above me. A bucket of water and ice sat in the middle of the main living room, with cans and bottles in it, and a group of much older boys stood by the window, blowing their smoke out into the cold night.

Beyond the main room, I saw Lizzie, the other girl from Bunkers, walk through to the kitchen, where two more boys were leaning against the fridge. They were both slender, with almost identical dark hair, cut short around the sides and slightly longer on top. They both had loose T-shirts and tight jeans, and held bottles of beer in their hands. One of them had a tattoo going across his left elbow; this was Jack Dooley. Jackdaw himself. The host. So far, every single kid I'd seen in this building – girls included – had been someone who normally I'd be afraid of because they were older and had a reputation for getting pissed or getting high. But each of those kids had either smiled at me and said 'Hi', or not bothered looking my way because they were busy smiling at someone else. Now, when my eyes caught Jackdaw's, I was sure that run would come to an end – but like the others, he winked, tilted the tip of his bottle my way, nodded and then grabbed hold of Lizzie to give her a big hug.

Another wave of happiness ran across me. I existed. But I wasn't important! How great did that feel? Just a wink, a gesture to say 'hi', and then on with whatever else was in his world.

The motion and rhythm of the room was mine and everyone else's at the same time. Each voice seemed to carry through me, but I couldn't hear any of them. Ella was smiling and swaying gently, while her sister kept either waving at people she knew, or throwing a middle finger at people she knew and liked. I could stay all night, I thought. I *would* stay all night. I belonged. It was all fine. And that was when I saw Gaby, and then it all took an immediate, spiralling and awful turn.

*　　*　　*

She was half way down the stairs and shouting aggressively at someone. Whoever they were, they'd found a Gaby, a Gabe or a Gabo that didn't exist to either me or Ella, or anyone else she knew.

This Gaby, was poised on the steps like a soldier trying to attack uphill without a hope, only instead of armour, she was wearing a long, black dress that clung tightly to her thighs and was making it hard for her to keep her stance. She had one foot on a higher step, and was hurling abuse up at whoever was around the corner. I couldn't hear the words, but whatever it was, she really meant it.

The rhythm was slowing in my head, swinging back and forth as if it wanted to race off, out of control. When I saw who Gaby was yelling at, something jolted in my chest and it took all the noise of the room around to hide the sound of my gasp.

Skunk George was stepping towards her. He had higher ground than her, and the cool sneer on his face knew it. Skunk's purple shirt had been popped open at the top, and one of the buttons was hanging off on a loose piece of cloth. He was pointing at the tear, and now I could see, and hear, what he was saying.

'You owe me a new shirt, rich bitch!'

'I owe you a knife in the temple!' Gaby yelled back, her eyes blazing, possessed.

Something thumped into me, and I fell out the way. It was Ella, shoving me aside as she ran up the stairs to come between them.

'Gabe!' she yelled. 'Gabe! GABE! Leave it!'

Just as Ella was getting in front of Gaby, I saw who else Skunk was with. Joe Poundes was up on the landing, and he yelled down, laughing:

'Hey Gabba-gabba. Get over yourself. You know you'll be chasing us again if we want you to be.'

Skunk laughed.

My rhythms were fading, and I tried to listen for help – from somewhere, anywhere.

Ella pushed Gaby against the wall, then turned to the boys; a fierce, cornered, sharp-clawed animal ready, it seemed, to do anything she needed to.

Then Gaby's eyes lit on me, and the situation dropped even further out of Ella's control. Immediately, the second she recognised me, Gaby went off all over again:

'No!' she yelled, straight at me. 'No-no-no, no, NO! No WAY!' She was pointing straight at me. Ella began whispering something in her ear and pushing her hard against the wall again, and then Maya grabbed me hard and I was pulled into the kitchen.

'Er, you don't need to be in there right now,' she said, even calmer than Ella in the other room.

'But...'

'Trust me, Lukee. Just hang in here. Ella can handle that. Those boys are terrified of her, and she can mellow that crazy mate of hers fine. It happens a lot.'

'What?'

'That stupid "Gabe" girl. She does that all the time. Don't worry about it. Probably won't even remember who you are in ten minutes.'

'What d'you mean?'

Before Maya could answer, Skunk and Joe Poundes pushed through the kitchen, looking annoyed and puffed up. My skull was flashing white hot as they reached me. Poundes shoved forwards, as if to ram his forehead through me, and I flinched so hard that he and Skunk both laughed, then Skunk too stepped close and said, slowly, too quiet for anyone else to hear:

'Bit of a thing for Gabbo eh, Lukee boy? Ain't no PSE lesson now, brah. Crazy bitch is all yours if you're that desperate. Gonna be her "after-everyone-else", then, is it mate?'

He shoved me against the fridge, and then turned to a call from further along the kitchen:

'Oi! George!' It was DK. 'What you doin', son? It's friendly in here tonight.'

'We're *being* friendly, DK,' said Poundes, and then the two of them walked away, quickly, out the back door, and DK turned back to his friends. I drew breath, slow and deep.

'They're *such* babies,' laughed Maya, as if the whole thing was somehow over. 'I said earlier, didn't I? The weedy one's older brother, Jake – haven't seen him yet tonight – is a mate of DK's, so they're never going to do anything serious. But that's why those gimps from your year think they can hang around here. What did they say to you?'

I wanted to tell her, to repeat it, to say I needed to be outside now except I couldn't go in case those boys might be there. I didn't speak at all, though. Maybe I didn't really feel like trying to make too much sense of anything in case it brought more reality to the situation. I tried to hone my head into the music, but it too was changing.

Gaby marched into the kitchen.

'Where is he? Where is he?'

Her eyes were still totally wild. Ella was just behind her.

'Hey, DK,' Gaby yelled. 'Where'd that *prick* go?'

DK turned to face us all again, looking tired, as if these younger kids were starting to threaten his buzz. 'Who?'

'Skunk. Where is he?'

DK laughed and gestured towards the back garden. 'Probably jumped a fence by now with you calling him out like that,' he groaned.

'His brother too.' Gaby's voice was rising to a shriek. 'Where's he gone? They together?'

'Doubt it. Who cares?'

'Leave it, Gabe,' said Ella holding her elbow.

Held back by Ella, and unable to run off after Skunk and Poundes, Gaby caught my eyes again and became immediately still, calm, full of thought. 'Who the fuck is this,' she said, and then, before I could do anything, she spoke straight at me, her voice back under control:

'If *you're* part of this,' she growled. 'I'll kill you.'

Then she shoved Ella away and stormed out into the night.

The thing, whatever it was – the devil in me, call it what you want – was properly boiling now. It was low in my stomach, but rising quickly. Ella ran after Gaby, and Maya tried to calm me again, still with no idea:

'Wow. You've copped all the luck there, Lukee dude. What a dick. That girl better say sorry when she comes round! Come on, let's go and sit down.'

She led me to a sofa, and fell back into it, laughing.

'You guys have got some *out there* friends,' said Maya. 'Want another beer? Stay here and I'll fetch us one. She gripped my knee to push herself back up, and the sensation gave me an electric jump. Still, she didn't notice anything about me. I wanted to shout *STAY* but nothing came out, and Maya walked off calling, 'Boys, who's got anything to drink?'

I closed my eyes and breathed. The music had shifted again, as if the electricity in my blood had polluted it. There was a soft moment of strings, buzzing with synthetic noise, and then this horrid jingle kicked in, as if some computer had taken over a keyboard and was trying to destroy it from inside. A sampled voice started shouting something about 'dimensions' and then the song cut out altogether, replaced with *my song*, midway through!

This was it. I was either going to be saved by music or taken away. I screamed, but no sound came out. The song lasted a line, then went all techno. Still my lyrics, but remixed to oblivion. And I was out the front door, into the roads that led back to shore, past the turnoff to my street and onto the dunes, with 'Lucifer son of the morning' racing centrifugal circles inside the cap of my still-heating skull.

I couldn't tell you if it was my legs moving me – or if I was even really there by the sound of it – but as I passed the dune the troop of men was just starting to emerge from within it. I whizzed around, maybe even in the air, and from up above with a drone's eye view watched the fixed face of their leader emerge from the fine sand, still wet from the goo below, one steady pace after another. They should have had the power to calm me, but I was too hot, too far gone from anyone else's world.

I yelled at them: 'It's you, isn't it! Gigi CARRANERO! It's YOU! I've got my doubloon tonight and I know you can hear me! I know GABY-GABE-GABOO. Wanna meet her?'

The men kept moving. There was no response, no shift in pace, nothing to suggest I was there.

'You'll stop in your tracks if I get her,' I yelled, then turned and ran back towards the roads and Jackdaw's place.

I don't know how long it had been, but there was no music left and no lights at the front. I ran around the side and there, on the back lawn, was Gaby. I recognised the guy she was with immediately. Skunk's older brother, even under a porch light, was easy to spot. He had a softer, calmer face than Skunk, but the resemblance was one-hundred percent clear. It was a face which could have even looked kind, if it wasn't for the fact he was hugging Gaby close against him, whispering in her ear. She looked like she was crying.

Out of the dark, a voice spoke.

'Out of here now, retard, or I am going to paint the floor with you.'

Joe Poundes stepped into my vision, from behind the hedge joining Jackdaw's house to the neighbour.

I slid away, walking back to the dunes as fast as I could without actually running, all the while shaking my head around in circles and breathing in hard to hold off the tears.

At the dune there was nobody, so I turned for the beach, step-step-stepping into a jog as I got near. The last two figures in the procession were just sinking below the surface, and I couldn't see if the one backing them up was Gigi or not.

I yelled names inside my head:

Mr Carranero!

Gigi!

And then:

Alex!

Cee!

These were the people I needed to get to, now. Tonight had been because of their advice. It was their fault. What the *hell* were those two doing messing with my life like that?

I ran at the shoreline, at the patch where the men should be, and the warmth was almost there – fading, but just enough. I waded in, waist, neck, then plunged.

The voices, and the beat too, throbbed through the sea, faint, but still only just away – and surely there to be caught up with.

I yelled underwater. 'WAIT!'

'No worries, LLJ,' came a reply, and the warmth grew around. My arms went over my head and I turned downwards, pushing with my feet as the ocean got deeper, heavier and hotter. The cool little trickles brushed past my face.

'Wait!' I shouted, again, and then caught the current of voices, this time many of them:

We are *waiting…*

Chapter 20

It was sand at the exit this time. In through sea, out through dune. Only this exit wasn't a dune at all, I realised once I'd finished clawing my way out the other end. The pile of sand I came out of was stacked up on a flat quayside, right in the middle of a massive harbour at night, bathed in orange, man-made half-light.

My eyes were already adjusted to the dark, so I immediately saw Alex. I had come out of a mound of sand and gravel about twenty feet tall, and he was standing there at the bottom, watching as I dragged my legs out of the dust. His feet were planted on firm ground – concrete, I think – and he looked reluctant to step up onto the mound to help me down.

'Luca!' he said, arms outstretched to hug me.

'That all went *totally* wrong,' I shouted at him, my legs giving way to some kind of horrible tiredness and dropping me to the tarmac.

'Luca, i'ss okay. You look worried. This is not necessary. Everything, i'ss okay.'

'Says who?' I looked ahead, along the floor and noticed yellow painted lines.'Okay… Listen, okay? Many, many changes. I try to explain. But you must listen, because very important.'

'Listening to you has got me…'

'Luca, Luca. Listen.'

'And where is this? I'm not doing anything till you tell me where I am.'

253

'You are in Africa,' he said, softly. 'And quiet because i'ss the night and people are sleeping!'

'Africa? Not possible, man. Come on. Japan last time. This isn't right. Where's Cee? I've got a big fat thanks-but-no-thanks to give for all *her* help.'

'Yes, you meet *Chie-eh*, no?'

'Fff…' I went to curse her name hard, but Alex grabbed my mouth and clasped his hand over it.

'No-no-no, Luca. No. Listen. Chie-eh make to help. Very many things to tell you. Come with me.'

He helped me to my feet, and started guiding me along the wharf.

'This is South Africa,' he said. 'We are in *porto* of Durban! Very exciting place. And… You must to guess…'

'Guess? What?'

'Father is here with me! I *so* happy! Luca! Everything is working after you come to Cartagena. Policeman is coming to my corner of the road after two days when you leave. He tells me that he will try to find father, because very good to give good stories for his boss about helping the *artisanos* of our city.' He winked at me, then added. 'So the police put out information and then they *arrest*!'

'Arrest?'

'Yes. Arrest for sleeping in farm and bring him to city again. Very kind to arrest like this. Normally arresting is horrible, but not this time. I come with my mother to see, and the policeman tell my father, "You go free to family but no return to farm. We keep arrest secret, and you must return to *good* work!"'

'He was in a farm?'

'Yes. He try to farm to save money for family but police bring him back and make him scared to go to farm again, so no farm for father, and no death for father on farm!'

I wiped my eyes, and realised there was sand in my

eyebrows and hair. 'But… You're in Africa?' I said.

'Yes! After some more weeks, father finds fire eater and juggling job… On big, big ship! He needs me too, as helper. Many tourists come to Cartagena on big ship and we working as small, two-persons circus on ship.'

'You mean a cruise ship?'

'Yes! Here is terminal.'

We rounded a corner, and there, moored along the next quay was a boat so big I lost my balance to look at it. Rows of windows, balconies and decks were stacked so high above our heads we couldn't see the top even from here. A wide ramp had been lowered to the ground some way off from us, and my eyes followed it onto the lowest level, where some dim lights shone over a wide open entrance.

'This is Alejo's new home! We are two weeks in Port of Durban before more people on ship, then more one month sailing – one day on land for every three nights – then big sailing journey to Cartagena and can spend three weeks with family, then more two months sailing. Life is *good* now and this is Luca's kindness doing!'

'It's not really much to do with me,' I said.

'Everything to do with you. And also guess.'

'You mean guess what.'

'I am swimming now, in the warm water like you, and this is how I am meeting Chie-eh!'

'She told me,' I said, remembering I'd come here to be angry with them both.

'It is good. I have been many times now and always learning important things.'

'I know. She told me about you. I knew it was you she meant.'

'I lose my fire-eating stick under the warm place in the sea one time, but this is no problem because we have more, and now I am…'

'Alex, how long have you been on this boat? Like, working with your dad?'

'More weeks now. Maybe three months?'

'But it wasn't three months ago I came to you in Cartagena? It was only a few weeks ago…'

'Time funny through the sea, no?'

'So far it seems normal to me. I worked it out. I'm always showing up places at the time of day it's meant to be. I was in Japan in the morning when it was night in Wales, and I was with you in the evening when it was night in Wales. Plus, isn't most of Africa on the same time as Britain?'

'Time is different,' Alex repeated. 'I learn this because I *listen*! You must listen too.'

'Listen? D'you mean the voices under the sea? I can always hear stuff, but it never tells me anything.'

'No? I'ss clear for me. And for Chie-eh.'

I rolled my eyes.

'Must say "no" to being angry with her, Luca. She is right, Chie-eh. The girl, Gabrielle, she have something very important you can help with. You are helping people, but *she*, Gabrielle, is most important person to help. This I try to tell you now.'

'Why?'

'Luca, maybe you not hearing the voice very good because not now *wanting* to hear very good. Listen. You can see very well. Me? I never see men walking on the beach or in the sands. Same for Chie-eh. She never sees men too. You can see, but not hearing. Me, I can hear. I know who the man is that you see. He is *antepasado*, umm… ANCENSTOR! Yes, I remember word. He is father to father of father of Gabrielle! His name Gianni. Ghost of Gianni.'

'I'd worked that out,' I said.

'Man is very lucky to be ghost. In many countries people spend *mucho dinero* trying to find ghosts of *antepasado* but never is anyone coming. Gabrielle and Gianni, and family, they are all very lucky. But must not tell her this. Better she never know, I think.'

'Why?' I asked.

'Her head. Just maybe better this way. Gianni, he worried Gabrielle is not girl who will like him, so he wants it secret.'

'She *would* like him!'

'How are you knowing this? You cannot hear him. How do you know even *you* will like him?'

'I can tell,' I said. 'I can see him, remember!'

'Okay, maybe we can share stories and it helps us understand. Now listen to me. You hear *me*, no?'

'Obviously.'

'Good. So Gianni must follow, how do you say the word – like when racing cars go round and round?'

'A track?'

'Yes. Track!'

'Or circuit, maybe?' I rotated my finger in a circle through the air and Alex nodded. 'Okay,' I said. 'I get it.'

'Yes, circuit. I'ss same word in Spanish. Good. *Circuito*. Yes, he is on a circuit. This circuit is under the water and under the sands. It makes a circle though the earth, and is making the way for him to pass from one place to another place. You, and me, we have been using the circuit to travel now!'

'What, through the warm water? You mean it's going, like, through the earth?'

'Luca. Where are you?'

'Well, you say Africa.'

'So circuit goes through the earth.'

I thought about his logic. 'Yeah, but that's not really, like, possible.'

'Why not?' said Alex, his face lighting up. 'Circuit is opened from bad, bad spirit that Mr Gianni has found when

257

he was living on earth. Now he must fight it with good and kind things. This man was pirate, and he help his friends do many bad things to all our countries. He and his friends hurt Cartagena de Indias and people with their kidnap and bad gold. But now he is not able to die, and he is on circuit, into sea, out of sand, or into sand and out of sea, going big circles under the earth, and i'ss possible to follow. This is what happen when we swim! We follow Gianni on circuit!'

'So who are the other men?' I asked. 'And why am I the only one who sees them? Why doesn't Cee come across them in Japan, or why have you only heard them but not seen them?'

'Yes. Other men! They have the same problem as Gianni. Each one is choosing younger people who are living now, from all over the world, to help them. This is where you are chosen, and me, and Chie-eh. We are only Gianni's choices, though, and the other men might be choosing people in a different time. It is Gianni who needs us all, and this is why he is the one you notice. It is simple and his plan shows how clever he is. He was in all our home villages when he was alive doing bad things.'

'Tokyo's not a village.'

'Village, or town or city. You know what I mean. Gianni was doing his business in these places, and now he must help make something better in these places. But *you*... You, he needs to make Gabrielle's life better. He cannot help her directly, I don't think. Like I said, if he is *antepasado* it is selfish for him to be helping his own family – even if his help is nothing to do with money or power. If he can help you at same time, though, or me, or Chie-eh...'

'What links us, though? Is it our parents?'

'I think this is good possibility, Luca. It makes us friends, that we have this funny life where we are all wiser than our fathers. Chie-eh is the same. My father is funny, though. I like him being less wise than me. It makes me smile once I am used to it. Maybe you should find your father funny, too. Except that...' He paused, and looked down.

'Except that what?'

'I tell you in a minute, something important. First though, let me tell you what I don't know. I don't know, Luca, why you are the only person *seeing*, Gianni. Maybe just the way you are made. You see. I hear. And what I do know... I know exactly who the men are that you see with him.'

'The other dead guys off the *Pictor*,' I said. 'Maybe that's why they show only at Chapel Shores. It's so near to where they drowned.'

'Ah, maybe. Hey, you are learning with me now! Yes. Some are from same boat as Gianni,' said Alex. 'Some from other boats but who knew him when they were all alive and doing horrible things. These men also are bad from long ago who now must help Gianni. All of them are, how you say... *endemoniado*...' and he made horn shapes with his fingers.

'Demon?' I tried to guess, then realised what he meant. 'Oh, *damned*!'

'Yes. Damn. They have curse. They must walk this circuit to help their children and children of their children and friends of children of their children to do many good things to help, to help... Opposite of make or do?'

'Undo?'

'Yes, undo. To help undo most bad things from the times when they are alive as men. Young people living today, who they choose to call, are in a new chain, a new *circuito* – a *circuito* of kindness! The world needs this. But it is also why I am thinking "no" to telling Gabrielle. It's more kind, I think, not to tell her you are helping her. Unless you are forced, of course. But maybe you decide this, when you are seeing her again.'

'*If*,' I said. 'It wasn't looking too clever when I left to come here tonight.'

'I am sure this can be put in reparation,' he said. 'Luca. I think you are here now because something more important is happening, and this is the bad we must help to make good for Gianni and the men who *you* can see and *I* can hear.'

'This gonna be another visit to the local police then? Or maybe the harbourmaster?'

I turned away from him and walked to the edge of the quay. We were about a hundred metres off from the cruise liner, and the surface below was oily, shining back the lamps above. I saw my reflection, looking down, and watched it slightly rise and twist as small movements of energy shifted through the captive water.

Alex tapped me on the shoulder.

'No, Luca. This is more important. We also must help you, now. Chie-eh tried but it is not finished. Gianni tells me to tell you to speak to Gabrielle, because she is in his family and he must help her. But you don't come, so I give the message to the girl in Japan and something not go very well, so you fight with the girl.'

'I didn't even really get the chance to do that,' I said. 'She was so angry with me, man!'

'Yes, but can make reparation always. Not to worry about this now, Luca. Now *I* must help you.'

He turned me gently around, and pointed to a tight alley through two tall dock warehouses. We walked through it, to find a small cargo ship the other side. Alex began whispering.

'Luca, Father and me, we have been in port for ten days, and this is good for making friend with other boys living near. This boat here is very important. I have make friends with boy whose father is helping to load. This is not friends like you and me, or you and me and Chie-eh. This is not boy who swims. But nice boy. He not realise the important thing he tell me, and I only realise when sitting here in night and listen to the voices in the *marea* – how you say – yes, tide. Our journey is blessed by Gianni and he helps me find this boy, because…'

I interrupted. 'What are you trying…'

'Listen, Luca. This is very important, Luca. This time is not my father who is in danger. This time it is *your* father.'

My own flow of blood zapped me, quickly and quietly, and my heart thumped twice, hard, to send it back on its way. The veins in my arms warmed, and the cold of the night bounced off.

'Luca, now is very important to listen. I explain.'

He pointed at the cargo ship, and I looked. It was white across, apart from a red cabin towards the back and stood brilliantly still, as if asleep and unable to hear us. The orange glow of the lamps above acted almost to freeze the boat, though, as if it was sitting in some glass box in a museum for us to look at – like we'd broken in during the night and could only see it with a security light. I studied it for any sign of life as Alex continued:

'This boy, his father is loading boat here, and they have truck coming long, long way, from north. From…' – his voice dropped to an even softer whisper – '…from *Congo*!'

I felt the prickling in my blood again, and now the sting was on my lungs, too – for the first time since visiting under the seas.

'Go on,' I said.

'Luca, this boy who makes friends with me. *His* father is also working in ways that makes the boy sad – just like our fathers. This time the boy's father is not farming in hills for militias or doing the things you don't like. *This* boy's father is moving metal across the sea. He goes to voyage for one month every time, and always the same places. He goes to Europe. The ship, it goes to United Kingdom and *Inglaterra* too, where they will tell the *Inglés* that they are selling *oro* – gold. This was a trade Gianni did horrible things with, and it is one of the most important ones for him to make right now.'

* * *

In the far off distance, I listened for the sounds of the city beyond the port. A motorbike accelerated somewhere far away, and the small chains of moored boats clinked in the night breeze. I looked at Alex. 'No,' I said. 'Come on, man. That doesn't mean that...'

'Luca, listen. Gianni, he has helped me to find this boy, too, for *you* to know that your father is in danger. This gold, they sell to the *Inglés* as *doblón*. I'ss same word for you, no?' Alex said it again, slowly, and I realised he was right. *Doblón*... Doubloon.

'This *doblón*,' Alex said, his voice below a whisper now. 'They will say it is from very old *galeón* on the bottom of the sea, but it is not. These *doblóns*, they are not gold. They are another metal – *tungsteno*.'

'Tungsten,' I said, remembering Ella Bowen laughing at its name in BTEC last year.

'Yes. Metal is heavy like gold, but not gold? Also found deep in the land under Congo.'

'I think that's right,' I said, trying to recall what we learned that day in class but then immediately only able to see Ella and the stuff that had happened just an hour or two ago.

'Yes, so this is same metal, Luca. This boy's father and his business partners, they have coloured with very small outside of gold, after making everything else with *tungsteno*. The *doblón* is only made in Congo this year, and is not made from gold, and it is not old from a *galeón*. They will also sell other metal which they pretend is gold, later, when people pay too much money. The other gold is the same *tungsteno* too, but they will say it is all gold. They will say they have melted the *dobl*óns in one, as *lingote*.' He shaped a small rectangle with his hands.

'Ingot,' I said. That's the word he meant. How come every English term for types of gold seemed to be the same in Spanish?

'This is very real,' said Alex. 'This boy is kind and one day I will take him to hear the voice, helping us to change the bad things our fathers can do. I have been sitting here too, Luca, after he told me, and hearing the voices in the water saying to me this boy tells a story we must believe. The boy is expert in metal and he tells famous stories in Congo about the metal which is causing war in his country because it is needed in portable phones, and the bad men who are moving the metal out of his country. These men are very, very...'

'Dangerous,' I finished. 'Yeah. I know.'

'Luca. I am expert only in being a statue and in watching my father eat fire,' said Alex. 'So I cannot say for sure about these words or our fathers' stories. But this boy, Luca, he *is* clever. I am sure he is sleeping on this boat now. He cannot come out in the night with me. He is also afraid, Luca, because the men his father is selling *lingotes* with in Europe are very bad and will also be hurting people if there is a problem.'

I squinted hard to push away the images flashing across the backs of my eyes: my dad and Jeff running from someone, the dark point of that automatic weapon's chamber. My dad and Jeff getting caught, my dad getting... I squeezed the visions out of my head just in time, but their imprint was still there, somewhere. Once more, I looked up at the boat ahead. The oranges of the port safety lights were turning red, then white, then red again. With them went my mind, I thought about running at the ship and kicking it or hitting it or doing something else pathetic and pointless. I closed my eyes to stop that, too, and turned away before opening them again. Alex turned with me.

✳   ✳   ✳

'We are going to move very fast, Luca?' he said.

'Yeah. We are. Well, *I* am anyway. I'm, like, assuming it's okay that I don't stay much longer then?'

'Of course. Luca, you must go home. I am sure of this.'

'Me too,' I said, catching my shortened breaths and holding them in. We were walking back towards the quay I'd arrived on now, and the pace was quickening. Alex could feel my urgency.

'Luca,' he said, as we quickened and now breath grew shorter for both of us, '*if* you are coming again to see me, then I very much like for you to meet my father some time.'

'Sure,' I said, between another pair of short gasps.

'*If* you are here again,' he repeated. 'If not, remember you are important to the world if you are kind. *If* she is in your life again, be kind also to Gabrielle. And also, i'ss very important you know, Chie-eh is your friend and she also think you are important and you must make sure you and your father and your life is happy because you *can* do this!'

I was scrambling up the sand, and could feel it getting warmer.

'Thanks, Alex. I know. Look, thanks. I mean it.'

And he stepped into the warm sand and hugged me hard. He held it so long and so firm that his legs were sinking in with me, and I had to push him away as I felt the ground give below. The warm pulled at my waist, and it was so dry and so soft I wanted it to rise up and sink all of me. The tear on my face collected some of the grains before the whirling and the winds and the dryness dragged it away.

Then came the water, and it was as warm as it had ever been, and I was deep under and listening, and hearing too much to think or remember, but this was the right way to swim, because the sea was telling me, using *his* voice.

So many things to put right. So many things that could still go wrong or had gone wrong. So much power and so much knowledge. So much good in my heart. I was looking forward to home, and daytime, and the chances to think clearly and to make the right decisions – because from now on I would be confident. I *knew* what was right, and how to be happy. I knew how to help others be happy. I just needed to get back and find the chances to do it.

Except that this time I never walked up the beach back home again. This time I don't know how I got onto dry land in Chapel Shores, and I'm worried that I'm never going to work it out now.

Either that, or I think I might not want to know the story.

This time the next thing I knew after the warm, warm water and the coolness of the mini-currents was when they wheeled me into that clean, white room – held under, not by soft, dark saltwater, but by cold, fragrant hospital blankets and pinned to that mattress on Dr Wentloog's ward.

'He's safe now,' said another voice – a blur of police uniform – to someone else just beyond my vision.

Chapter 21

They woke me with some kind of cold cloth on my face. My mum was crying and she had angriness behind her eyes – either that or fear. Sometimes they seem almost the same emotion in my family.

'Lukee, Lukee, Lukeeeee...' she kept saying. 'What were you *doing*!'

But it wasn't a question.

'Why? Why?'

Not questions, either.

My dad just looked dumb. He didn't have the stuff to deal with this, clearly.

Okay, so I'm still maintaining this wasn't much of a thing to deal with, but that certainly wasn't the way the police told it to them.

Alright. I'll give them that. They had been woken up in the early hours of the morning by a copper who went for the full-on, worst-case-possible approach:

Your son's been...

Ah, come on. I mean, really?

Dr Wentloog took his time to introduce himself that first morning. With it being a Saturday, he'd come to work in no particular hurry, and decided to interview everyone else but me before making his mind up what needed to be done.

Still, though, since my parents didn't have the balls to do it, he did come in and tell me face-to-face. Well, to the side of my face, because he sat so far up the aisle besides my bed that eye contact was almost impossible if I didn't want to twist my own neck off. I shouldn't use language like that, now, should I? They'll all panic again.

'Luca,' he said. 'I'm Dr Wentloog, a clinical psychologist working with the local health board. I specialise in child psychology and traumas, and my main field is children your age.'

'Child me again and I'm out of here,' I wanted to say, if I'd had any voice to do it with.

'Now, it's perfectly normal for you to be thinking you can't recall where and why you were picked up in the way that you were.'

'Eh?' I wanted to say, scrunching my face as rudely as I could, but didn't.

'But from all the accounts given to me this morning, the picture is clear enough. We are going to need you to stay a few days here, at least, and this is for *your* safety, until we can work out how to help you avoid the kinds of thoughts you were having last night.'

The lights over my head swirled, as if some dark spiral had begun pulling the roof of this place up and away. I felt myself lifted out of where I was sitting, and my parents in their seats revolving too, frozen and elevated alongside me like a scene from *The Matrix*. The need to get angry was washing through the room and out the door, in the window and out the hole in the roof.

'You've had some sedatives, Luca,' said Wentloog. 'So the anxiety isn't going to be able to happen. You might feel some of the thoughts that gave you the panics, but the actual bodily symptoms are under control. There's a time for something like this, and right now, it is the decision I am making. You parents approve, too.'

My mum was shaking gently again, and still my dad looked blank.

'We hope there's going to be no police consequences for the party that was happening,' said Wentloog, 'which is a good thing as that could have caused resentment towards you from school peers, but we are offering support to Gabrielle Carranero and Joseph Poundes.'

Again, the hole in the roof spun, and tore at the darkness above. A whirlpool above me raised us all off the ground again. No change in blood pressure. No quickness of breath. My temples tingled. Nothing was happening, apart from feeling that I wanted the old, familiar reactions back.

Wentloog opened a curtain; daylight poured in; and the hole in the ceiling closed forever.

'I'm going to talk with you about your own version of events from last night,' he said, 'although I do think it's likely you won't remember for a little while. In any event, what you were saying when you came in overnight, about there being individuals leading you out to sea, about their being willing to accompany you, about a "land" underwater that you've been to before. Well, at this stage I have to exercise caution that this isn't just an attempt at what we call "malingering"; telling *us* something you know we will consider irregular or unstable to lead us away from the worse possibility.'

He turned and talked to my parents, and the tingling took over. The hole in the roof was a sinking hammock within the bed, and I closed my eyes to try and balance. Tiredness was waiting behind those eyelids. I opened them. The doctor and my parents were still talking.

Then I remembered the absolute urgency of my mission to tell my dad about the gold – right as my mum walked back over with that pitiful look in her eyes.

'What were you doing?' she asked again. 'Lukee, they *pulled you out the sea*! That Carranero girl, and the boy. They watched you wading into the ocean in the middle of the night. What on *earth* were you doing? Oh, my god, I'm imagining things. Why would you *do* that? It would *kill* us both!'

She looked at my dad. He took a deep breath.

'None of you understand anything,' I wanted to yell, but still the words, and the release of being able to say them, were only in my mind, along with, 'And he needs to listen to me or we're all gonna get it.'

The night came in and they plugged me up again, something in my arm, something in my mouth before a drink, food which tasted like plastic toys and a sleep that was full of boring dreams about nothing anyone cared about, myself included. It was as if someone had poured washing powder or disinfectant through my imagination, and turned it into clear, grey cloth – a fresh roll of plastic tarpaulin to line my dad's van one day in a future I knew I needed somehow to stop.

A morning of some sort drifted through the already open window, and Wentloog was back, asking if I wanted to see a visitor who had been asking constantly to see me, and I said 'No, I'd rather…' and then managed to stop short of the kind of language which might send them all into another massive flap-about.

Lunch… and more who-cares, before an afternoon of sunlight blew past the window and the doctor promised to 'catch up' soon before going home early probably to laugh about me to his mates.

He came twice more on the day after, twice more the day after that. He let me argue with him about whether I meant any harm, and then told me to see my friends before him, if it helped. I told him it wouldn't, and that I didn't have any friends – which was *exactly* the kind of thing Wentloog loved you to say in those early days, because it gave him the moral high ground immediately.

'You can't value yourself lower than the value others place on you. It's poor self-awareness, Luca. People do and will *like* you, and it's no safety mechanism to push them away.'

I groaned and asked to be left to sleep.

'Trusting others, Luca,' he said, 'is a good first stage towards being trusted more by us.' He stood up, so I could see more of him in the corner of my vision. 'We have to start this journey somewhere. You can't sit in this position forever.'

*　　*　　*

'Luca, you've got to stop saying that now. It's going to cause trouble.'

Eyes open again. Now my mum had come in to replace my Dad – because *he* didn't want to hear it anymore.

'Mum! You've got to listen to me. I can't believe you won't let me explain! I'm telling you both, that deal Dad wants to do…'

'Luca, shh…'

'Oh my GOD. Come *on*. Why would I make something up?'

'That's what we're looking to find out, isn't it?'

'But you *have* to believe me. I *know* that this is true.'

'Luca. Please?'

My mum looked too tired to be angry. Least she'd stopped being upset, though.

'Lukee, you don't need to say it again, anyway, to *anyone*. You told every single person you could find once the police took you. You told them all the same thing. That you were friends with kids who lived underwater and that those kids had warned you about all sorts of things.'

'But Mum…'

She stopped, and took a breath. 'Okay. I won't say anything else.'

'Go on! You're accusing me of making stuff up but…'

'Lukee…' and she paused again, before deciding to go ahead: 'I was kinda hoping you'd… you know… *taken something*. I mean… you *can* tell me if you had done, right? You might not think it, Luca, but I've been around. In India I've seen people in all sorts of states…'

'Mum!'

'I know, I know. Dr Wentloog confirmed you had hardly even drunk anything. Gabrielle and that boy from the party were a tiny bit more out of it, but they were okay too. Least *they* didn't hear you say any of the other stuff.'

'They didn't?'

'No. They were with the other policeman. Gabrielle and that boy were…'

'Well, it doesn't matter,' I said. 'You can tell them every single word anyway,' I said. 'I don't care who hears it. The only thing that matters is that you get Dad back in here now.'

'Lukee, he won't come back in until you stop with the gold being from some war zone nonsense. He's worked hard to get to the brink of that deal and…'

'It's not gold!' I yelled – or did as best as I could to yell, given the fact my face and head felt numb from whatever had been pumped through my blood stream to keep me under orders.

My mum shoved the bed hard, then she stood up and looked away. When she turned back her eyes had tightened.

'You're gonna get stuck in here for ages if you can't shut up about this, Luca. Trust me. You need to say it was a dream, or tell them there was some clever pills going round at the party that don't show up on tests… Actually, don't say that coz the police would probably raid the Dooley household for no reason then… But whatever you do, you need to drop the bullshit and now!'

'But…'

'Seriously, Luca. We're all gonna be in such a pickle if you can't just shut up about these imaginary kids and the under-the-sea rubbish. It's not…'

'Not what?'

'You know.'

'Come on. Say it.'

'It's not *normal*, Lukee. It's not what that guy out there needs to hear…' She jacked her head in the direction of the corridor that Wentloog would emerge from every now and then, and stepped closer to the door. She peered out, then stood sideways, half way across the room.

'I don't care,' I said.

'Exactly. And *that*, is precisely why you're in this position where other people are going to tell you what to do for a while!' Now she was turning to face me straight on again – before spinning clean around and then walking out the door.

The room seemed to be empty of air, as if it all poured out with her, and I waited for the buzz, the anger, the worry. But… but… Who could I try to argue with or shout at?

The beat had gone, though. Good beat, bad beat, odd beat or new beat; they'd all disappeared from my head – maybe out the door along with her and the draught that had taken the room's air. Or maybe they had slipped out earlier, while I was waiting between the bouts of sleep?

You guys have to listen to me, I thought, then tried to say it through a yawn. *No, no, no…* But that dragging weight of sleep had found its way back in through the half-open door.

No. No. No. You have to listen.

I laughed, softly at myself. Listen to what? I wasn't making any sounds. My eyelids dropped back over everything that could make a difference, and maybe – right then – that could have even been what I wanted.

No. No. No.

*   *   *

It wasn't long before I'd lost count of the exact day. It would be really cool to have been out of it for – I don't know – three weeks, maybe? But the way that place got to work on you, it was probably only a few days before that total clueless feeling kicked in. Day or night, all that mattered was being somewhere you didn't want to be.

Slowly, they started letting me not get too zonked out so that I couldn't speak properly. That meant only giving me something light to stop me getting the thumping heart and the short breath, and that I was, officially, according to Dr Wentloog's notes anyway, ready to start 'learning who I was' – or some similar crappy psycho-phrase of his that nobody would ever want to repeat.

I was out of bed too, showered and allowed into a side room to watch telly or read – which was far more important than my sessions of getting patronised twice daily by the doc.

Still, it was only when Gaby and Ella walked in that I really got my first sniff of the real world. Or should I say the *new* real world, because I'd been right in the thick of the old one for too long – and that was half the problem. Actually, it could have just been a wake-up call because Ella was soaked in some sort of weapons-grade perfume, and had coloured her nails an extra time while waiting outside. That's enough to make anyone switch their brain on high alert.

'Wow,' I said, when I saw who had come to visit me. 'No!'

For some reason, I tried to protest, even then.

Ella led the way, though, and they came and sat up close, both of them. Gaby was trying hard to find her own meaning in the floor, but Ella wasn't going to let her do that for long. 'He's ahead of you, Gabe,' she said. 'Not down there.'

When Gaby looked up, she shook her head, then loosened a tear.

'You are a proper muppet, LLJ' said Ella, on the edge of laughing. 'I wasn't there, but these guys reckon you were *on one*!'

I did more of a sniff than a laugh.

'Oh, and I ain't gonna be very serious about this stuff, LLJ. I'll tell you that now. Yes, you're mental. But who isn't? Plus, that doc's more of a prick than *any* teacher in Chapel Shores Comp, and if I don't keep this light, then Gabe by here is gonna be in as deep as you.'

Another sniff from me. 'Thanks, Ella.'

'Also, is E4 the only channel you can get in this room?' She pointed at the TV which I hadn't yet concentrated on enough to even notice it was on.

'Er... Maybe?'

'Coz if it is then I'm gonna need to move my seat. That's *Come Dine with Me*, isn't it. I get hungry watching that show. Can't you make them turn it off?'

'Probably.'

'Eh. Doesn't matter.' And she shifted her chair noisily round to face me. It made a grinding noise on the floor that caused Gaby to wince.

'Right then,' said Ella, sitting back again. 'So, now you can tell me what that crap was about on Friday, and then Gabe is apologising, and then we're telling you what we know. Bet that sounds fun?'

'Kind of. Ah, there's not much to say though... I'm fine. I wasn't...'

'Oh you *were*,' said Ella, immediately. 'But it's the first and last time, because if it ain't them *I'll* finish you off.'

'I wasn…'

'Zip it,' said Ella. 'If you can't tell us something sensible, then we'll go first. Eh? Gabe? What d'you reckon?'

'Uh, yeah,' said Gaby, vacantly.

'Well go on then,' said Ella, nudging her hard.

'Alright, alright,' came the reply, and Gaby looked up. 'Lukee, dude, Lukee… I'm so sorry. Oh, my god. This is heavy. I mean… Like… I just… You know. Sorry, like.'

'That's fine. He accepts,' said Ella. 'Now. We got to get shit straight for this kid ASAP or he's gonna try and walk out the window or something, so we need him not mental, and in the clear, right now. Are we on the first floor? Is there a drop out the window?'

'Ella, man, come on.' Gaby tried to interrupt, but got nowhere.

'Right, Lukee. Listen to me. If Gabe can't fill you in, *I* will. Now, first things first, you are a dweeb for doing what you done. Scared the shit out of Gabe, bothered me with it. And poor Poundsey! Jeez. He almost followed you in.'

'He did,' mumbled Gaby.

'Yeah, he did. Boy's hardly gonna make it on *Bondi Rescue*. But, still, he tried his best, for sure. Anyway, that's besides the point.' Ella turned to Gaby. 'Go on. This is *your* stuff. Time to get on with it. You know what I mean.'

'Not really,' said Gaby.

'You promised. Don't chicken out now.'

'Luca,' said Gaby, trying hard this time. 'I came after you. I wanted to say sorry then. But… Ah, man.'

'Yeah, man,' mocked Ella.

'Piss off,' said Gaby.

'That's more like it. Now come on, give him a bollocking first. That helps get you going.'

'Luca, you got the wrong end of the stick massively,' said Gaby.

'But did I though?'

'Yes. You did. The whole way. Thing is,' she paused and took a deep breath, before coming out with it: '*I've* been here before, too, see.'

The empty space in my head, where the worry should be, tried to pulse.

'You've been *here*? What d'you mean?'

'Exactly that. I've been in here too. In this place. To stay. That doctor's got a file to prove it if you ask him. Do I need to spell it out? I was…'

'I'm leaving you two alone to do this, if it's gonna get all girly and heavy,' said Ella, standing up and flicking her shiny, blonde ponytail over her shoulder.

*   *   *

Of course she had. *This* was why those kids under the sea, and the voice that instructed them, had been trying to get us two closer. Gaby was right. I had got the wrong end of the stick – and here was why it didn't matter one bit.

Gabrielle Carranero, Gabe, Gabo, the artiste, the rich bitch, the girl who wouldn't talk to me or Ella if she didn't want to, was in the deep end, way over and above anything I knew of.

This girl was a long-term 'friend' of Dr Wentloog – even if Ella didn't like the guy.

Missing school? The blow-out in PSE? The stuff I'd heard my mum's friends saying but hadn't been brave enough to ask about. The way Gaby needed to fly to the mists of Bunkers Beach with no notice at random times of day? The girl had been living with full-blown flare-ups of bad-brainitis for ages now, and she'd spotted me getting the thinkies in school way back when it first happened – when my mother had made me have that stint at home.

'I bet half the people we don't like, maybe even more, get like this sometimes,' she said. 'Trouble is you and me only bother ourselves with it.'

'But you want to bother other people now?'

'Well. Kind of. Don't you think they deserve it a bit?'

'Uh…'

'Ella's a dick about it, anyway,' said Gaby. 'Says grow a pair and don't go thinking this makes us special in any way, but really she's super-sensitive. The thing is, those boys, Poundes, Skunk George and them, they never had a clue, but after what happened to you on Friday night, then when I lost it again, Ella – she's known for a while about me – well, she laid into Joe Poundes and told him about my personal shit. Which I am still probably gonna kill her for. Even though it seems to have done one good thing for the rest of the world. Now that guy's suddenly on the waiting list to be you and me's best friend forever. I reckon there's nobody on earth right now more sorry and ready to make up for their ways than him.'

'Joe Poundes?'

'I know, mad in't it?' She laughed, a sort of tired, but happy giggle. 'They were ragging on me because they knew it got reactions, knew about my anxiety, except they just thought it was me being a brat – which is kind of fair enough if no one ever told them anything more. But that's changed now. They don't just know about it now, LLJ – they *understand* it. I reckon that Poundes boy grew up more on Friday night than he will in the next ten years.'

Here it was – their idea of what had happened, and it made total sense too: me showing signs for months – the breathing, the nervous glances – stuff Gaby easily recognised but couldn't psyche herself up to asking me about. Then came her losing it at Jackdaw's house and getting even worse when she looked up and saw me right there, gawping at her.

'You're different, Lukee. It was somehow, like, so much worse to know that *you* were seeing it,' she said.

Then came her getting her head together again at the party, quickly, and realising I was probably going into a spin myself because of how she'd gone off at me. Gaby's second chance to catch up with me that night went wrong too, then, when I appeared out of the dark as she was hugging Skunk's older brother. Before she could call to me to say whatever she needed, she'd wobbled again herself and the rest was all too far in motion to be pulled back.

Why couldn't she just *say*? Why hadn't she just told me about it all, before? Especially if she thought it was something we might have in common. All those afternoons in the mist at Bunkers... But then again, I hadn't said anything either, had I? I mean, how would you bring something like that up? 'Hey Lukee. Are you having problems in your head, like I am?' Of course she'd never have been able to just come out with it. This was why she'd kept the weird boundaries she did.

Anyway, after that second incident at the party – after I'd run off again – she followed me to the shore with the boys. Joe Poundes, who had only moments before said the cruellest thing to me, was now learning by the second how serious that crap could be – only to see me wade into the sea.

But the men? Why hadn't *she* seen them too? I needed to bring it up.

She was still on the bits which didn't matter, though.

'Okay, so I'd had a slight relationship with Skunk's bro,' she was confessing. 'It was, like, months before, and we were still good friends. He's a different deal altogether from Skunk. And Joe Poundes had been hassling me for ages about it, and coming onto me in school saying I should see him sometime – like he does to all the girls. Well, like he *did* to all the girls, before his epiphany on Friday. Anyway, I used to put him off, and as you know I was being pretty cold to *all* the boys – including you. And to Ella, as well.'

She paused, took a deep breath, and added, 'I didn't talk to anyone last few weeks cos I was, like, way more shaken up by the Gigi news than I let on, and then I had an episode of my own.'

A moment of calm drifted around the room, as Gaby let me hear those last words over. *Episode... Shaken up...* Then she said, 'So, anyway, Skunk, not having a clue, made up a rumour I'd done some stuff with his older brother, and then told all the boys for some reason only ever going to be understood by the moron himself. You'll be pleased to know, by the way, that Skunk got a proper whack off his older brother later on Friday for that, after the party and after you'd been brought in. Trouble was, the damage had been done though. Those boys in our year, Poundes and them, loved winding me up about Jake George, obviously. And at that party they saw me and guessed it was a chance to rag on me again. Poundes went to up to me and took the piss, and the rest you know.'

'Do I?'

'Well, yeah. Oh, except that Skunk's older brother took over to calm me down. Like I said, he's a nice guy, and he sort of knew the deal with my moods, too. So we're hugging coz we're dealing with some stuff, and remembering breaking up but still not bitter and he's telling me his little bro's gonna get it! Then you show...'

'But, Gabe, I was coming back because...' The men, the men! Gigi himself! I had to tell her.

'So we saw what happened at the beach,' she explained. 'You were standing around and then just headed into the water, so from somewhere the police got called – and Joe Poundes shit himself because you had totally gone under. Then he went in himself and was flapping around for ages before he pulled you out, and you were, like, floating in the sea and shivering like you were already half dead. Jesus, Lukee. It was intense, man. Like a mirror going up to me, the way I've felt a million times, and I was *not* into it, not one bit.'

'But Gabe, Gabe...'

'Man, Poundes feels *terrible*! The last few days that guy has been so keen to find out if you're okay, it's unreal. So you've done all of Chapel Shores year Elevens a favour in one way. All the bad in Poundes has taken a hike.'

'Gabe. Listen. Gabe. I can't believe you didn't see something else, too? Come on, think. You've painted him just like it was. Come on, I know you must have been close to seeing it. Or hearing his voice, then, even if you couldn't see him.'

'See what, Lukee?'

'Him!'

*　　*　　*

'Ha. It's *beautiful*! It's so... so... *simple*. The best things always are, eh, Lukee? And there's me thinking I did those sketches only for me.'

'Except you did show one to...'

'Well, yeah, but that's you. I didn't plan to share it at the time I did, though.'

'Really?'

She took the news about Gigi Carranero like it had been told to her by Dr Wentloog in one of those meetings he would have with us in the weeks to come – you know, like it was something interesting to get told about your own brain, or your own world, but nothing *really* major. To her, this kind of announcement seemed… well, pretty straightforward. As if she'd sort of known it all along.

'The pictures I painted,' she said. 'They were coz something flashed through my head when I tried to imagine him. But that *was* definitely how he looked. I knew it at the time. Something kept telling me I'd got him right – as if I'd seen him somewhere. Wow. Can you imagine how much it would have cooked Dr Wentloog's little mind if I'd miraculously sketched the same figure as you were seeing – and Wentloog had found out? God, I'm glad I only ever made up a load of woolly stuff when he was making me keep a logbook. Gigi, though! Of course it was him! Is he still around, d'you reckon? Or have you scared him the hell away from Chapel Shores for ever and ever?'

'Dunno,' I said. 'We can always go out one night to see?'

'No,' she laughed. 'We will *not*!' Then she winked. 'Well, not for a while, anyway. And not without Ella, or someone else who's not mental like we are.'

'It wouldn't happen for Ella though,' I said. 'They'd stay in the sea, or in the dune.'

'Then it wouldn't be happening at all,' said Gabe. 'If she doesn't see it, we shouldn't be seeing it. Plus. How do we know that loop under the sea isn't going through the Underworld anyway?'

'We don't. But why would it? I mean, look. I'm safe.'

She laughed.

'Plus,' I said. 'Aren't they maybe showing themselves just to the people who are willing to see?'

'You think *Ella* wouldn't be up for seeing nineteen ghosts including the legendary Gigi? She'll try anything once.'

'Yeah, but she might not *believe*,' I said.

'True dat.'

'Gabe. You believe me, don't you?' I asked.

She took a short breath in, then blew it out hard through her nose, shuffling in her seat and fixing me with her eyes.

'Hell yes,' she said. 'I'm with you all the way to the *brink*, LL Cool J.'

I looked towards the window, to see if outside had started to look more real again yet.

'Oh, but one thing I do need to tell you,' she said. 'Just some advice.'

'What?'

'Luca, don't ever tell them, out there, that version that you just told me. *I* believe you, but if you do tell Wentloog this, then they'll cert you for sure.'

I smiled. 'Sensible all the way,' I said. 'I'm not *that* far off it. I can see it's a no-brainer not to give them the real deal.'

'Good,' she said. 'But I'm getting Ella back in so we can hatch a plan for tuning your old man, though. He's in a pickle if you ask me. That Alex kid – he's got to be talking about the same stuff for sure as that knock-off gold your dad and that cheeser mate of his are about to buy.'

'Jeff, you mean.'

'Yeah. Jeff. Right, Lukee. We need a plan of attack there, and soon. Poppa Lincoln's your after-lunch meeting, and it's gonna be a career-breaker.'

'Fine. Whatever. Thanks.'

She was standing up to leave.

'Oh, Gabe,' I asked, as she took her first step back.

'What?' She stopped short of the door and faced me again. Her face looked open, and ready to listen.

'Gabe. Back there, at Jackdaw's – I know you probably don't like this, but it's been bugging me – you said something to me in the kitchen, as you ran by, like. You said, "If you're in on this, I'll kill you", or something like that.'

'Jeez, Lukee. Your memory!'

'I bet you remember the important things too.'

'Well, this thing *isn't* important,' she said. 'That's just me when I'm possessed. Think of it as if someone else said that to you. Someone who doesn't usually exist, and who never says or does the right things. I'm working on getting rid of that person for good, though. We need to *imagine* her away. Seriously, LLJ – imagine that didn't happen. Please? For me? Coz if we imagine it that way hard enough, the two of us, then it'll become true. It actually could disappear from history. Stop existing. Can we please try to do that?'

'Okay,' I said. 'It's a deal.'

Chapter 22

Right then, let's see how this goes. Let's see if I'm any good at it.

> So, the weather was nice, and it was sunny outside. When my parents came to see me in the afternoon after I'd met the girls, I asked to see my dad on his own.
> I did this because I needed to be honest and tell him how...

Ha ha ha. I'm *crap* at it, aren't I! Thing is, that's all I need to do; just let flow a bit of nice, safe stuff about how I'm learning some simple lessons about the hazards of being young. That I need to keep his little blue book with me in order to cope with the pressures of growing up and being ready for the adult world etcetera, etcetera. Come on though, would anyone in my place *really* give someone like Wentloog the real version of how I faced my dad like a day later?

From Dad and the doc's point of view, this was the biggest issue of the lot. I suppose it makes sort of sense, if you try and see it from their perspective. Son throws hammer at his dad, goes to school the next day like nothing's wrong, isn't in when parents get back – from the *pub*, of all places, which is kind of dodgy when they've got a son who freaked out the night before like I had done – and then the next they hear is that call they got from the police.

So, yes, maybe it was reasonable for my dad to be as nervy about this one as I was – but either way, this is the non-Wentloog version of how that one panned out in the real world:

Me: Dad, what the f…

Him: Luca, what the f…

Me: I'm fed up with this now.

Him: I'm also fed up with it.

Me: With what?

Him: With whatever you're fed up with.

And it flowed from there. One moment we're dancing around whatever it is we have to say and then, next minute, I hear him saying how glad they were when I was born, and how the gold would allow him to provide for me, how that's all he ever wanted to be able to do, and how he'd give anything to just be able to understand each other again like every other parent and their kids.

Obviously, even a fifteen-year-old kid under surveillance from guys in white coats is wise enough to know that every other parent and kid in the world doesn't find everything easy either. Once I told him this, he seemed to almost leap out of his seat – we were in the room with the TV, which I'd left on purposely – and started talking fast and happy.

'You're right, Lukee,' he said. 'It's so difficult. For all of us, isn't it! So let's all stop lying and just say what we want from each other.'

And then old Stevie Lincoln-James went full-on with the story of his life like I'd never had it before. I don't know why he said that about lying, first, but it is amazing the light that truth can shine on the world. There's no need for gilded metals or precious jewels when people can say what they mean. He went on a bit about having a kid so young – which kind of made me doubt the bit about being glad for half a second – before he said how he must have made loads of mistakes because he didn't know better, like 'Lucifer son of the morning' and all that.

That was when I tried to tell him, again, that those guys selling the gold in Birmingham seemed dodgy – which made him straight away say that he'd already paid in a grand now and he didn't want to lose that... Yeah, stupid, isn't it? I was still trying to talk about that deal when he had much bigger stuff he wanted to bring up.

'Luca,' he said, looking straight at me like he had something big to ask. 'What's the purpose of it?'

His eyes were right on me, dark and lost.

And so I laughed. I don't know how, or why, but that was the only thing I could do to answer him. I mean, who asks their teenage son a question like that?

For a moment, his face flicked through being angry, then shook for a nanosecond like it was going to cry. And then – of course he did – Steve Lincoln-James looked straight at me, and started laughing too.

It took us – the laughter – floating us around the room. It had us yelling and giggling and shouting at how stupid everything else was other than the fact that the two of us were there, together, and happy to be so.

The money, I thought, again, as he leant back in his seat again.

'Dad. What's a grand when they want you to pay in another trillion sometime soon?'

And then the laughter passed and we seemed to be on the same topic, without really knowing it:

Me: But I'm still fed up.

Him: What with?

Me: Not knowing.

Him: Not knowing what.

Me: Not knowing if we're gonna have money or if you really are glad I was born.

And that was what got us both. This time it wasn't laughter. This time it was silence, and things I'll never, ever forget – how he suddenly looked more human than I'd ever seen, and how he turned for a few minutes into a kid as young and as scared about the future as me. How he sat there admitting he didn't have any ideas, and how we sort of agreed it could be fun not having any idea as long as we were willing to be honest about it.

'I'll think about it,' he said, and he promised he would.

He did more than that, though. My dad had pulled out of the gold deal and forgotten his stake by the next morning. In fact, he did a whole lot more. He went looking for work that paid by the week, month or even year, only a couple of days later – and when Jeff nagged him to come back in and push on with the gold deal he did something Steve Lincoln-James had never, ever done in his life.

'Cutting my losses, Jeff,' he said.

Whatever Jeff said back down the phone, it had no chance.

'Salaried work now for me,' said my dad, some shiny day later, looking at me across the same visitors' lounge, this time with the TV off, as my mum packed up for me to come home. 'My boy needs to know the bread is coming home with him. Need him to be proud of me, innit. Not that he wasn't, with the sole-trading, like, but maybe something new is on the cards, buddy. Maybe it's time. You understand, don't you?'

I'm sure Jeff Rafferty *didn't* understand, but that didn't matter to my dad. Stevie Lincoln-James had my mum right behind him, and anytime soon he was going to have me in his corner too. I mean, why not?

Of course, in a perfect world, Gaby – when she wasn't fighting with or threatening a set of parents herself – could have maybe asked her folks to fit him up with something quite respectable. Something shirt-and-tie, with a plan and responsibilities. Something that matched a life that meant you had people to look out for. She could also have helped make sure the Carraneros spotted that, from all Dad's time selling and talking crap, he had a bit of 'charisma'. Gaby's parents might have then thought he'd be good for a 'front of house' job in one of the family's new hotels or gyms – one of the ones up the motorway that had been bought with Gigi's evil money. The same money that me and humble little Gabrielle were now sworn to a lifetime of goodwill to try and repay – without actually giving it all away to those posh families he probably nicked it from in the first place, obviously. That was surely how Gigi would have wanted us to play it. Yeah, the same money me and her were going to repay with random acts of kindness for as long as we lived – something Joe Poundes would also be doing from now on.

But this might not be a perfect world. I will be ready for that, too. That's the point of getting the real version of it all down somewhere, somehow, isn't it? This is about facing up to the things that go right *and* the things that don't. Still though, why not try to make it a bit better every day, anyway?

Why not? Because I like what Gabe said about old Gigi when she first drew him – so much that I reckon it's actually true: once you imagine it, then that's how something might actually start to look.

Chapter 23

She kept drawing. She just stayed away from drawing anything like him. It seemed simpler that way. Anyway, with me sat next to her in Art now, she didn't want to risk setting off any of the stuff the teachers had been warned about in my 'file'.

'Keep that picture back for a better time, anyway,' said Gaby. 'It'll count for more, one day.'

Kleener, Wentloog, all the other professionals who pretended to care – they had a file on her too, of course. It's just that hers wasn't as fresh as mine, complete with references to the blue notebook that held all and none of the answers anyone teaching me might one day need if I decided to go off on one again. Yeah, we must have made quite a pair, sat there with pastels and paints in Rogoff's room, trying to get on paper, canvas and into wire frames the mad stuff from inside our heads. Gaby's vision was worth more marks maybe, but I knew by then to value whatever came out of my mind just as much.

'What d'you think of Ella's plan, then, LLJ?'

We had three weeks left in Year 11 now – plus exams – before the summer rolled out ahead.

'What? The End-of-Life Beach Party?'

'Yeah. She's given it a kinda morbid name, don't you reckon?'

'That's what it's gonna be, according to Ella,' I said.

'I *know*. Did you ever imagine her getting antsy about the end of school?'

'She's fine with it. She's just called it that to rip into all the serious kids who are gonna get spaced out by the whole school thing finally finishing after all these years.'

Gabe agreed: 'It's the end of *their* lives, maybe. For Ella, it's just gonna be the start of turning slowly into a clone of her sister.'

'That's not a bad thing, is it?' I suggested.

'Maya? She's *bonkers*, LLJ.'

'What, and Ella isn't?'

'Nah. If she was, she'd never have come up with calling the end of school the end of *life*!'

'Fair point.'

Gaby leaned over the table to carefully smear a charcoal edge on the 'self portrait' she was finishing today. It was her own face but with all the shades in negative, and held tight by a pair of hands. Her normally light hair was scratched in the darkest strokes, while her eyes burned white hot in contrast. She'd done a series showing the reversal of light and dark happening. The first pics were of her normal face in black and white, before an eight-image strip where the shades gradually swapped places until the one she was finishing today, which shone with brilliant black. Each pic had been stuck into a wire frame, with a sculpture of hands holding them up out of a plank that supported the whole thing. For the last picture, though, the wire hands had grabbed the head hard by the temples and were squeezing it. The way the 2D and 3D came together made you feel kind of dizzy. She wanted it that way.

I watched her teasing the charcoal with her thumb, then leaning back to check her work.

'End of life,' she chuckled. 'How are you about that stuff, anyway, Lukee?'

'What, the end of...'

'School. End of *school*. Obviously.'

'Fine,' I said. 'Whether I get Maths or not, there's plenty to do out there in the world.'

'Like what?'

'Ooh. Depends what I'll be able to fit into my schedule,' I laughed.

'Oh yeah, I forgot. All those meetings with Wentloog, eh?'

'Yeah, can't wait,' I said, rolling my eyes but smiling.

'Hey, Lukee, did he get you to do one of those blue book thingies in the end?'

'Sort of. Did you have to do one as well?'

'Yeah, but it wasn't worth much to anyone, I don't reckon.'

'Nah, mine neither.'

'The meetings are okay too,' she added.

'Yeah, I'm not too bothered by it,' I said. 'And he's gonna have to get in the queue too, anyway.'

'What? Behind all your busy volunteering stuff?'

'Exactly. There's dolphins to save from those Japanese trawlers. Congolese metal miners to protect from mobile phone makers. Fire eaters and farmers to keep safe from armed militias…'

'Dude, you're only folding secondhand clothes down the local Oxfam branch! How d'you know they're gonna save the dolphins or pay the fire eaters more?'

'They help in the Congo,' I said, 'and anyway, we need to learn the ropes from somewhere before we set up this worldwide putting-everything-right organisation with your dad's inherited kidnap money. Charity shop floor's a start, isn't it?'

'It is. I'll give you that, LLJ.'

'What are you doing about the "end of life", anyway, Gabe?' I made the inverted commas with my fingers. It seemed safer to say it that way.

'Nothing at all. Just gonna let it come for me and then probably panic when it's time to make a decision.'

'That's perfectly normal,' I said.

'I know. Sad innit. Remember when I said you and me were passing each other on the way to and from being normal?'

'Oh yeah!'

'Well, we messed that up, didn't we! "Swapping Places"... What was I thinking?'

'I dunno.'

'Hey!' she said, jumping up from her chair, excited about something. 'That's what I'll call these pics! I've got my project title: "Swapping Places" – like from being normal to not normal.'

'That's a good idea.'

'The people who look at it can decide which is which.'

'You mean which pic? That's easy, Gabe. Normal... Well, it's all of them and none of them,' I said, and she banged me with her shoulder, like she'd always done.

'That's *such* an LLJ thing to say,' she grinned. 'Come on, bell goes in a minute. Let's go and find Ella. I wanna hear more about her plans for the end of life.'

'Gabe, shh. Rogoff hears you say that and takes it the wrong way, she might call You-know-who and then we're both going away for a *long* time.'

'Good point. Better warn Ella, then. That mouth of hers. It's gonna get us all into trouble one day.'

'What more trouble than...'

'Ah, come on, LLJ. Of course we can get in more trouble than that. I thought we were all just getting *started*?'

*   *   *

293

She chose the longest day of the year, Ella, to call the End-of-Everything Beach Party officially 'on'. And, guess what, she also managed to find the one day of the century when Bunkers had no mist at all and a gloopy, red sunset. Instead, I remember the silhouettes of her and her sister, the boys they went round with and a few other randoms, all lining the square shapes of the toppled concrete, as that burning ball lit up the western horizon.

For hours the night stayed warm, and that fading swipe of yellowy dusk held on to its traces of the summer day. The stars dropped into view softly, as the heat slowly evaporated into the emptiness overhead. Somewhere beyond, the sea chopped carefully at the shore, reminding us all it was there with its steady, rhythmic rounds.

It was on the way home, and only just before turning at the halfway rocks, that I got the idea. What if...

And right then, feeling embraced by the warm, summer night, I knew the answer.

The shore carried on bending round, until the streets that led to my house showed up on the left. Turning right instead, towards the gravel path, I could make out the rises and dips of the dunes as an extra shade of dark coming up ahead. The mini-hill was still there, but the hedges and plants on its brow were full of leaves now, and I heard them shake gently in the breeze that was pulling off the land behind.

Without the moonlight, everything had to be done by feel – but my eyes still made them out as soon as I came over the pebbles and onto the sand:

Nineteen of them, uniformed and stood to attention, all waiting just beyond the shoreline. In water up to their waists, they waited shoulder-width apart, spread out either side of one figure who had stepped forward just a little more than the rest.

You're still here! I said, and old Gigi began to raise his right arm.

The darkness was fizzing around him, and I could only make out his movements a moment after he'd made them. With his wrist drooping low, elbow rising first, he lifted his hand up, along the centre of his chest and across his face. When it reached his head, another part of the night seemed to rise with it. His hat. He was lifting his hat. Then, from the way his silhouette crumpled slightly, I could make out the softest of bows, before the hat went back into place and he straightened into a perfect salute.

I raised my right arm too, and as I did the other eighteen lifted theirs with it. When my hand got to the side of my head ready to salute, I stopped, and waved instead. Eighteen hands sent the same signal back.

Have we done it? I asked, whispering so quiet it could only have been for me to hear. *Of course not.* And I stepped closer to the shore, taking off my shoes and leaving them on the pebbles behind.

The foam lapping against the tide-line carried on marking out the beat of the night, as I waved again. This time Gigi joined them too, as he stepped backwards and took his place in the line.

The water reached my toes, and they tingled with its gentle cold. I stood and stared, as the figures grew fainter on my horizon. The sea pulled gently back, and my toes dropped into the wet sand. When the next shore-pound swished over, my feet adjusted to the temperature around. I waved once more, as the eighteen figures followed Gigi downwards, easing themselves gradually into deeper water. Again, they waved back – hands rising slowly over their heads so that the last I saw of them was just those turning palms, sloshing through the inky surface of the summer sea, before they were gone and darkness, too thick to reveal the ripples left behind, washed in all around.

I kept my shoes in my hands as I walked back over the dunes towards home – a route I knew so well I could do it without sight. Eyes on standby, I concentrated only on the other senses, picking out the cool sand underfoot, the wind shaking the sharp dune grass and the smell of the wild flowers that lined the path back home.

The dim porch light had been left on, easing my eyes into the safety of our house. I picked the key out of my pocket, heard it click into place in the door. Inside, I tiptoed up the stairs and rolled straight into bed. Shortest night of the year. The one we'd chosen to celebrate the End of Everything. If I'd looked out the window, I might have even noticed the horizons had swapped places. The west, over Bunkers, would be drenched in darkness, while the east began to breathe out the next cycle of daylight.

It was going to be a bright one, too. But we all knew that, right?